Murder at an
English Séance

Books by Jessica Ellicott

MURDER IN AN ENGLISH VILLAGE

MURDER FLIES THE COOP

MURDER CUTS THE MUSTARD

MURDER COMES TO CALL

MURDER IN AN ENGLISH GLADE

MURDER THROUGH THE ENGLISH POST

MURDER AT A LONDON FINISHING SCHOOL

MURDER AT AN ENGLISH SÉANCE

Published by Kensington Publishing Corp.

Murder at an English Séance

Jessica Ellicott

KENSINGTON
PUBLISHING CORP.

KENSINGTON BOOKS are published by

Kensington Publishing Corp.
900 Third Avenue
New York, NY 10022

ISBN-13: 978-1-4967-4016-8

Printed in the United States of America

Murder at an English Séance

Chapter 1

Edwina took a final look at the stack of typewritten pages on the desk in front of her and nodded her head, as if to convince herself that she was, in fact, ready to send the manuscript off to a publishing house for consideration. Her heart thumped wildly in her chest as she lowered the stack of crisp, white pages into a box and proceeded to wrap the parcel in brown paper.

She had procured the address for the publishing house weeks earlier, but somehow the idea that she was sending her novel off to be critiqued, and most likely rejected, by a stranger still somehow took her by surprise. It had seemed to her that she had been working away on her story for ages, and she could not quite believe that she had not only written the entire thing but had revised and corrected it until she was sure she could do no more without another person looking it over.

And although Beryl, Simpkins, and even her friend Charles had proven staunch supporters of her fledgling literary efforts, she could not bring herself to let them know she had finished the task. After all, one of them might ask to read it. The very idea made her slim frame shudder, from her neatly trimmed bob to her sensibly shod feet.

No, this was a part of the experience she would keep to herself, at least for the time being. Not that she thought it likely that she would be able to keep the news of it to herself for long, not with the way Prudence Rathbone, the local postmistress, alerted everyone in the village to the business of their neighbors. Edwina's hand shook as she poised a pen over the wrapped parcel with the intent to inscribe the publisher's address.

Chiding herself for her bout of nerves, she gave her head another shake and began by printing her return address. Before she could talk herself out of it, she added the address for the publisher and capped her fountain pen. The ink had feathered only slightly on the brown paper, and to her eyes, the destination appeared legible. She tucked the parcel into a drawer in her large wooden desk and firmly shoved it shut.

With her nerves still jangling, she got to her feet. Crumpet, her faithful little dog, stretched and hurried from his bed placed beneath the desk, eager to follow her wherever she was bound. She paused in the hallway and plucked her old straw gardening hat from the hall tree and shoved it onto her head. There was nothing like time amidst her beloved plants to soothe her troubles away.

Simpkins, her former jobbing gardener turned housemate, had spent considerable amounts of a newly acquired fortune on renovating the gardens at The Beeches. The war years had been hard on estates everywhere, with a downturn in the economy as well as a crippling shortage of staff to keep things in trim. For several years, the garden had been as much a source of sorrow and regret as it had pleasure. But over the last few months, it had come back into its own and even enjoyed some improvements due to Simpkins's generosity and skills.

Crumpet capered around her feet before pausing to roll around on his back in the velvety green grass. Even though it was early October, it was the warmest one in thirty-five years, and there was still a lingering feeling of summer in the air. The roses bloomed and bloomed, despite the lateness of the season, their sweet fragrance drifting on the warm breeze. She could not remember a time when they had persisted so long into the autumn.

Michaelmas daisies and stonecrop offered up a fine show of late blossoms as well. Grasses topped with waving plumes swayed in a new border near the edge of the potting shed that Simpkins still retired to for a portion of each day. He might have moved into the house, but old habits die hard, especially for a man as set in his ways as Simpkins. She crossed the lawn and peeked into the shed to see if he was within. Inside, there was nothing to see but tidy rows of clay pots and sacks of daffodil and tulip bulbs awaiting their turns to be tucked up into the prepared garden beds.

Perhaps he was having a bit of a lie-in. After all, she had been abed for some time the previous night when he and Beryl had returned from the pub. He was not as young as he used to be, not that any of them were, and from the sound of his cheerful crooning, she had concluded that he had perhaps partaken of an ill-considered quantity of strong drink. She was not one to do so herself, but she had an inkling that such an overindulgence might incline one to keep to bed late the next day.

Beddoes, her cherished housekeeper, bustled out of the scullery door, a wicker basket piled high with linen resting on her hip. Edwina knew better than to offer to assist her in pinning the wash to the clothesline stretched between two poles at the far side of the kitchen garden. Beddoes was an old-fashioned, proper sort of servant who would take enormous offense to such a suggestion, and Edwina would not wish to insult her.

Instead, she made her way in the opposite direction to the summerhouse to sit. She would have appreciated the distraction that hanging out the wash would have provided from her thoughts about the fate of her novel, but she would not risk her housekeeper's wrath. Beddoes was likely not yet recovered from Beryl's insistence in helping out with a major bottoming out of the house a few weeks earlier that had almost resulted in her resignation.

She leaned back against the wicker settee, marveling that the temperatures were still warm enough to enjoy the outdoors without even a lightweight jumper. Crumpet hopped up onto the seat next to her and pressed his wiry body against her leg. She stroked his fur absent-mindedly as she considered when might be best to attempt to slip away to post her manuscript without Beryl offering to accompany her. She looked back over her shoulder toward the house. She couldn't shake the feeling that someone was watching her.

Beryl stood at the window, watching, as her dear friend came into sight. Edwina had been behaving secretively lately, and Beryl could only surmise that it had something to do with her novel. It had been some months since she had become aware of her friend's passion project and even less time since Edwina had admitted to the truth of it. Her friend was a very private person, and although Beryl could not understand keeping one's light under a bushel herself, she did realize that was Edwina's way. There had been a recent flurry of typewriter keys clacking loudly at all hours from the office of sorts Edwina had set up for herself in the library. But over the past two days, such noises had ceased. When she had lurked outside the firmly shut library door from time to time, she had heard nothing whatsoever. She sincerely hoped that the silence did not mean that Edwina had come to some sort of impasse with her book.

It was just as well, Beryl thought, that Edwina was so preoccupied with secrets of her own. After all, Beryl had something up her own elegantly costumed sleeve. Edwina would surely raise objections if she knew ahead of time what was in store for the pair of them. Beryl knew that, once it was a fait accompli, Edwina would find herself hard-pressed to make more than a routine objection. She waited until she noticed her friend was settled in the summerhouse and then moved swiftly away from the window and down the stairs. Following the sound of humming, she tracked Simpkins to the kitchen, where he sat with his hobnailed boots firmly ensconced beneath the well-scrubbed kitchen table.

Beddoes, the imperious housekeeper, was mercifully nowhere in sight. Over the last few weeks, she had become less of a thorn in the domestic servant's side, but that did not mean things were at all easy between them. Beryl gave her a wide berth whenever possible, and considering the nature of her desire to see Simpkins, she was particularly grateful for Beddoes to be elsewhere. After all, it was abundantly clear that the housekeeper's loyalties lay exclusively with Edwina. It would not do for her to overhear what Beryl had in mind. Simpkins looked up from his plate of toast and marmalade and gave her a toothy grin. He wiped his lips with the back of his hand before speaking.

"I'm just trialing the latest offering from Colonel Kimberly's. Grapefruit and ginger it is," he said, holding a piece of toast aloft for her to inspect. "Would you care for a piece?"

As much as Beryl was in the habit of accepting provisions whenever offered—a habit long-standing of her traveling lifestyle, in which one never knew how often a meal would be available—she shook her head firmly. There was no time for such pleasures when an adventure was afoot.

"No, thank you. I'm sneaking off to deal with that errand we discussed. I want to head out before Edwina sees me leave. If she asks, you haven't seen me, all right?" she said.

"You know I make it my policy never to tell untruths to Miss Edwina," Simpkins said, taking another bite of his toast.

"And you know I make it my policy never to mention to her

what you get up to in the potting shed of an afternoon, just you and a hip flask. Neither of us wishes to disabuse Edwina of her belief that you spend your time in there coaxing along new seedlings and sharpening your secateurs, now do we?" Beryl said.

Simpkins drew himself up to his full, lanky height and managed to look offended. "There's no need to take that tone. I won't spill your secret, and I expect you not to spill mine."

"Both of us know the value of not spilling a drop, now, don't we?" Beryl said, giving him the warm smile for which she was justifiably famous. Many's the time she and Simpkins had carefully, one might even say gingerly, managed not to waste a single bit of a flask they passed between the two of them well out of Edwina's sight.

"So, today's the day then, is it?" Simpkins said, clearly not willing to hold a grudge.

"Indeed, it is. And not a moment too soon, I might add. I've been feeling rather restless since we returned from London, and I think this might be just what the doctor ordered."

"Miss Edwina hasn't been herself lately either, now you come to mention it," Simpkins said. "I hope she's not feeling a bit down because of the encroaching winter."

Simpkins had been a part of Edwina's daily life for far longer than Beryl had. As the jobbing gardener who was the son of the previous gardener, he had been raised at The Beeches, Edwina's family home. While he was the same age as Edwina's mother, he had known Edwina for her entire life. During the years when Beryl had been traveling throughout the world on one adventure or another, setting land- and air-speed records, Simpkins had been at The Beeches, with his hobnailed boots firmly planted on his native soil. If anyone would know how shortening lengths of days might affect Edwina, it would be him.

After all, with both of her parents and her brother in their graves, there was no one else who knew her quite so well. An involuntary shudder rose up along Beryl's spine. She hated to consider that her friend might find herself back in the unfortunate state in which she had discovered her almost a year ago. When Beryl had arrived at The Beeches in response to an advertisement for a lodger, she had been shocked at the state of both the house and her old friend. But in the intervening months, both the property and its mistress had come warmly back to life. Beryl thought it likely that her plans would continue to provide a bright spark in both their lives.

"I think it may have a bit more to do with her novel. I haven't heard much in the way of typing lately, and I wonder if she's come to some sort of a crossroads."

"You don't suppose she suffered from some sort of writer's block, do you?" Simpkins asked.

Beryl shrugged her broad shoulders. "I really couldn't say. All I know is the sound of typing has entirely vanished over the last couple of days. And she's been wandering about, looking somewhat far away. But as she isn't actually off the premises, I need to skedaddle before she starts asking questions. Remember what I said—not a word."

Simpkins nodded and raised a piece of toast in a sort of salute. Through the kitchen window, Beryl caught sight of Beddoes heading toward her, a wicker laundry basket balanced on her slim hip. She turned on her heel and hurried off to the front hallway before either the maid or her friend could catch her.

Chapter 2

Edwina collected her best hat from the hall tree and arranged it carefully on her head. Her manuscript, wrapped carefully in brown paper and twine, was secreted down into the bottom of her market basket. No one would pay any attention to her parcel as she made her way toward the post office. She had been relieved not to encounter Beryl as she returned from the garden, finally resolved upon heading for the post.

Her little dog, Crumpet, gazed up at her with a look of expectation as she turned away from the hall tree and took up her basket. She considered whether or not she would be best served allowing him to accompany her. Generally, she found his companionship very welcome, and indeed distracting, if she had troubles on her mind. That said, she didn't particularly wish to think of her novel as any sort of trouble. And she did think it possible that she might wish to make a quicker escape than was possible when encumbered by a curious and constantly sniffing dog. She determined to make it up to him on a walk later in the day, and steeling herself against his recriminating glances, she told him to stay.

The walk into the village did not take very long, especially when she was not accompanied by Crumpet's constant insistence on stopping every few feet to investigate. In almost too little time, she found herself within sight of the post office. Her stomach trembled with nerves as she considered the barrage of enquiries, she was certain Prudence Rathbone, the postmistress, would feel duty bound to make. As the most confirmed gossip in the village of Walmsley Parva, Prudence would be certain to make much of the address on the parcel. It wasn't as though Edwina could simply slip it into the drop box. No, such a thing would need to be weighed and the postage calculated. In order for that to be done, the address would have to be noted.

Confronted with that reality, she felt unequal to the challenge. The gravitational pull of a fortifying cup of tea was impossible to resist. Almost without thinking to do so, her feet carried her toward the door of the Silver Spoon Tea Room, and before she could stop herself, she pushed open the door and stepped inside the cheerful space. Minnie Mumford, the proprietress, glanced up from her task of placing a towering tray of freshly baked scones and tiny tea sandwiches in front of an unfamiliar woman. Edwina could smell the aroma of the scones from the doorway. Her stomach gave a loud rumble, and she realized, with a start, that she had not bothered to partake of any breakfast. She glanced at the clock on the wall and realized it was almost eleven. The perfect time to tuck into a bit of a meal, even if one was suffering from a nervous tummy.

"Good morning, Edwina. It's good to see you," Minnie said, as though they did not find themselves on committees and organizations together several times a week. It must be the stranger who was responsible for Minnie's excess friendliness. Not that the owner of the tea room was ever anything but pleasant and welcoming. How could she remain in business if she were not? After all, unlike the post office, one did not absolutely need a tea room. No, Minnie was always amiable. Edwina gave the stranger a second glance.

"Likewise, Minnie. Those scones certainly look good this morning," Edwina said. "Although, to tell the truth, yours always do," she said. Minnie gave the briefest of nods, as if in gratitude for Edwina's endorsement.

"How kind of you to say," Minnie said. She turned to include the other woman in the conversation. "Please allow me to introduce Miss Maude Dinsdale. She has recently moved to the village."

The woman looked up at Edwina appraisingly. Apparently satisfied with what she saw, she nodded her head and gave Edwina a polite smile. The woman appeared to be of average height and build, with mousy-brown, slightly graying hair and a gently softened jawline. Edwina would put her at approximately forty-five to fifty years of age and possessed of an altogether unremarkable demeanor. Her dress was conservative, if not slightly outdated, and in no way designed to attract particular notice: a serviceable navy-blue blouse and matching long skirt, from what Edwina could make out as the other woman sat with her legs tucked beneath her at one of the many small tables clustered about the tea room. Sensible shoes with a high degree of polish clad her feet, and she sat with her ankles neatly crossed. Upon her head was a modest but flattering hat that Edwina took particular note of, being a millinery enthusiast herself.

"It's nice to meet you, Miss Dinsdale. I'm Edwina Davenport. It's always a pleasure to welcome newcomers to the village," she said.

"How kind of you. And, please, call me Maude. Would you be willing to join me?" Maude said. "Minnie has been telling me all about you."

While Edwina felt slightly taken aback by Maude's statement, it should not truly have come as a surprise. While Prudence Rathbone was the most determined gossip in the village, Minnie Mumford came in a close second. That said, Prudence's inclination was to spread the most titillating and unflattering bits of information between villagers. Minnie simply liked to know what was going on and had no real interest in making anyone out to be a bad sort. Edwina was quite sure that anything Minnie had disclosed about her would not be unflattering or embarrassing in any way.

"It would be a pleasure," Edwina said, as she pulled out one of the chairs at Maude's table and settled herself in it. She drew off her gloves and placed them in her market basket before tucking it and her precious parcel close by her chair on the floor.

Edwina ordered a pot of tea as well as a plate of scones and sandwiches of her own. Her stomach rumbled again, and she hoped it was not loud enough for her dining companion to hear.

"Minnie tells me that you are a private-enquiry agent," Maude said, a note of awe tinging her voice.

Edwina still felt a jolt of pride every time she was able to acquiesce that that was indeed the case. It had only been a few months since Beryl had wended her way back into Edwina's life, bringing with her an air of excitement and a sense of adventure. With her friend's urging and the convergence of circumstance, Edwina had found her life transformed from that of a quiet country spinster into a detective with a growing business and track record of success. It hardly seemed possible that, in so little time, her life would be so completely transformed, but indeed it had. She sneaked a quick glance at the basket by her feet and wondered how much more her life might expand should her novel become published. She glanced back up at her companion and nodded.

"That's right. I run an agency with my dear friend, Beryl

Helliwell. And what is it that brings you to Walmsley Parva?" she asked.

Before the woman could answer herself, Minnie piped up. She plopped the plate of scones and sandwiches onto the table in front of Edwina before speaking. "She's a psychic medium, here to refresh herself from her recent activities in London," she said almost breathlessly.

Whatever Edwina had expected Minnie to say, a psychic medium was the farthest from her thoughts. Edwina did not hold with such things herself, in particular, and had recently been put off from that notion altogether by the discomfort such activities had brought to an old friend. The cook at the finishing school Beryl and Edwina had attended as young girls, and where they, in fact, had first become acquainted, had found herself regretting her decision to employ a psychic medium in the hopes of contacting her dearly departed grandson, one of the many unfortunate casualties of the Great War.

No, Edwina was not as enchanted as Minnie by the notion of a psychic medium in their midst. Still, it would not do to appear unwelcoming to a new neighbor. And perhaps the woman was not truly a charlatan but rather a misguided individual who was eager to provide comfort to the bereaved.

"How did you come to choose our little village?" Edwina asked. She loved Walmsley Parva with all her heart, but even she had to admit it was not a place well known across the country.

"I met Hazel Moffat whilst we were both on holiday in Bournemouth a few weeks ago, and she spoke so highly of Walmsley Parva that I determined it was just the sort of place I had been looking for after spending several years moving about from pillar to post."

"Maude has consented to offer séances now that she is here," Minnie said.

"Really?" Edwina said, hoping that her voice betrayed none of her skepticism.

"Are you familiar with the world of spirit?" Maude asked.

"I'm afraid that is outside of my purview. I tend to be one who feels more in step with the world of the living," Edwina said. Which was entirely true. While she prided herself on her imagination when it came to the creation of her novel, in her day-to-day life, she preferred to be more firmly rooted in the practical. In fact, her sensible nature and interest in the truth had led to her being offered the position of local magistrate. It was a duty she undertook with a strong sense of purpose. She could not imagine weighing up psychic evidence in a court of law.

From the eager look on Minnie Mumford's face, it would not seem that the tea-shop owner shared her view on such things. In fact, Minnie took it upon herself to pull out a third chair at the table and to sit herself down beside them. Over the next few minutes, as Edwina attended to her rumbling stomach, Minnie peppered Maude with question after question about séances she had conducted and spirits she had encountered. Before long, the poor woman looked as though she was ready to flee. Edwina found herself feeling rather sorry for her.

Any attempts on Maude's part to steer the conversation into other realms were roundly thwarted by Minnie, who could not be dissuaded from her enthusiasm for all things otherworldly. By the time Maude had drained the last drop of tea from her cup she was casting furtive glances at the door. Edwina took pity on her and removed her serviette from her lap and placed it on the table in the universal sign of completion.

"Maude, have you visited the local post office to set up your new address?" she asked, arching one eyebrow high enough to indicate conspiracy.

Maude was capable of taking a hint. She placed her own serviette across her plate and pushed back her chair. "I entirely forget to take care of that bit of business. Would you be able to direct me to the post office?" she asked.

"I'm just heading there myself." She gestured toward Minnie

as she rose and grasped the handle of her basket. "Minnie, please put this on my account, and I'll settle up with you later." Before she could convince herself to back out of it, she hurried toward the door and off in the direction of Prudence and the post office, with Maude in tow.

The post office stood almost too close to the Silver Spoon Tea Room for Edwina's liking. Her basket felt heavier with each step that she took, and she shot glances toward the discreetly covered parcel again and again as she and Maude made their way along the pavement. Edwina regretted leaving Crumpet at home. Her little dog could always be counted on as a distraction. His exuberance and enthusiasm for walking, as well as his indefatigable interest in investigating whatever happened to be along their path, took up much of her attention when they went out together. Left with only gentle nattering from Maude Dinsdale and the rapidly approaching post office, Edwina's thoughts churned in her head almost as quickly as the sandwiches in her stomach. She deeply regretted having consumed anything as she laid a slim hand on the post office's doorknob and encouraged herself to turn it.

Maude was close on her heels, and there was no chance of turning back without being forced into a clumsy sort of lie. How foolishly she was behaving, she told herself, as she lifted her chin and turned the knob. Prudence was an unrelenting nosy parker, but Edwina did not let her fear of the other woman's inquisitive nature hold her back from attaining her goal. That said, she was grateful for the way in which Prudence swiftly turned her gaze from Edwina's familiar form to the novelty that was Maude.

"Good morning, Edwina. Who is this that you've got along with you?" Prudence asked, widening her thin lips into a broad smile and exposing her large teeth.

"This is Miss Maude Dinsdale, recently moved to Walmsley

Parva. I told her you would be happy to assist her in having her post routed to her residence here in the village."

Prudence looked Maude up and down and seemed favorably impressed by what she saw. While Prudence was someone who feasted on novelty, she also seemed soothed by those who met her expectations. A woman of the age Maude appeared to be, and as yet unmarried, should be a homely sort of woman. Not for her should there be modern hairstyles or the latest fashions from London and Paris. Her shoes should be the sensible sort, just such as those that Maude had upon her feet. Even her demeanor, friendly but not overly so, would have tallied with Prudence's expectations. Edwina hoped that Maude would not regale the other woman with a description of her occupation before Edwina had managed to slip out the door. After all, she had had quite enough of it during their impromptu meal together.

"I'd be more than happy to take care of that for you. If you'll just come this way," Prudence said, gesturing toward the counter located next to a glass case filled with confections. The post office served as a stationery and sweet shop, in addition to handling the post and selling stamps. It was a business started by Prudence's parents, and she had presided over it single-handedly for many years.

"I should like to take a look around the shop first, if I may," Maude said, swiveling her head to take in the vast quantity of merchandise. "Everything is so pleasantly displayed and appealing."

Edwina thought, to her surprise, that Prudence's cheeks had taken on a rosy hue. Of course, the postmistress was no more immune to compliments than was anyone else, especially if they were so well deserved, but Edwina could not remember another time when she had detected such a reaction. Perhaps, Edwina thought to her chagrin, Prudence was so rarely in receipt of positive comments that she did not know how to handle them. In fact, Edwina thought, she could not remember the last time she had dealt one out to the other woman. Prudence was not someone she found it easy to warm to, despite their many years of acquaintance. Perhaps it was those numerous years that had caused it to be all the more difficult. After all, theirs was a history that did not lend itself toward fond memories.

Edwina's mind drifted back to the weeks before Beryl had arrived and the constant prying Prudence had made into Edwina's financial situation. It had been amongst the most unpleasant times of her life, and Prudence had been largely to blame for her discomfort. It was bad enough not knowing where the money to pay off one's debts might come from. It was far worse to have such speculations spoken aloud by a neighbor to everyone within earshot. Just the thought of Prudence's reaction to her desperation left her feeling filled with steely resolve. She carried her basket to the counter next to the brass till with surer footsteps than she would have expected.

"I'd like to send a parcel while you have a moment," Edwina said, hoping her voice did not tremble.

Prudence hurried to the proprietress's side of the counter and positioned herself directly in front of the basket. Edwina lifted the parcel from its depths and placed it on the counter between them. She hooked the handle of the basket over her forearm in a pretext of avoiding seeing the expression on Prudence's face. When she glanced back up, the remnants of the postmistress's surprise remained as firmly fixed on her features as one of the many postal stamps placed on outgoing mail.

Prudence tapped a long, bony finger on the address printed clearly on the brown paper. She clucked her tongue loudly, which Edwina took to be a measure of the other woman's astonishment. Generally, Prudence managed to keep her tut-tutting to herself. As Edwina watched Prudence from behind lowered eyelids, she was surprised to see the other woman shifting from one foot to the other in her excitement, like a small child waiting to be allowed an iced lolly or a piece of taffy.

"Thornsby and Laughton, Publishers," Prudence read aloud as she dragged her finger across the address. At least, Edwina thought, it was legible. She had been concerned her hand had not been steady as she'd printed it on the brown paper. "Now what in the world could you be sending there?"

"I'm sure you must realize that, given my dual roles as a private-enquiry agent and the local magistrate, there are many things I cannot discuss publicly," Edwina said, surprising herself at how quickly the possible explanation for her parcel tripped off her tongue. She wished she'd thought of it as she had headed out of the house that morning. It would have saved her so much agony as she made her way to the post office.

Prudence fixed a gimlet eye on Edwina's face. For a heart-juddering moment, Edwina thought Prudence would outright accuse her of fibbing. But the other woman simply raised one eyebrow higher than the other and tapped the address with her finger once more. It was as though she was willing the parcel to tell her all its secrets.

"I suppose that means we have much in common. I am duty-bound not to divulge the information that comes across my counter either," Prudence said with a conspiratorial wink. It was all Edwina could do not to burst out giggling. The notion that Prudence ever prioritized keeping what she knew to herself was enough to leave her rolling on the floor. She could hardly wait to discuss it with Beryl.

"I see we understand each other completely," Edwina said. "If you would be so kind as to put the cost of postage on my account, I would appreciate it." Then, with a curt nod to Prudence and a cheery wave to Maude, she made her way to the door, feeling far better than she had when she entered. Now if only she could keep herself from worrying about whether or not the parcel would arrive undamaged and how it would be received.

As she continued along the pavement, she spotted Jack, the newsboy, shouting about his wares and waving a newspaper above his head in his customary style. She advanced quickly toward him with every intention of purchasing a newspaper. After all, she did like to support the boy's ambitions, and she knew his family could use every penny of his earnings. She swiftly exchanged a few coins for the latest addition of a London newspaper. In giant letters above the fold appeared the headline announcing the most recent developments in a military airplane disaster, the investigation of which had been ongoing. A shudder ran through her body as she remembered the appearance of an airplane during a case she and Beryl had solved recently. She folded the newspaper neatly in half so as to shield the headline from her vision and tucked it down into her market basket.

Chapter 3

She had taken the train, a form of conveyance she usually avoided at all costs. After all, as a world-renowned racer, Beryl did not prefer to leave to others the piloting of any vehicle in which she found herself. She had no confidence that there were many people more competent to be in charge of any form of vehicle than was she and thus disliked the role of passenger. In fact, it was one of the few experiences that unnerved her. She wished there had been some way to achieve her aim by using her beloved motorcar, but the train simply was the most practical. An involuntary shudder slithered up her spine as she considered that she might just be turning into the sort of person who made decisions based on what could be considered sensible. It was a good thing that she had this particular errand to run, despite her discomfort.

Still, the ordeal would be worth it. She had only a few miles to travel, after all, and the prize at the end of the journey was well worth such a brief tribulation. She entertained herself by watching the quintessential English countryside through the window of her first-class coach and imagined how Edwina would react to her errand.

*   *   *

In less time than Beryl had feared it would take, the train slowed, then came to a stop. Outside the station, only a few people milled about, either waiting to board or expecting to meet an arrival. She hurried to the door as soon as it opened and strode out onto the platform. Up ahead, the dark head of Desmond Montrose towered above most of the other people moving to and fro about the platform. His face broke into a wide smile as she made her way toward him with eager footsteps.

"I don't suppose you would like to find a bite to eat before I take you to her, would you?" Desmond asked.

She hooked her arm through his own.

"I've no interest whatsoever in food, and you well know it," she said. "You have always been the most tremendous tease."

"Guilty as charged," he said, clasping her hand with his free one. He steered her toward an awaiting motorcar, almost as lovely as her own, and settled her into the passenger seat. She tried not to grind her teeth as she once again took on the role of passenger rather than pilot. That said, Desmond was a more than capable driver, and she found herself admiring the way his strong, long fingers wrapped the steering wheel. Part of her wondered if she ought to have accepted his offer of a meal together. Perhaps they might have rekindled some sparks of interest from their youth.

But although she was very fond of handsome men, they couldn't hold a candle to her true purpose that day. Desmond leaned forward as they approached an open field, and as they crested a low hill, it came into sight. Beryl's heart raced in her chest, and her hand was on the door handle even before Desmond brought the motorcar to a complete stop. She turned toward her companion before pushing the door open.

"This isn't some sort of elaborate prank, is it?" Beryl said. "If it is, I shall never forgive you."

Desmond shook his head slowly. "It most assuredly is not. After all you and Edwina did for my company back in London, it's the least that I could do."

With that, he pushed open his own door and retrieved a bag from the back seat of the motorcar. They both stepped onto the field, with its closely cropped grass. Beryl forced herself not to break into a run as she approached her heart's desire. There, gleaming in the morning sun, sat a brand-spanking-new airplane. With its two seats, one behind the other, trim shape, and bright red paint job, she could already imagine cutting quite a dash while soaring over the hills and fields of Walmsley Parva and the surrounding countryside. It had been far too long since she had been aloft, and her hands itched to get at the controls without delay.

"I suppose you know how to operate it without any further instructions from me," Desmond said.

"I should be very disappointed in myself if I didn't," Beryl said. Desmond helped hand her up into the cockpit, then offered her the bag he had retrieved from the back seat of the motorcar. "What's this then?"

"Look inside and see for yourself."

She followed his instructions and slid her hand deep into the paper bag and retrieved a jaunty leather aviator's helmet from its depths. It was dyed in the most exquisite shade of bright red to match the plane. In fact, it matched her red silk aviator's scarf as well.

"It's simply divine," she said as she settled it firmly upon her head, tucking her hair back and covering her ears with the flaps on its sides. "It's enough to make Edwina jealous. She's always been one for a beautiful hat."

"I had heard as much from Miss DuPont. Perhaps you ought to take another look inside the bag," Desmond said.

Beryl reached back into the depths of the bag and pulled out a cobalt-blue aviator helmet that precisely matched her own. It would suit Edwina's coloring and personality to a T. It might even be enough to persuade her far-from-adventurous friend to go for a ride in their new acquisition.

"She will absolutely adore it, even if she refuses to wear it any higher up than the second floor of The Beeches," Beryl said. She placed it back inside the bag and secured it beneath her seat. "Now, if you won't think me terribly rude for cutting things short, I simply must take this beauty out for a spin."

Desmond backed away and stood waving as she started up the motor and began trundling along the field, gaining speed in preparation for takeoff. She felt the familiar dip and lift of her heart along with her stomach as the wheels left the ground, and suddenly, she found herself aloft.

In the months since she had arrived in Walmsley Parva, her life had taken on a far different character than any of her preceding years. With the gentle undulations of daily life in a small village, Beryl had found herself easing into what had become a familiar routine. She had never experienced something quite like it before, and while she had come to appreciate how much value there was in being someone who was part of the community, she had sorely missed the more unpredictable aspects of her days as a celebrated adventuress. Or perhaps that was not precisely correct. She had missed the surge of adrenaline that went with pushing a vehicle to great rates of speed or careening around hairpin turns up and down steep mountainsides.

But, in reality, she had experienced a great deal of adventure while becoming a regular fixture of village life. Her venture with Edwina in creating a private-enquiry agency had proven one of the most adventurous things she had ever undertaken. The thrill of the chase and helping to make a lasting result for someone else had proven surprisingly satisfying. Although it surprised her to say it, she wouldn't trade her life in quiet Walmsley Parva for all the exotic adventures in the world.

But it did her heart enormous good to view the Kentish

countryside from above. With its rolling fertile fields and orchards, it presented a chocolate-box-pretty sort of perfection, especially when viewed from above. The hedgerows dividing fields one from another and clustering groups of cows or sheep looked picture-book quaint from so great a height. Any of the unpleasantnesses of reality were blurred, and all appeared in order. As she drew closer and closer to her destination, her excitement grew.

While she was certain Edwina would not warm immediately to the idea of owning an airplane, she thought it likely would grow on her, just as so many other things had done of late. It truly was remarkable how much Edwina had come into her own since Beryl had arrived, just under a year previously. As she circled the village green, spiraling ever closer to the duck pond, Beryl recognized the faces of Walmsley Parva residents looking up at her in shock. As she made her final descent and roared along the turf, coming to a neat stop just before splashing into the pond, she locked eyes with her friend Edwina, whose look of shock was more extreme than she would have predicted.

Suddenly, above her head, she heard a loud droning noise. Her heart thumped loudly in her chest as she glanced up at an object in the sky, just above the village green. Edwina could not quite believe her eyes. Surely that could not be Beryl screeching to a stop ensconced in an airplane. It had been one thing to endure such a shock from the likes of Desmond Montrose. It was quite another to endure it from Beryl herself. Edwina knew full well that Beryl was an accomplished aviator. After all, Edwina had created an entire scrapbook with clippings of her feats of derring-do, including those in an airplane. But there was something quite different in seeing Beryl's antics with her own two eyes, rather than through the much-less-overwhelming manner that was a newspaper clipping.

It had not helped matters that Beryl had flown the plane in dramatic loops before landing and skittering to a stop next to the millpond. Adding to that was the headline in the newspaper Edwina had hardly been able to bring herself to read. If members of the military could be involved in such a tragic disaster, could not the same sort of thing happen to her dear friend? It didn't bear considering. Her legs felt as though they had turned to aspic as she wobbled toward the now-silent airplane. Beryl sprang from the cockpit and landed with a surprising amount of grace, considering the age of her knees and ankles, an enormous smile spread across her face.

"So, what do you think, Ed?" Beryl asked, spreading her arms out expansively and gesturing toward the airplane. "Isn't she a beauty?"

"How in the world did you come to be in possession of such a thing?" Edwina asked. She could not bring herself to admire the airplane, despite its neat appearance and gleaming red finish.

"It was a gift from Desmond Montrose. Think of it as a sort of thank-you for the help we gave him last month in London," Beryl said.

Her heart raced. It was one thing to imagine Beryl with the temporary use of someone else's airplane. It was quite another to consider it would be available to her on a permanent basis. There would be no end to the worrying.

"But where will you keep it?" Edwina asked, her voice beginning to squeak with anxiety. She could not stomach the thought of such a contraption being parked anywhere on the grounds of The Beeches. Every time Beryl would prepare to take off or land, the damage to the gardens would be unthinkable.

"I'm sure something will be sorted out. So, are you ready to take a ride in it yourself?" Beryl asked, taking a step toward her. Edwina backed away, holding her hands out in front of her defensively.

"Certainly not."

"It's as much yours as it is mine, after all. I didn't solve that mystery by myself, and Desmond wished to thank us both."

"I'd rather he had thought of something more suitable, like a bicycle for you so that we could have gone out riding together," Edwina said. For all Beryl's love of things with wheels, she never did seem to warm to cycling and left it exclusively within Edwina's purview. Edwina uncharitably considered that it must have more to do with Beryl's dislike of rigorous exercise when she could make her way through the use of the combustion engine.

"It's a very generous gift, and there's one more thing that perhaps will convince you," Beryl said, extending a paper bag toward Edwina. "Go on, look inside."

Edwina took the proffered package and peered inside it. For all she knew, Desmond had offered a snake along with the airplane, and there was no way she intended to place her hand in the depths without checking first. But there, in the bottom of the bag, sat an intriguing object. She pulled it out and looked it over carefully. She glanced up at Beryl, who tapped herself on the head.

"Is this an aviator's helmet?" Edwina asked.

"Exactly. It's just the same as mine, except for the color. Wasn't that thoughtful of him?"

Despite her disinclination to take to the skies, Edwina had to admit the helmet was charming. Crafted of supple leather and dyed a cobalt blue, it was unlike anything she had ever placed on her head before. She could imagine herself striding along the streets of Walmsley Parva cutting quite a dash in some sort of jaunty trousers, a jacket with multiple pockets, and the helmet firmly in place. Still, there was nothing to say she could not wear it whenever she chose, regardless of her intentions of climbing into the airplane. She would have to write a note of thanks to Desmond. As Beryl said, it was very generous, and there was nothing Edwina delighted in more than a new hat, unless it was a new skein of wool for a knitting project.

The entire matter had rattled her more than she cared to admit. She certainly did not wish to feel pressured into climbing into that plane, charming helmet or no charming helmet. There was only one thing to do to soothe her nerves and to avoid an uncomfortable conversation with her friend. She thrust the helmet back into the bag and passed it to Beryl.

"This is not a matter which brings out spontaneity in me. I'm going to the Woolery, and I'm not sure when I'll return," Edwina said, turning on her heel and crossing the village green with as much dignity as she could muster, given the fact that the adrenaline which had washed through her body seemed to be easing off and leaving her weak and trembling. Her market basket still held the newspaper, and every time she glanced downward, she was confronted by the thought of the terrible plane crash that had claimed the lives of so many.

She could hear Beryl calling out for her from behind, but she did not slow her footsteps. It was unlikely Beryl would follow her to the Woolery. She was not known for her pleasure in shopping in general, but she found the yarn shop especially tedious. The notion that someone might spend so much time producing an item that could be simply purchased at a shop in a finished state made no sense to her whatsoever.

By the time she reached the familiar entrance to the shop, the strength had returned to her limbs. She mounted the single step up to the door and pushed it open firmly. As she stepped into the cozy space, she felt her heart rate begin to slow. The baskets overflowing with plump skeins of soft wool drew her toward them like a magnet. She plunged her small hands into the nearest container and pulled out a ball of luscious periwinkle angora. She rubbed it against her cheek and sighed deeply. From the other end of the store, she heard the sound of footsteps.

"Good morning, Edwina," Phyllis Linton said. "I had the

same reaction to that very yarn." Phyllis, a trim, quiet woman in her thirties, had moved to the village a few weeks earlier. She and her husband were amongst the dozen or so new faces to appear in the village after armistice was declared. Edwina was not sure what had brought so many newcomers, but she suspected it was a desire for a bit of peace and quiet after so many years of chaos. And who was she to blame them for finding her beloved village charming enough to stay.

Not that everyone did so. There had been quite a lot of turnover of people from the larger cities thinking they would enjoy country life who found out rather quickly they did not. After all, the Silver Spoon Tea Room, as nice an establishment as it was, was the only restaurant in town other than the pub. There were no theaters, only one cinema, and the small number of shops, while sufficient for her own needs, by and large, did not dazzle those persons who were far more accustomed to shopping in the far more impressive department stores of London.

But Phyllis was one of those who seemed to think village life suited her. She had not proven to be much of a joiner thus far, but Edwina held out hope that after she had been there long enough, she would find her own niche in the Women's Institute, the church fete committee, or even the choir. After all, one of the benefits of village life was that one got to know one's neighbors.

"It is quite beautiful, although I'm not sure what I would make with it," Edwina said, placing the skein back in the basket with some reluctance.

"I expect it would make up into a very fetching hat," Phyllis said.

"You know, I believe you're right," Edwina said, reaching for the skein once more. She checked the tag and realized she would need at least two in order to complete the project. Before she could decide, Mrs. Dumbarton, the proprietress of the

Woolery, emerged from the back room with a carton filled with more yarn. She greeted Edwina as she placed it on a large table that filled the center of the room.

"Well, let's see if there is something in here that will take your mind off your troubles, Phyllis. I just received a shipment from a yarn merchant to the north, and I would have to say it's amongst some of the finest wool I've ever gotten my hands on," Mrs. Dumbarton said.

Edwina wondered what sort of troubles Phyllis might need her mind distracted from. She had not heard any rumors about town concerning the Lintons. Not that Edwina participated in gossip as a habit, but in her role as magistrate and as a private-enquiry agent, she often needed to have her ear to the ground as to the goings-on amongst her fellow villagers. The Lintons kept mostly to themselves and seemed to be upstanding persons. She would hate to think that something unfortunate had befallen them.

Phyllis inched toward the table, as if willing to keep her emotions in check. She lifted from the carton a russet-colored ball of heathered yarn, just the sort that would make a very dependable jumper for years to come. The color would suit the younger woman admirably. With her auburn hair and slight smattering of freckles, it would prove very flattering.

"A new project is just what I need," Phyllis said, rubbing her thumb back and forth across the yarn.

"Well, of course, it is. After all, with the heartbreak such as yours, an all-encompassing distraction is what's in order," Mrs. Dumbarton said. "I still haven't gotten over the loss of my own dog, and it's been three years, so I can only imagine how terrible you still must be feeling."

Phyllis bobbed her head and burst into tears. Loud, choking sobs wracked her slim frame, and she dropped the ball of yarn and gripped the edge of the table instead. Edwina could hardly believe what she was seeing. No one ever cried in the Woolery.

It was not that sort of place. Although, to be fair, Edwina could well understand why the other woman would be so bereft. She herself pushed away stray thoughts that occurred to her now and again about her own dear dog's age and how many more years they might have together. Mrs. Dumbarton patted Phyllis on the back and stood there beside her until her sobs subsided. Overcome with embarrassment at creating a scene, Phyllis hurriedly asked for a dozen balls of the russet wool to be placed on her account and tucked them one by one into her shopping basket.

As soon as Phyllis was out the door, leaving the bell jangling in her wake, Mrs. Dumbarton shook her head and sighed deeply.

"I didn't mean to set the poor woman off. I only mentioned it as a helpful suggestion."

"I'm sure Phyllis knows you meant no harm. But such things can be so difficult, it's not surprising that she was overwhelmed by emotion," Edwina said. "Do you know what happened to her dog?"

Mrs. Dumbarton shook her head. "I don't know any specifics other than the fact that the poor dear thing passed rather suddenly."

"I haven't heard anything about it, and frankly, I'm rather surprised. After all, I was in the post office this morning, and I would have thought Prudence might have said something." It wasn't like Prudence to miss the teensiest scrap of gossip.

"I don't know that the Lintons have said anything to anyone about it. I only know because Maude Dinsdale told me about it," Mrs. Dumbarton said.

"Are Phyllis and Maude close friends?" Edwina asked.

"Not that I'm aware of. I believe she heard from the dog itself during one of her séances," Mrs. Dumbarton said.

"Did Maude tell you that herself?" Edwina asked.

"I do believe that she did. I must say I was rather impressed by her ability to communicate with not only people but animals too," Mrs. Dumbarton said.

"Was Phyllis attempting to contact her dog?" Edwina asked.

"She wasn't actually there. The dog piped up and complimented Hazel Moffat on the beauty of the grounds at the property the Lintons are renting from her. It was all very moving."

Edwina did not wish to argue with Mrs. Dumbarton on any subject, but certainly not something as likely to cause a rift as a belief in the hereafter. Perhaps it was her own reluctance to be in contact with her own mother after her passing that made her so incredulous. But no matter the reason, she certainly did not wish to leave Mrs. Dumbarton feeling mocked or dismissed. She would keep her opinions on the subject of spiritualism to herself. She redirected the conversation to the quantity of wool required for a floppy tam and was able to exit with her purchase without revisiting the topic.

Chapter 4

Beryl had expected Edwina to take the news poorly, but she had not expected her to be quite so upset. As she watched her friend wobble off toward the Woolery, she regretted springing such an unexpected surprise on someone so unlikely to enjoy such things. Beryl knew that Edwina was not ever a particularly spontaneous person, and she realized that it had been most unkind not to prepare her for something so out of her realm of comfort.

Still, she was determined to make it up to her as soon as her friend calmed down. She promised herself she would refrain from overtly encouraging Edwina to use the airplane. Nor would she even try to insist that Edwina try on the aviator helmet. No, she would wait for her until she reappeared, no matter how long it took. Given Edwina's propensity for feeling every scrap of yarn in the shop, it could prove to be quite some time. She told herself that she would mix up a batch of her bracing gin fizzes as soon as they returned to The Beeches. Nothing put Edwina in a rosy frame of mind like an American-style cocktail.

The only question was where to wait for her friend to exit the yarn shop. She needed to find a spot where she could overlook the High Street with some degree of ease, but she did not wish to stand looking about like some sort of street urchin. Besides, it had been an eventful day, and she wanted to get off her feet. She peeled her aviator's helmet from her head and realized that the perfect option would be to pop into Alma's House of Beauty for a quick bit of attention to her hair. As lovely as her new hat had proved to be, it had done nothing for her appearance once it had been removed. She crossed the street and, after only a few more steps, found herself standing in the entryway of the village's only beauty shop.

Alma Poole had proven to be both a savvy businesswoman and a staunch supporter of women's rights. As soon as the penchant for having one's hair bobbed was confirmed to be more than a passing fancy, Alma had taken herself off to London and learned how best to add the art of haircutting to her other skills. Most women were not enthusiastic about appearing in a barbershop to ask for their hair to be trimmed. Such events were often accompanied by crowds of men jeering as the women sat in amongst them awaiting their turn beneath the shears.

Besides, barbers were not all that interested in hairstyles exclusively meant for women, whereas Alma most certainly was. In short order, she had provided the women of tiny Walmsley Parva with the sort of beauty salon experience one could only expect in a major metropolis. As a result, her business had thrived.

Added to that was the fact that Alma, as part of her good business sense, had come up with the notion of providing a betting pool for the village's women. Men were strictly forbidden from participating, and the bets were laid on far more fascinating things than which cricket team might triumph at a match or which horse would come in first at a given race. Alma's betting pool focused on things like the next local lad to wind up before the magistrate's court or which young lady would be next to marry. Guesses as to the names of eagerly anticipated offspring or the number of arrests Constable Doris Gibbs might make on any given Saturday night were also topics of interest.

When Beryl had first moved to town, she had been surprised to realize her name had cropped up as the favorite, week after week, on the list of who would be next to meet their maker. Truth be told, she had been somewhat chagrined that anyone would expect her to be so incompetent at her exploits as to do herself harm. Over time, she had dropped back down to third or fourth favorite, a sure sign that she had made progress with the locals, in her opinion.

Hattie, the shampoo girl, looked up from where she was sweeping at the far side of the shop when Beryl entered. She raised a finger and then bent to apply herself to a dustpan and broom, sweeping bits of hair into the broad pan. Within only a moment, things were spick-and-span, and Hattie crossed the room to greet her.

"That was you up in the airplane, wasn't it?" Hattie asked.

"It most certainly was," Beryl said. "Which is exactly why I'm here. You can see that, between the wind and my aviator's helmet, the flight didn't do my appearance any good." Beryl raised a broad hand to her head and ran her fingers through her platinum-blonde hair.

"Were you hoping for a shampoo and set?" Hattie asked.

Beryl looked up at the clock hanging on the wall. Surely, Edwina would not exit the Woolery before such treatment could be accomplished. She nodded. "I would need it to be a quick one, but yes, that would be just the thing."

Hattie led her toward the shampoo sink and eased her down into the chair. The cascade of warm water and soapy bubbles drove any strain that Beryl felt straight out of her. By the time

Hattie had ushered her toward the dryer, positioned perfectly in view of the High Street through the plate-glass window, Beryl had started to dismiss the incident with Edwina from her mind. Which was a good thing whenever the young shampoo girl was around. Hattie was inclined to chatter incessantly but was not the sort to fail to notice if her conversational partner was not picking up the other end. After a great number of questions she posed on the subject of airplanes and flying, Beryl was able to change the subject.

"Do you have any interesting plans this week?" Beryl asked, hoping to steer the conversation away from aeronautics. As much as she was enthusiastic on the subject, it wasn't helping her to forget about the shocked look on Edwina's face. The tranquility she had felt in the shampoo sink had faded away once more, and she felt almost desperate to steer the conversation elsewhere.

Hattie, sitting in the chair opposite, leaned forward eagerly. "As a matter of fact, I do. I'm going to a séance hosted by a newcomer to the village, Maude Dinsdale, this week."

Beryl was not entirely sure how to respond. She had often attended séances, as it was all the rage in her social set from time to time. And, as someone who was always up for an adventure and prided herself on having what she considered an open mind, she was eager to take part. That said, she had often left such sessions feeling slightly grumpy and as though her intelligence had been insulted. While some of the mediums she had seen gave a seamless performance and offered a surprising degree of clarity on the other sitters' lives, she could not quite shake a vague sense of distaste.

Then there were the mediums who were almost laughably transparent in their flimflammery. On more than one occasion, she had witnessed the unmasking of a self-proclaimed channel to the spirit world. Still, the look on Hattie's face was not one she wished to wipe away. The girl seemed entirely in earnest about her enthusiasm, and she had given no indication she solicited anyone else's opinion on the subject. Besides, in a small village like Walmsley Parva, such a thing could simply amount to a bit of excitement in an otherwise quiet existence. As long as Hattie was not being milked out of much money, there was probably very little harm in any of it.

"How interesting. Is there anyone in particular with whom you wish to speak?" Beryl asked. She knew from her own experiences how many of Hattie's peers lay in the cold mud in France. She would hardly begrudge the girl a bit of comfort about any lost friends or relations.

"I'm hoping to hear from my sweetheart, Reggie. He was lost in 1917, and I didn't feel like we had the chance to say a proper goodbye," Hattie said.

Beryl wondered if Hattie would become one of the surplus women found on both sides of the Atlantic. Beryl was not sure if it was a blessing or a curse how many women were forced to reconsider their roles as the opportunity for marriage and family was snatched away from them by the double calamities that were the war and the flu epidemic. Beryl had not heard that Hattie was routinely walking out with any young man in the village, and she thought it likely it was not because the girl had no such interest in doing so. She seemed an entirely ordinary sort of young woman, and that would likely include interest in a young man of her own.

"Have you ever been to such a thing before?" Beryl asked. Even if she didn't think it could do much harm, she did feel slightly protective of the girl. After all, she had led quite a sheltered life, and the supposed medium was a veritable stranger to the village.

"No, I haven't. Miss Dinsdale invited me when she came in to get a wash and set of her own just yesterday. I've never considered doing such a thing before this," Hattie said.

"Are you taking anyone with you for moral support?" Beryl asked.

She thought such things were best undertaken with someone

who could place a restraining hand on one's pocketbook, should a request for donations arise, as they invariably did. Hattie's eagerness did not bode well for her ability to fend off such solicitations.

"I never even thought to do such a thing. To tell the truth, I didn't want to mention it to my parents, who wouldn't hold with something they would consider foolishness. I'm not sure my friends would give it much credence either," Hattie said.

"Whenever I go off on a new adventure, I make sure to have all my kit in order and to carefully select my traveling companions. You might wish to do the same," she said.

At the very end of the street, Beryl caught a glimpse of Edwina's familiar figure. Her shoulders had pulled down from around her ears, at least a bit, although she kept glancing upward as if expecting to see another airplane drop down from the sky. Beryl reached her hand out and touched her head. It was still rather damp, but it couldn't be helped. It would be a far better thing to allow her hair to dry out and about in public than it would be to miss the chance to walk back with Edwina.

All at once, Edwina paused. A man standing at a nearby shop had hailed her, and the two appeared engaged in conversation. Beryl did not recognize the gentleman, but Edwina did not seem alarmed. If it took her another five minutes to traverse the street, Beryl's hair would be satisfactorily dry.

Hattie was speaking again. "Miss Dinsdale said that anyone at all was welcome to attend. Perhaps you'd like to join me?" Beryl glanced across at Hattie. She did not particularly wish to be involved with the farce of contacting the dead, and she had no idea what Edwina would have to say about such a thing. Remaining noncommittal was the best course of action. Besides, Edwina was once more moving up the street. Beryl ducked out from under the dryer and stood.

"What a kind invitation. I shall have to consult my diary. When did you say you would be in attendance?"

"Tomorrow at two o'clock. It's my half day."

"I shall consult with Edwina and let you know. Would you please put the wash and set on my account? Edwina is coming up the street, and I need to speak with her before she heads out of the village."

Beryl felt a great need to rush out of the shop, but it was not on account of Edwina. A man in a dark blue suit had crossed the village green and was approaching her airplane.

"There's no need to confirm ahead of time. Just know that you're welcome to be at the old tailor's shop at two o'clock tomorrow afternoon. I hope to see you there."

Chapter 5

Edwina felt the spring returning to her step, although she could not keep herself from glancing furtively up at the sky above the village from time to time. It was almost as though she had developed a nervous twitch. Still, her mind turned just as frequently to the periwinkle-blue angora safely tucked into her market basket. She was already imagining how fetching it would look perched atop her head when she went out for a stroll once the weather finally turned cool. It was the warmest October on record, and if she got moving that very evening, she might well expect to complete a project as small as a woman's beret in only a few evenings' time.

Just thinking about a hat made her remember the blue aviator's helmet Beryl had offered as a bribe toward accepting the horrors of an airplane in their lives. Another shudder wracked her slim frame as she recalled the sight of Beryl turning loops above the village. An accident involving her dearest friend did not bear thinking about.

Up ahead, an unfamiliar man was tacking some sort of notice to a board on the side of the tobacconist's shop. As she drew closer, he stepped back from his handiwork and caught a glimpse of her from the corner of his eye. He turned and offered her a courteous nod. Although they had not been introduced, she felt no compunction at returning his nod. After all, she was a modern sort of woman and did not require a formal introduction by a third party before she could speak to a strange man.

Although, to tell the truth, she had certainly been raised not to allow such overtures on the part of the other sex. Her mother would be turning in her grave to think Edwina might be seen on the High Street chatting casually to a strange man for all the village to see. If anything, that thought caused Edwina to slow her feet even more and to offer the man the barest hint of a smile.

"Good afternoon, miss," the man said. "I don't believe we've had a chance to meet. I'm Arthur Dinsdale."

"I believe I've met your sister, Maude," Edwina said.

"Yes, she's my sister, all right. A lovely girl is Maude. As a matter of fact, it's on her behalf that I'm pinning up these notices," he said, gesturing toward the paper neatly attached to the notice board. Edwina took a step forward and squinted at it. While she didn't like to consider that such a thing might be true, she had noticed her eyesight was becoming a little less sharp than it had been in the past.

There on the notice board in front of her was an advertisement for a series of upcoming séance opportunities offered by Maude. At the very bottom, Edwina could not help but notice there were printed the words CONTRIBUTIONS APPRECIATIVELY ACCEPTED.

"She seemed very pleasant when I met her at the tea room. She was telling me all about your reasons for moving to the village," Edwina said.

"A bit of a fresh start is what we both felt we needed. But, then, doesn't everyone, after all that we've all been through in the last few years?" he asked.

Edwina was not sure she could agree. It never would have

crossed her mind to uproot herself from her beloved village. Although, truth be told, she had been most grateful when Beryl had arrived on her doorstep, bringing along with her a breath of fresh air and new ways of seeing things. She could not claim to have been any more immune to the effects of the war and the following influenza epidemic than anyone else. After all, her mother, who had been an enthusiastic hypochondriac for years, had succumbed to the ravages of the pandemic. And the faces in the village had changed substantially, not by their addition so much as by those who were missing. She could not blame the Dinsdales for wanting to put unhappy memories behind them had they endured such losses themselves. But she would not ask them any such thing. To do so would be seen as rude in the extreme.

"A change of scenery often does the heart good. I understand that you are eager to get stuck right into village life."

"We most certainly are. Maude has always been a social sort, and I'm just happy to go along for the ride. I understand there are any number of things one might get up to in a village even as small as this one," he said.

Edwina was not sure if she was right to bristle. Had he in some way implied that a place like Walmsley Parva would not be able to provide sufficient entertainment to its newcomers or long-term residents alike? The very idea irritated her. After all, between the events at the church, the plentiful country walks, and places to pick fruit or to fish, the bounties of the reading room and the enthusiasm of the various clubs and organizations, Edwina herself did not have time to partake in all the village had to offer, after all these years. Even someone like Beryl had not shown any sign of boredom in the months since she had turned up on Edwina's doorstep. Still, it was always the best course to behave graciously.

"Well, you and your sister are certainly adding one more thing to the local offerings by providing the opportunity to attend a séance. That's not something I ever remember seeing in the village before, at least not with someone who claimed to be a professional medium."

"I see you're not entirely convinced at the notion of contacting the realm of spirit," Arthur said.

"How so?"

"Well, the word *claims* pretty much sums it up, I've found. Have you had no sort of interest in spiritual subjects before now here in the village? I would find that hard to believe, considering how popular such things have been throughout the country and even the world."

"I had not intended to give offense. I just meant that no one else in my experience has claimed any level of professionalism." Edwina hoped that she had softened the blow she had not meant to wield. "We have, of course, had any number of amateurs dabble in such things over the years. We've had many parties with table tipping and the use of the planchette, but I could not say I recall anyone who would feel confident enough to put up a notice as to their services before now."

Arthur seemed mollified, as a broad smile stretched across his face. "You'll have to forgive me if I'm a bit prickly. It just seems that there are so many skeptics in this modern age, and it can wear one down after a while. Maude has such a gift, after all, and it pains me for others not to acknowledge it."

"Then we are most lucky to have both of you in our midst," Edwina said, hoping to have entirely pacified him. It felt a bit like a lie, and she was surprised at how easily it tripped off her tongue. Beryl had had an influence on her usually truthful nature. Still, there was no profit in making a newcomer feel unwelcome, especially one who had done nothing to offend her.

"I hope that means we can count on you to attend a séance very soon." Arthur gave her a slight bow and raised his hand as if to say goodbye.

She was spared the need to reply, and gladly, as she had no

idea if she would be in the least interested in attending a séance. She wasn't quite sure how she felt about such things and was even less convinced after having chatted with Maude in the tea room. Up ahead, she noticed Beryl hurrying across the street and back toward the village green. It would be better to have it out with her on the subject of the airplane sooner rather than later. The bounce had completely drained out of her step as she followed her friend.

Just as Beryl had suspected, the man was headed straight for her airplane. And, as predicted, he had reached out a hand, clearly with the intention to leave his fingerprints all over the shiny finish. She increased the length of her stride and called out to him before he could lay a finger on her newest acquisition. She didn't suspect it likely a stranger would be willing to spend his afternoon buffing it over with a soft cloth.

"May I help you?" she called, as if she were a shopkeeper addressing a potential customer. The man turned and dropped his arm, leaving her sparkling cherry red finish unmarred, at least for the moment. As she drew closer, she spotted a familiar look of recognition crossing the man's face. It was an expression she had seen many times in the past, although, to be honest, it had happened less and less frequently of late.

After all, she had not been featured in the papers for her exploits, at least not those involving feats of derring-do in airplanes or race cars. She had still appeared with some degree of frequency alongside Edwina as that rarest of creatures, the female private-enquiry agent, in no small part by the efforts of her off-again, on-again romantic interest, Archie Harrington.

"Aren't you Beryl Helliwell?" the man asked.

"That's right," she said.

"Is this your airplane?"

"It is indeed. Are you an aeronautic enthusiast?"

"I'm interested in all sorts of machinery, but especially those that can move quickly," he said, beginning to work his way slowly around the plane. "This one appears to be especially attractive."

Beryl was not sure what to make of him. His tone was light and flirtatious, something she had grown used to in her dealings with men, especially when no other women were present. She looked him over carefully, wondering if he might be worth considering for a short-term fling. Although she generally preferred men who were more interesting and unusual in appearance, there was no denying he was a traditionally attractive man, with his wavy, sandy-colored hair and square jaw. His medium build and average height neither intrigued nor repelled her, but he carried himself with a sort of athletic grace that she admired. As she followed him around the plane, she added him to a category in her mind that she called possibilities.

"I happen to think so too. Not only is she nice to look at, but she also handles like a dream."

The man raised one eyebrow and smiled at her. "I expect the same could be said of you."

The man had suddenly slid from the list marked possibilities to one that she thought of as likely. After all, a man who could engage her in playful banter was far more attractive than any physical attribute might suggest. And although she had enjoyed her time in Walmsley Parva, she could not say she had been subjected to generous doses of witty repartee from the male population. In fact, if she were to think seriously on the subject, the closest thing to it that she had encountered from locals involved her frequent verbal jousts with Simpkins. And it had been rather longer than she preferred since her last weekend away with a male companion. She smiled back.

"How perceptive of you," Beryl said. "I'm afraid you have me at a disadvantage, as I have no idea who you are."

"Let me set that to rights." The man extended a hand and grasped Beryl's own firmly, but without the bone-crushing vigor so often displayed by men who found her forays into what they perceived as male territory to be a bit disconcerting. "I'm Anthony Linton. I've recently moved to the village, and frankly I'm surprised to see a woman as celebrated as yourself ensconced in this quiet little backwater."

Out of the corner of her eye, Beryl spotted Edwina making her way along the street. She paused at the tobacconist's shop and appeared to be engaged in conversation with a man standing in front of a notice board. As attractive as Anthony Linton might be, Beryl had no intention of being caught in conversation with a stranger on the subject of any deficiencies in Edwina's beloved village. That would hardly help her to get back on a firm footing with her friend. Before she had arrived in the village herself, Beryl would have understood his sentiments. Now she found them frankly ridiculous after having spent so many months in Walmsley Parva. In fact, if pressed, she would have to admit that the village had provided far more excitement than had any of her globe-trotting adventures. After all, what could be more intriguing than tracking down those intent on criminal activity?

"I have found this village to be a hotbed of intrigue and excitement. Perhaps you will discover it to be so yourself, should you find reason to be here for any length of time," she said.

Anthony gave her a wink. "I may just have done so. Any chance of a ride in your plane?" he asked.

"Perhaps. But there are several people in line ahead of you, so you shall have to wait your turn. Do you plan to be here long?"

He began prowling about the plane once more, bending and leaning close as if to inspect it minutely. She wondered if he were more familiar with airplanes than he had admitted. Since the war began, she had met many people who had unusual knowledge they could not discuss due to the secrets laws. She counted herself amongst them and knew not to pry too closely into such things.

"I hope to be. I've rented a cottage from Hazel Moffat for at least the next few months. If I find village life suits me, I hope to extend my lease indefinitely," he said, straightening up and looking Beryl up and down with a leisurely gaze.

Beryl glanced up to spot Edwina nodding vigorously at the man standing at the tobacconist's shop. As much as it sounded as if Anthony had moved off the subject of the village's deficits, she was not particularly eager to be overheard engaging in any flirtatious banter with him by Edwina. As much as she enjoyed that sort of thing herself, it caused Edwina to squirm with misery every time she witnessed it. Her friend was not exactly prudish, but she had a strong sense of propriety when it came to romantic matters. She seemed to feel they should never be discussed in mixed company, nor should they be witnessed by those not directly involved in them.

Ever since Beryl had arrived in the village, she had been campaigning to convince Edwina of the feelings her long-term friend, Charles Jarvis, held for her. But each time Beryl raised the subject, Edwina pooh-poohed the idea and changed the topic of discussion. Beryl still was not sure whether her friend simply found the entire notion of a romantic entanglement repellent or if she simply had no interest in Charles specifically. Beryl's heart ached for the long-suffering Charles, who attended to Edwina like a courtly knight in a children's fairy tale.

Before Beryl could reply with something suitable, she heard a woman's voice floating toward them. The flirtatious smile slid from Anthony Linton's face, and he took a step backward, placing a decided distance between them. The woman whose voice it had been crossed the village green and came to a stop beside him. She was, Beryl thought, approximately the same age as Anthony and appeared to be of a similar sort. With typical English coloring and an average figure, she would not have stood out in any crowd. That said, she was a pleasant-enough-looking woman, except for the fact that she appeared to have been crying. Her eyes were rimmed red and slightly swollen.

"Have you finished with your errands?" the woman asked. She turned and looked expectantly at Beryl before returning her gaze to Anthony. Beryl was familiar with that look, and so Anthony's next words came as no surprise.

"I was just waiting for you, my dear. Please allow me to introduce my wife, Phyllis," he said, looking at Beryl with no trace of a smile on his face.

The woman crossed her arms over her chest and gave Beryl a curt nod. "And you must be Beryl Helliwell. I had heard a rumor you were living in the village. In fact, it was mentioned as one of the inducements to get us to settle here."

She glanced at her husband with what Beryl would have described as a slightly soured expression. That did it. Beryl was more than happy to enjoy all sorts of unconventional arrangements, romantic or otherwise, but she did have one golden rule. She did not poach married men, at least not without the expressed permission of their wives. And from all appearances, Phyllis Linton would not be interested in granting any such thing. Anthony slid onto another of her mental lists: *Not to be touched with a barge pole.* She had been right not to encourage him to get his fingers all over her plane—or anything else, for that matter.

Edwina had left off her conversation with the man and his notice board, and was making her way steadily up the street. It appeared she had no intention of even glancing toward the village green or the new airplane. If Beryl was to discuss matters with her before returning to The Beeches, she would need to hurry after her. Besides, it gave her the perfect excuse to leave Anthony with his wife. She certainly did not want to stoke any animosity between them.

"It's a pleasure to meet you. I understand you've rented a cottage from Hazel Moffat. I hope you will be very happy here," Beryl said. "If you will excuse me, I need to catch up with my friend."

Edwina's irritation faded. She never stayed angry with Beryl for long. After all, the two of them had been dear friends for decades, and what had Beryl really done wrong except to surprise her? By the time that they had walked the distance from the village center to The Beeches, Edwina was entirely mollified. She even accepted the cobalt-blue aviator's helmet, as a show of reconciliation. She waited until they reached their home to try it on, as she could not bring herself to be seen sporting new headwear for all the village to see without getting a chance to view it for herself. In the hall, they parted ways, and Beryl glanced back over her shoulder, delighted to see Edwina admiring how she looked in the mirror hanging above the entryway table. As she turned this way and that, Beryl thought that, with any luck, she might just be imagining herself climbing up into the airplane and going for a spin.

Chapter 6

Beryl had arisen early enough to join Edwina for a full English breakfast, an unusual state of affairs she hoped would be interpreted as a conciliatory gesture. Simpkins had outdone himself, as he was so wont to do. The dining room table practically groaned under the weight of his travails. Sausages, eggs, grilled tomatoes and mushrooms, two sorts of toast and, horror of horrors, kippers. Beryl would never come to understand any sort of enthusiasm for consuming fish at breakfast, at least not where English was the official language. As broad-minded as she was about so many things, including not turning her nose up at food she did not have to prepare herself, just the sight of a dish of kippers forced a shudder up between her shoulder blades. It was a sight she felt she never would become immune to.

Edwina politely refrained from pointedly commenting on the early hour of Beryl's rising and instead focused on spreading a piece of toast with one of Colonel Kimberly's justifiably famous preserves. As Beryl reached for the pot of Damson plum jam, Crumpet jumped from his place at Edwina's feet below the table and began barking furiously as he raced from the room. Even over the sound of his barking, Beryl could hear the sort of vigorous knocking she always associated with police raids.

She happened to have a great deal of familiarity with such things, as speakeasies had been one of her favorite sorts of haunts before her decision to move to England. After all, the company had been convivial, even if the spirits had been lamentably of the bathtub-gin variety. Edwina lowered her piece of toast and dabbed daintily at the corners of her mouth before Beddoes appeared in the dining room doorway followed by a red-faced Muriel Lowethorpe.

Muriel was looking decidedly poisonous and breathing heavily. It was shocking to witness someone generally possessed of as much self-control as the vicar's wife appearing so emotional. Simpkins scraped back his chair and stood as Muriel entered the room, and Edwina gestured toward one of the empty seats at the table.

"May I offer you a cup of tea or some breakfast?" Edwina asked, darting a glance of concern in Beryl's direction.

Muriel crossed the room in three long strides and yanked the chair offered to her out from under the table with the sort of violence one usually saw displayed toward unwanted weeds in the garden. She sank down into it heavily, as if her effort to arrive had taken a physical toll on her. While Muriel was not one to be a great stickler for manners, at least not when they got in the way of good sense, Beryl was surprised to see her appear so early in the morning. It would be far more likely to find her toiling away at the church, either inside polishing the brasses, bossing the ladies' auxiliary, or browbeating the flower arrangers into taking on more shifts than they would have preferred. She might even be found in the churchyard, applying her strong hands and arms to the aforementioned unwanted weeds clustered about the headstones of the long forgotten.

But to find her paying a call to someone who happened to

still be at the breakfast table seemed extreme, even for Muriel. It certainly felt that way to Beryl, who had yet to even pour herself a cup of coffee, let alone feel the invigorating effects of caffeine flowing through her veins. Still, it must mean something important was afoot, and as Beryl reached for the coffee-pot and held it aloft in silent offer to Muriel, she felt intrigued at what that might be. Muriel shook her head.

"I'm not here for refreshments. I'm here to hire you," Muriel said.

While it should not come as any great surprise that Muriel would have a reason to hire them, considering their very first paid case had come from Muriel's husband, the vicar, Beryl still felt a jolt of surprise. While she would not say that Muriel was far more intelligent than her husband, she did seem to be much more capable of dealing with the vagaries of life and thus unlikely to require their services. It was hard to imagine Muriel being a victim of any sort of crime. She was the type to get to the bottom of it herself, confront the perpetrator, and then bash the culprit on the head with an object she might find close to hand.

"What seems to be the trouble?" Edwina asked, sending Beryl another concerned glance.

Simpkins nudged the plate of sausages in Muriel's direction in a sort of sympathetic gesture. As Muriel did not seem inclined to help herself, Beryl speared one and commenced to tuck in. Whatever the vicar's wife might wish to impart, Beryl was certain it would be best heard on a full stomach. She plucked a piece of toast from the rack and reached for the jam.

"I want you to take on this nonsense concerning Miss Dinsdale and her séances."

"Has she done something to upset you?" Edwina asked.

"I should say that she has. Her devilish mumbo jumbo has cost us the services of our organist."

"How has she managed to do that?" Beryl asked.

She took a sip of her coffee and tried not to pull a face. Simpkins had remarkable skills in the kitchen, but he had still not mastered producing a strong, smooth cup of coffee. His efforts either created pale, watery cups of brew, or something so thick and bitter it put one in mind of creosote coating a chimney. Today's offering was the latter variety. She reached for the sugar bowl, despite her best efforts to adhere to a slimming regime, and stirred in two heaping spoonfuls before adding a generous splash of cream.

"Last night, at the end of choir practice, Hazel announced that Maude had offered her a position as an accompanist on the piano for her séances. When Wilfred heard of this, naturally he was most distressed. He told Hazel that she would have to choose between being the devil's handmaiden at the séances or playing as the church organist."

"I assume that Hazel chose the job with Maude rather than with the church?" Simpkins asked.

Muriel let out a loud grunting noise. "I'm sorry to say that she did. And to make matters worse, she stormed off in a huff, saying she had no interest in even attending the church if that was the way Wilfred was going to be about it. That's not the sort of trend we wish to see continue."

Beryl raised an eyebrow. Edwina's face had grown pale. She toyed with her fork and knife, as if her hands itched for the soothing comfort of her knitting needles. Beryl knew that, in the past, the church had served as the center of village life in Walmsley Parva, just as it had in so many villages and towns across the nation. But as it had done in other arenas, the Great War had ravaged the citizenry's relationship with its houses of worship.

When the decision had been made not to attempt to retrieve bodies of the fallen from the battlefield and return them home for burial, the church had lost its value as a place to honor the dead. With such great numbers of young men cruelly taken from them through violence or by the influenza epidemic, there were fewer marriages to be performed at churches. With fewer marriages, there were fewer births and christenings, and the entire matter had become one of great concern to people who clung to traditional values or those who were amongst the most faithful of the populace. From the way she had spoken of her involvement with the church, Beryl would have assumed Hazel to be a stalwart in the congregation.

"I'm very sorry to hear this," Edwina said.

"Then you will be even more upset to hear this last bit. Despite her claims of disastrous health, Mrs. Corby has volunteered to replace her."

"Surely you're joking," Edwina said. "The few times she filled in for Hazel in the past left some churchgoers with impaired hearing for the rest of the day. You can't possibly be considering her for the position, can you?"

Muriel shrugged her shoulders and sagged back against her chair. "What choice do we have? It's not as though there is anyone else in the village who even knows how to operate the organ. Add to that the fact that it's not in our best interest to continue offending members of the flock at the rapid rate they are scattering."

"But how is it that you think we can help with this matter?" Beryl asked.

"I want you to expose Maude Dinsdale and her brother as the frauds I know them to be. If it comes to light that they are nothing more than charlatans, it is my fervent hope that Hazel will return to us both as a Christian and as a superb organist."

Simpkins helped himself to a heaping serving of kippers and added tomato and mushrooms for good measure. "That she is. Many's the time I've sat through a poor excuse for a film just to listen to her play the accompaniment."

Beryl would have to agree. Hazel volunteered as the church organist, but she worked as the accompaniment to the silent films they showed at the Palais in the village. Oftentimes, in such a small community, the musical accompaniment left a great deal to be desired, but in Walmsley Parva, the cinema experience was first-rate.

"Apparently, that's where Maude first heard her play. You don't think she darkened the door of the church now, do you?" Muriel asked.

Beryl wasn't about to pick an argument with a potential client, let alone a pillar of the community and one who was so distressed. That said, she felt it was unfair for Maude to assume that someone who purported to be a spiritual medium could not also share the vicar's wife's faith. In Beryl's opinion, there was no discordance between those two practices, although she knew that many traditional churchgoers might disagree with her.

She exchanged another glance with Edwina and bobbed her head ever so slightly. Edwina did the same before turning to Muriel. "Of course, we would be happy to investigate, but you must understand that we can only provide you with whatever evidence we turn up. There is no way we can guarantee to expose Maude as a fraud if we discover nothing untoward."

Muriel shoved back her chair and stood. "I'm sure the evidence is there and will be easy enough for a pair of capable detectives like you to find. After all, I don't hold with any of this nonsense that there's any truth to chatting with the dead. I've come away without my chequebook, but I will be happy to pop a retainer into the post this very afternoon."

"You're in as much of a hurry as all that?" Simpkins asked.

"I am if you don't want the already half-empty church pews to be completely devoid of congregants. I would hope you will have results before Sunday morning."

With that, she turned on her heel and strode out the door as quickly as she had entered the room. This time, Crumpet wisely remained beneath the table.

"It's already Tuesday. However, we are expected to deliver results as quickly as that?" Edwina asked.

"Fortunately, while I was waiting for you to visit the Woolery, I stopped into Alma's House of Beauty. Hattie invited me to attend a séance she is going to this afternoon," Beryl said.

Chapter 7

What did one wear to a séance, Edwina wondered, as she stood in front of her armoire, flicking through her wardrobe. She couldn't imagine it required the formality of a funeral, but she did not think that it called for the same degree of respect required for a trip to the butcher or even a W.I. meeting. Finally, she settled on the same skirt and blouse she had worn at the last session she conducted at the magistrate's court. After dabbing her nose with some pressed powder and assuring herself that her sleek bob was in no way disarranged, she headed down the stairs in search of Beryl.

With only half an hour left before the séance was due to start, she found herself agitating to get out the door. While she would not accuse Beryl of being someone with a habit of tardiness, she was always prepared to make up for any wasted time by driving her motorcar. Edwina was not eager to give up the chance for a walk into the village. After all, she frequently found her nerves jangled by Beryl's driving, and she would have to admit she felt vaguely unsettled by the notion of attending a séance.

It wasn't that she had strong feelings, one way or the other, about whether or not it was possible to speak with the dead. It was more the fact that she felt she might be surrounded by true believers when she herself was not one. It left her with a vague sense of disquiet as she considered that the British had a general loathing for intensities when it came to religion. After all, the Reformation might have been centuries past, but it was a lesson hard-won and long remembered. No, the type of fervor associated with spiritualism was not something Edwina was eager to embrace, even if she were to be convinced of its veracity.

Edwina was still choosing which hat to wear when Beryl descended the front staircase looking her most exotic and glamorous. She clearly had had no difficulty in deciding what to wear. A flowing teal silk caftan fluttered behind her as she moved. Upon her head she had wound a matching turban with an ornate jeweled brooch fastened to its front. Edwina felt a surge in her chest and realized she wished she had the sort of personality that would permit her to wear a turban without feeling as though she were attending a fancy-dress ball.

Very little about Beryl's life left her feeling the least bit envious. On the whole, just imagining participating in her jungle treks or motor rallies left Edwina unsettled and faintly nauseated. That said, she did often find herself wistfully viewing Beryl's sangfroid in regard to all forms of headwear.

From miner's helmets to gifts from foreign dignitaries involving quantities of exotic feathers, Beryl wore them all when and where she wished, without the least appearance of self-consciousness. Edwina bit her tongue, turned away from her friend, and plucked her best hat from the hall tree. Surely, she could at least extend herself that far.

Despite any misgivings that Edwina had for motorized transport, she couldn't very well imagine traipsing into the village accompanied by Beryl sporting such an ostentatious outfit. Not that she would ever dream of decreasing her friend's pleasure in whatever it was she chose to wear. She glanced up at the clock placed on the wall and sighed.

"I'm afraid we're running ever so slightly late," she said, tapping her foot impatiently. Crumpet pranced over to inspect the spot on the floor where she had, in his opinion, indicated something he ought to notice.

"We shall have to take the motorcar if you wish to be on time," Beryl said, making an effort to disguise her glee. Clearly, she was still trying to make up to Edwina for the incident with the airplane.

After crouching down to give Crumpet a scratch behind his ears, Edwina followed her friend quickly out the door. While they should have easily made it into the village on foot if they were willing to walk swiftly, Edwina did hate to be late. Once they agreed to look into the matter for Muriel, Edwina had telephoned directly to her friend Charles to invite him to attend the séance as well.

She knew she could always count on his solid good sense and unflappable nature. She thought perhaps it would aid the case to have yet another pair of eyes on Maude as well. If the medium was, in fact, using chicanery to convince her sitters, she would likely be well skilled at doing so. It would not hurt to be able to evaluate her from multiple angles.

They pulled up in front of a building that had previously housed the village tailor shop but had stood vacant since the war. The tailor had been drafted into service and never made it back from the front. It had grieved Edwina no end that such a mild-mannered man had perished so senselessly. It was also a great loss to the community to lose its tailor. Charles had lamented that very fact on more than one occasion. Just as she thought of him, he wandered into view, moving along with his typical loping stride. As she reached for the handle to push open the door of the motorcar, he appeared alongside it and opened it for her, sketching a gallant little bow.

"My, don't you look lovely in your best hat and magisterial ensemble," he said as he straightened up and handed her out onto the curb. He waved a hand in salute to Beryl as well and did credit to his profession by preserving a straight face as she floated into view. The sun winked off the jewel tones of her brooch and momentarily blinded Edwina, who caught the toe of her sensible shoe on an uneven bit of paving stone. She landed heavily against Charles, who reached out a capable arm to save her from a fall.

"You aren't feeling unsteady on account of the upcoming ordeal, are you?" Beryl asked, breezing past.

Edwina shot Charles a grateful smile before following her friend through the door of the shop. She slowed her pace as she tucked her hand into the crook of Charles's elbow. As they entered the transformed space, it took a moment for her eyes to grow accustomed to the gloom. The windows of the shop had featured manikins displaying the tailor's handiwork in many previous incarnations. But now, heavy velvet drapes hung over the glass, blocking out every bit of light. As Edwina squinted, she could make out a table centered in the room, an oil lamp turned down low placed in the center. The pungent odor of lamp oil mingled with some sort of heavy incense, leaving her feeling vaguely nauseated. She was grateful for Charles's arm as she navigated the low light.

As her eyes became adjusted, she could see several figures were already seated around the table. Hattie, the shampoo girl from Alma's, sat beside Mrs. Watkins. Opposite them, she could make out Maude, and nearby sat Mr. Dinsdale, the man she had met pinning up notices. A melancholy tune filled the air, and as Edwina looked for the source of the sound, she spotted Hazel Moffat seated at an upright piano tucked into an alcove at the far side of the room. The pianist gave no indication that she had noticed them, for which Edwina was grateful. There was something disconcerting about seeing the church organist in such surroundings.

"We are so happy to have you join us," Maude said, gesturing toward the empty seats around the table. Beryl sat between Maude and her brother, while Edwina and Charles settled next to each other on the opposite side of the table. If Edwina had had her druthers, she would have arrived even earlier in order to have the pick of the seats. She would have preferred to distribute their points of view more equally around the table. It couldn't be helped, however, without causing some sort of a scene. They would have to do their best with what they had to work with.

"Thank you for allowing us to attend," Beryl said. "Your skills come highly recommended."

"How very kind of you to say. But it has very little to do with me. I am at the disposal of spirit and, of course, my spirit guide, Rosanna," Maude said.

"Do most mediums use a spirit guide?" Mrs. Watkins asked. The older woman had placed her hands on the table in front of her, fingers laced together. Even in the dim light, Edwina could see they were tightly clenched. Mrs. Watkins had tragically lost her daughter the year before in what would turn out to be Beryl and Edwina's first case. The poor woman had never gotten over Polly's death, and the grief was clearly stamped on her features. She had lost at least a stone in the intervening months and had not been a particularly plump woman to begin with. Her clothing hung limply over her frame, and her hair looked as though it could do with some of Hattie's ministrations.

"Many of us do, yes. I feel particularly blessed for mine to be such a helpful and agreeable sort." Maude shifted in her seat and turned toward the bulky item placed on a table pressed against the wall behind her. In front of it sat an ornate dagger and a gaudy metal chalice. They were the sort of things one often found at church jumble sales. Edwina fervently hoped that was not the case, considering their current use. The vicar would be most distressed indeed. She leaned slightly forward, not quite sure she could trust her eyes.

"Rosanna is an Egyptian princess. As soon as I passed her sarcophagus in a specialty shop in Alexandria, I heard her call out to me. We've had a strong connection ever since."

Edwina's stomach gave a lurch. The idea of a mummy speaking out from her own coffin was a grim thought indeed. She could hardly imagine what it would be like to poke about in the village bric-a-brac shop only to hear a disembodied voice calling out from a funereal urn. She did, however, envy, at least theoretically, Maude's trip to Alexandria. While she doubted very much she would enjoy the actual travails that travel involved, part of her longed to visit Egypt and to view its great pyramids and glittering Nile for herself. So often she had read books set in such a romantic place, and she often enjoyed daydreaming about visiting, despite the lack of any real desire to do so. As Edwina studied her, Maude did not seem to be the same sort of extraordinary figure Beryl was. If she could travel to the Middle East, perhaps Edwina might be able to make the journey herself without too much difficulty. After all, if anyone did not know any better and entered the room, they would have assumed that Beryl was the medium rather than Maude.

"Shall you begin, sister dear?" Mr. Dinsdale said, holding his hands out to either side, palms up turned.

"I don't know what I would do without you," Maude said, giving her brother a smile. "Please form a sacred circle by holding hands with those seated on either side of you. I can feel that Rosanna has something important she wishes to impart to us today."

With that, Maude closed her eyes and began to mumble slightly under her breath. Charles grasped Maude's hand with his left and Edwina's with his right. Edwina felt slightly disconcerted to be sitting in the near dark in such close proximity to Charles. She felt even stranger about grasping Mrs. Watkins's hand. It felt bony and brittle, her skin dry and papery. It fluttered like a trapped bird, and Edwina wished she could do something to calm her down without calling attention to doing so.

All at once, Maude's mumblings grew louder and more coherent. Her body began to writhe. A creaking sound filled the air, and Edwina noticed movement from the corner of her eye. The lid of the sarcophagus slowly lifted until it was completely open. To her astonishment, a greenish light seeped from within it. Edwina strained forward to get a better look. Despite the gloom in the room itself, the light emanating from the sarcophagus illuminated what appeared to be a bundled human form. Edwina flinched at the sight of it. Somehow it seemed shockingly disrespectful. She had heard of parties being hosted by well-traveled or well-heeled persons whose main entertainment for the event was a mummy unwrapping, and the very notion of it had turned her stomach. This seemed hardly less vulgar.

Maude's mumbling grew louder, and her thrashing became more intense before she stiffened. She sat bolt upright in her chair and swayed back and forth slightly.

"I see a book. Someone here has literary leanings. Rosanna wants you to know that whatever it is you have aspired to will come to fruition," Maude said.

Edwina felt her whole body quiver. Even with very little lighting, she was certain all eyes had turned toward her, although why she would think anyone besides Beryl and Charles would have an idea of what she had been up to with her book was beyond her. It was utterly irrational, and yet she could not shake the notion that a spotlight was beating down on the top of her head. What was the protocol in a situation such as this?

While she had had some trepidation concerning the content of the séance, it had run toward hearing from her dearly departed mother, not messages concerning her own secret desires. She felt utterly naked and all the more conscious of clasping

Charles's hand in the dark. He gave her hand what was surely meant to be a reassuring squeeze, leaving her feeling all the more uncomfortable. Beryl gave her a brief nod from across the table as if to encourage her to comment, but Edwina found her voice had utterly abandoned her.

The moment passed. Maude slumped back against the back of her chair once more and began to mumble even more slowly and incoherently than she had at first. Mrs. Watkins's hands began shaking violently. Once again, Maude sat upright, and this time, she tugged firmly on Charles's hand. She turned toward him and, in a voice utterly unlike her own, began to speak.

"Rosanna has a message for you from Polly," she said. Mrs. Watkins's hand stilled, and she leaned forward. "She wishes for you, Charles, to take care of her most beloved treasure. She says she knows she can trust you to faithfully fulfill the task without delay."

"Surely that message is for me," Mrs. Watkins said, her voice reaching an octave higher than normal.

Maude turned toward her, as if startled out of communication with her guide. She gave her head a slight shake. "Rosanna insists the message is for Charles."

"But I don't know any one named Polly who has passed on," Charles said, shrugging his shoulders.

"And I'm here with the express purpose of connecting with my daughter named Polly," Mrs. Watkins said.

Maude leaned back against her chair once more and shook her head slowly. "I don't create the messages. Rosanna does. She was most clear about what she had to say. Someone named Polly wishes to entrust something precious to Charles. If you'd like, Mrs. Watkins, we can try to contact your daughter as well."

Mrs. Watkins bobbed her head, and they remained in the circle for what seemed like ages, attempting to contact Polly

Watkins to no avail. By the time the séance had concluded, Edwina's hand ached from Mrs. Watkins's desperate grasp. It had reminded her a great deal of her mother when she had been putting on a performance about her ill health. She would writhe and moan and clench Edwina's hands and arms with a bone-crushing grip. She certainly could not fault Mrs. Watkins for being distressed by her disappointment, however. There seemed something particularly cruel about a message from someone named Polly that was not meant for her. It hadn't been helped by the fact that Charles insisted he had no idea who he might know with that name who had passed. Without warning, the sarcophagus lid slammed shut, blotting out the green light and leaving the room entirely in gloom once more.

Chapter 8

By the time they exited the room, mercifully leaving the heavy scent of incense behind them, Edwina felt thoroughly wrung out. Charles and Beryl stood at the motorcar, discussing events in hushed tones.

"I think it may be quite easy to prove that she's a complete and total fraud," Beryl said. "How could she have gotten the message so wrong about Polly? Even if she knew about a woman in the village with that name who had died, you would've thought she wouldn't have been so sloppy as to direct the message at the wrong party."

"Poor Mrs. Watkins. She was beside herself with agitation," Edwina said, looking over her shoulder to assure herself that the older woman had not yet exited the building. For all she knew, Mrs. Watkins was demanding that Maude continue to attempt to contact her daughter.

"I have to say, I didn't see anything that indicated chicanery," Charles said. "I wasn't particularly impressed by the value of what she had to impart, but I saw nothing overtly fraudulent in the room as far as props and that sort of thing."

"It was all very simple, wasn't it?" Beryl said. "There was very little showmanship to the entire session. I've been to these sorts of things before and found them to be fraught with ectoplasm and disembodied limbs running their hands up and down your legs or pulling your hair. But there was nothing like that in this case, at least not that I noticed."

"I think the only thing worth going for was the news that one of us may soon be a published novelist," Charles said, a teasing lilt threading through his voice.

Edwina's cheeks flamed red, and she did her best not to squirm. Fortunately, she was saved from needing to formulate a reply by Mr. Watkins appearing behind the motorcar. Mr. Watkins closed the gap with a limping gait. Beryl watched as Mrs. Watkins exited the building. Her expression was one of surprise and fear. Her husband raised his voice as soon as he spotted her.

"What is it that you think you're doing participating in such foolishness?" he said, stepping alongside Mrs. Watkins and grabbing her by the arm.

"Harold, please," Mrs. Watkins said, shrinking away from him. He renewed his grip on her arm and gave her a slight shake.

"We talked about this earlier, and I forbade you from coming," he said. "And now here you are, sneaking off and doing it anyway. How do you think that makes me feel? How do you think that makes me look?"

Beryl had no use for men who felt comfortable laying their hands on women, their own wives or otherwise. It was something she had seen in too many places across the globe during the course of her travels, and it never failed to bring out her temper. She was generally an upbeat, live-and-let-live sort of person, but she simply could not let such a thing pass without comment.

"As far as I'm concerned, the only one who's making you look disreputable is you, sir," Beryl said, taking a step toward him.

Without shoes, she would have been approximately his height. Given the fact that she had opted to wear a heeled sandal with her caftan as well as a lofty turban, she towered above him menacingly. Beryl had managed to hold her own against any number of angry and violent men over the years, not the least of which was her first husband. She could not stand to see the pained expression on Mrs. Watkins's face. She well remembered being the young woman who had first encountered such behavior on her honeymoon.

"You can't speak to me that way," Mr. Watkins said, raising his fist even higher. He came within a few inches of Beryl's nose.

"I suggest you desist immediately, Mr. Watkins," Edwina said, taking a step forward. Beryl glanced at Edwina from the corner of her eye. She looked just as she had when they were young girls and Edwina had faced down a bully at their finishing school. She had not grown any less imperious in the intervening years. Even if she had not taken on the job of local magistrate, Beryl thought it likely Harold Watkins would have responded to Edwina's tone of voice. Few people who heard her take on that particular attitude dared to brook her. He dropped his arm and hung his head slightly.

"See, that wasn't so hard now, was it?" Beryl asked.

She immediately spotted the error of her ways. Still, there was something in her that couldn't help but provoke him. She knew she ought to feel some compassion for the man who had lost his daughter and did not wish to revisit that grief through his wife's desire to contact a medium. That said, if he was willing to be so aggressive on the street in full view of the village, what was he up to at home? No, she really ought not to have poked him once again. She thought it possible Mrs. Watkins would be the one to pay once they finally arrived back at their cottage.

"I'm not the only one who's going about causing scenes and looking disreputable, I'll have you know," he said. "Don't think the whole village wasn't yakking about you and your blasted airplane yesterday."

"Harold, you promised that you wouldn't mention that," Mrs. Watkins said, taking a step toward him and patting him on the arm. He shrugged her hand off and scowled.

"I never said any such thing. Your airplane and all its noisy nonsense had my animals all riled up yesterday afternoon and long into the evening. It was a wonder the hens laid any eggs and the milk wasn't curdled when I went to do the milking this morning. I hope you don't plan to make that a habit, because, believe you me, someone will put a stop to it."

"Surely you can't blame problems with your livestock on noise from an airplane," Charles said.

"Is that your legal opinion?" Mr. Watkins asked.

Charles widened his stance and crossed his arms over his chest. "As a matter of fact, it is. If you were to attempt to bring some sort of action against Miss Helliwell, it is my professional opinion that you would have a devil of a time not having the case thrown out of court."

"I suppose it might be, considering she lives with the magistrate," Mr. Watkins said.

Beryl could see that Edwina had taken offense. The back of her neck was growing red, and she opened and closed her lips without any sound coming out. An apology was in order.

"It was not my intention to distress your livestock. I can see how such a thing might be troublesome for them, especially after the war years and all the turmoil airplanes caused at that time. I hope you will accept my apology," Beryl said.

Mr. Watkins harrumphed and turned his back. Mrs. Watkins

hurried after him as quickly as her short legs would carry her. Beryl couldn't help but wonder if the woman was in for a difficult night. She hoped that it would not be so, but she had a sinking feeling there was a menacing element to the Watkinses' marriage.

"Scenes like that don't exactly encourage one to head to the altar, now do they?" Beryl said, turning toward Edwina. Her friend was unsurprisingly silent. Charles dropped his arms away from his chest and spoke.

"I don't know about that. The fact that the Watkinses are still married after what happened with their daughter is practically a miracle. I think it's likely he simply does not wish to open up a barely healed wound by watching his wife attempting to contact Polly. You saw how upset she was during the séance."

Beryl watched as the older couple hurried away, Mrs. Watkins attempting to reach for her husband's arm but being continually shrugged off. She had not thought of them as well suited before his outburst just then. Perhaps his anger was, as was so often the case with men, rooted in fear. Mrs. Watkins had been bitterly disappointed that the message from Polly was not directed at her.

"I'm sure that Maude will come up with something to put her mind at ease before long. Perhaps it's just a ploy to get her to come back and pay once more. She seems like the type of customer who would be easy to keep dangling on the hook for some time."

"Do you think that's what it was about?" Charles asked.

"That would be my guess, having been to more of these types of things than I care to admit. They were all the rage for so long that it seems there was an endless stream of invitations wherever I went for several years in a row. I've seen exactly the situation where a medium whets the appetite of the most eager victim and then keeps them strung along for ages."

"But that is simply dreadful," Edwina said.

"I should say so," Charles said. "Do you think that's what Maude giving me some incomprehensible message was really about?"

Beryl nodded vigorously, feeling her turban wobble slightly as she did so. She raised a hand to steady it. "That's exactly what I think. There shouldn't be too much difficulty to exposing her."

Chapter 9

On the way home, Edwina was far too distracted to comment on Beryl's driving. The entire experience of the séance had been unsettling. As much as she was not inclined to give credence to the supernatural, she could not deny that she hoped Maude had some sort of fortune-telling ability when it came to the success of her novel. It would be comforting if she could believe that the message from the spirit realm were destined to become true.

On the other hand, what had happened with Mrs. Watkins appeared extremely cruel. Edwina could remember distinctly Mrs. Watkins's reaction to her daughter's death. So many of Edwina's acquaintances had placed hope in spiritualists since the war had begun. Edwina could well understand why they would wish to do so. How much comfort would it provide to someone carrying as much grief as Mrs. Watkins to know that her daughter, Polly, was well and happy on the other side of the veil?

It wasn't just the debate about the veracity of Maude's claims that had her feeling uncertain. She could not honestly say she had witnessed anything within the confines of the séance that led her to believe there was any trickery involved. Perhaps one might accuse Maude of playacting and appearing melodramatic as she started in mumbling and writhing. But that wasn't the same as proof of fraudulence, now, was it? She felt less sure that they would be able to get to the bottom of the case than she had in a long time. And as much as she didn't want Mrs. Corby to be in charge of musical accompaniment at the church any longer than necessary, Edwina was not so sure that the case was all that important in the grand scheme of things. After all, she and Beryl had gotten to the bottom of more than one murder since they opened their private-enquiry agency. And while it was true that often they were hired to look into other matters besides murder, this case seemed particularly small potatoes in comparison with some of the others.

Edwina was surprised at her own thoughts. To think that, only a few months previously, she would never have considered herself capable of being any sort of career woman, let alone one who felt herself above taking on certain sorts of assignments. But the truth was, she had come into her own ever since they had started the business, and she was looking at the world through new eyes. If she were to be honest, she would never have considered accepting the case if it had not been brought to them by Muriel. It was almost impossible to resist any sort of pressure from the vicar's wife, but Edwina counted her as a close acquaintance, if not a friend. She would not have wished to be the one to let her down, but given the opportunity, she never would have taken the case in the first place. As if sensing her distress, Beryl let up on the accelerator and glanced over at her.

"What's on your mind, Ed? You've been surprisingly taciturn since we climbed into this old bus," Beryl said.

"I don't feel as clear about this case as usual."

"What do you mean not clear? Does this have anything to do with Maude's assertion that someone in the room has a great literary future in front of them?"

Edwina took a deep breath and exhaled slowly. She still did

not feel ready to disclose to Beryl that she had sent off her manuscript. It was hard enough waiting to hear whether or not she had been rejected without having to share that news with anyone else.

"I suppose Maude mentioning that gave me a bit of a jolt. Do you think she could actually be the real deal?"

Beryl snorted. "I would be very much surprised if she were."

"But how many times have you regaled Simpkins and me with tales of mystical experiences you've had in far-off places? Why is it true that such things can be believed when they happen far from home, but not when they occur in the village?" Edwina shifted in her seat to keep her eyes riveted on Beryl's face. She wondered if there was any chance Beryl felt as conflicted as she.

"It's not so much that I think it impossible that unexplained occurrences could be a part of life here in England. It's more that the experiences I've had in other places have been connected to a community spiritual practice that do not involve the exchange of goods or money," Beryl said.

"So, you think Maude being paid for her time automatically discounts her as a true medium?" Edwina asked.

"I think that if anyone should be being paid for what we experienced, it was Princess Rosanna, not Maude. And besides, whoever heard of an Egyptian princess named Rosanna in the first place?"

Edwina had to concede that Beryl had a point on that subject. She had been surprised herself to hear the name Maude announced for her spirit guide.

"But isn't it possible that the guide gave Maude a name she knew she would be able to understand and to pronounce? After all, Maude speaks English and was not channeling any messages from her guide in a foreign language."

"You're making my point for me. Why didn't an ancient Egyptian princess have trouble communicating in English?"

Edwina felt she had an answer for that one. "Perhaps the afterlife is something like life before the Tower of Babel. Maybe the concept of separate languages is simply erased as soon as one passes to the other side." She rather liked that notion, as she enjoyed the thought of communicating freely with figures from all over the world at a sort of afterlife cocktail party. She would have thought Beryl would like the notion too.

Beryl snorted once more. "For such a sensible woman, I am rather surprised at you, Ed. I think it's far more likely that Maude is a fraud. Whatever her reasons for trying to pull the wool over anyone else's eyes, she is still not a genuine medium because no such thing exists."

"But how will we ever go about proving it? I didn't see anything during the séance to give me pause."

"I shouldn't worry too much about that. I've spoken with my friend Harry at length about how such tricks are pulled off and will be sure to employ his unmasking techniques the next time we attend a sitting."

"Who is this Harry that you esteem so greatly?"

"Why, Harry Houdini, of course," Beryl said, glancing over at her with one eyebrow raised, as if surprised by the question.

It wasn't that Beryl was a name-dropper exactly, Edwina thought. It was more that she thought nothing whatsoever of her important connections all over the globe and spoke of them casually because of it. Even so, Edwina could not quite believe that Beryl would have never mentioned a connection to Harry Houdini before that moment.

"Are you telling me you've actually attended a séance with Harry Houdini?" Edwina asked. She was so surprised she forgot to hang on to the door handle to steady herself as Beryl careened around the country lane.

"At several locations, in fact. Séances have been all the rage for some time, as I'm sure you well know. Harry invited me to attend one or two with him, and I returned the favor on occasion. He is particularly interested in unmasking fraudulent mediums. He's done so over and over and gave me a number of helpful tips on doing so myself, should the need ever arise."

Edwina suddenly felt hopeful for the first time since they stepped foot into the séance room. As much as she had confidence in their investigatory abilities in general, the notion that they might have access to a bit of extra knowledge from someone as esteemed as Harry Houdini wouldn't go amiss.

"What sort of things did he mention to be on the lookout for?" Edwina asked. She fished into her skirt pocket for her trusty notebook and small pencil. As she attempted to write the heading "Houdini's techniques" at the top of a fresh page, she realized how difficult it would be to make any notes with Beryl behind the wheel. She slipped both the notebook and the pencil back into her pocket, resolved to commit Beryl's answers to memory until they returned home.

"The handholding thing, for one. Mediums do that to convince the sitters that they couldn't possibly be responsible for making noises or touching the sitters when ghosts suddenly seem to be ruffling the backs of attendees' hair or pinching them."

"How does holding hands make it so they are free to attempt fraudulent acts?" Edwina asked.

"They shift and move like Maude did today and, in the confusion, remove their own hand and replace it with one belonging to a sitter next to them instead. Or they have a partner who has remained hidden until the commotion starts, and they take over. Houdini said they even have been known to use prosthetic hands in place of their own in order to get up to convincing bits of mischief."

"And that really works for them?" Edwina asked, not convinced that she would've been fooled by any such thing.

"What you have to remember is they entirely create the environment. The lighting, the incense, any sounds that may occur in the room, like the humming of a motor or the whistling of a teakettle, are all within their control. Besides, many of the people who attend séances are willing participants in their own deception. They want to be convinced or they wouldn't be there."

Edwina sat back and considered her friend's words. When they had first arrived at the séance table, she had been pleased that they were able to sit in positions that provided them with a variety of vantage points in order to observe what Maude got up to. But once she thought about it more carefully, she realized she had been so absorbed by the performance that she had forgotten to look anywhere but at Maude's face. It made sense that her brother could have been in charge of any special effects that took place.

"What do you think about her insistence that Charles was the one to receive a message from Polly?" she asked.

"I think she is the recipient of some bad information and couldn't back down after she had boldly stepped in the wrong direction. That said, usually I have seen mediums act less confident about an entire name. It would be far more likely for someone like Maude to tell Charles she had a message from a departed loved one whose name began with the letter P. Perhaps she's not as experienced as she first appeared to have made a mistake like that," Beryl said.

The pair sat in silence for the rest of the ride to The Beeches, but by the time they had pulled into the driveway and rolled to a stop, Edwina felt her confidence in their abilities returning. Perhaps Maude wasn't any more experienced as a medium than they were as investigators. Considering their successes over the past few months, she thought it could not be called arrogant to put her faith in them.

"All of this has left me feeling a bit thirsty. What do you say to whipping up a batch of gin fizzes?" Edwina asked. "I think we both deserve it."

"Funnily enough, that was just something Harry said to me the last time we attended a séance together. Perhaps you are some sort of psychic channel yourself, Ed."

Chapter 10

The next day, Beryl dressed carefully for a trip to a nearby storage shed near the village center. A button-down blouse and a pair of slim-fitting trousers, along with a pair of sensible walking shoes, were what her morning called for. She felt slightly guilty for sneaking out of the house once more without informing Edwina as to her destination, but she thought it best not to rekindle any animosity on the part of her friend. She released the brake from the motorcar and rolled it down the driveway, hoping the sound of crunching gravel would not alert her friend to her departure.

She hadn't felt so guilty in ages. In fact, guilt was something she rarely felt. When she wanted a thing, she almost never experienced regret. She simply could not see the point. Decisiveness was one of her defining qualities, and it left little room for self-doubt.

As she reached the lane outside the stone pillars marking the entrance to The Beeches, she gunned the engine and zipped off. Ed was going to have to make peace with the notion that they owned an airplane, whether she liked it or not. Perhaps it was merely a matter of logic to get her on her side. After all, there were plenty of ways to turn a profit with an airplane. She could set up a side business carrying parcels or post at premium prices for those willing to pay. She might sell tickets for interested parties to go for sightseeing tours by air. She could even pull advertising banners behind the plane for a fee. Even if she were opposed to riding in it herself, surely Edwina would see the sense of owning the thing.

Beryl had arranged to store it in a disused storage building, and she found her spirits rising with each yard closer she inched toward their new possession. Thinking back on her soaring flight above the village, she began to hum loudly and in her usual tuneless way. The sun shone overhead, the trees still held their lush green leaves, and birds sang from their tops with the sort of gusto one associated with early spring. It was truly a glorious day.

She pulled up in front of the building, and as she clambered out of the motorcar, she returned a friendly wave from the local photographer. While he was not her favorite resident of Walmsley Parva, she saw no reason to be impolite. With a spring in her step, she hopped down from the motorcar and strode toward the oversized shed. She was not the only one to have asked the owner for permission to use it as a storage space. While it was not overstuffed by any means, there were crates and bits of disused machinery stacked up in each of the corners. Beryl's plane took up the center of the large building, which suited her just fine.

The main features of the building were its oversized door, for easing the plane in and out, and its sturdy roof, which provided her airplane with the shelter from the elements she so desired. After all, she had no more inclination to allow its shiny finish to be marred by bird droppings and tree sap than she did by the greasy fingerprints of inquisitive local men. She left the door open behind her and climbed into the cockpit once more.

As she attempted to turn over the engine in order to take it out for yet another exhilarating flight above the village, this time steering well clear of Mr. Watkins's farm, her heart sank. The engine didn't even bother to cough, let alone leap into a throaty thrum. She tried again, but to no avail. After climbing down out of the cockpit, she lifted the bonnet and peered into the engine. Sure enough, someone had been in there messing about. She couldn't imagine who would have wished ill toward their new possession. Whoever had sought to cause damage had certainly done a bang-up job of it. It was as if someone with absolutely no knowledge of engines had set about hacking and prying just about everything in sight asunder. As far as Beryl could tell, there were even a few pieces missing. Who could possibly have done such a thing?

Her thoughts went instantly to Mr. Watkins's angry face and upraised fist. Had he been so furious with her for disturbing his livestock that he sought to ground her plane? Was he also angry at the way Beryl had put him in his place for threatening his wife? Sabotaging her airplane would be a perfect way to get back at her for publicly embarrassing him. But then another, far more disloyal thought, crept through her mind.

Was it possible that Edwina had been the one to sabotage the plane? Had she been so distressed by the acquisition of it that she could not stand to see it go up in the air once more? Beryl hated to think that her friend might be capable of something so underhanded, and she even despised herself for considering it, but the fact of the matter remained that, of all the people who knew she had the airplane, Edwina had been the most outspoken about her dislike for it. And the amateur nature of the damage certainly did not point toward anyone with mechanical experience.

Beryl wondered if Mr. Watkins might have been a little more selective in his sabotage. Someone with more knowledge of machines than Edwina would not have needed to be quite so in-discriminate in their destruction. In fact, she would have ex-pected Mr. Watkins to have at least a working knowledge of tractors, considering his time as a farmer. Wouldn't he have known how to disable the plane with far less effort?

If Ed had damaged the plane, what was to be done about it? Should she confront her about it straight on? Should she make subtle enquiries, as if conducting an investigation behind her back? Perhaps Simpkins would have some insight as to what she should do. It was as though all of the joy had been sucked out of her day. She climbed back down off the stack of crates she had cobbled together as a makeshift ladder and leaned against the plane. She simply had no idea what to do. Usually, when something like this happened, Ed would be the first one she would ask for advice. Obviously, that wasn't a possibility in this case. She almost wished that she had never accepted the plane in the first place. Almost.

Edwina had tossed and turned fitfully throughout the night. She had awakened extremely late, groggy and out of sorts. While she did not like to consider herself someone who was so easily influenced by outside factors, she had to admit the expe-rience of the séance had rattled her. From the awkwardness with Charles to the vulgarity of a corpse being used as a theatri-cal prop, Edwina had found it most unsettling. Her dreams had been filled with phosphorescent green clouds chasing her down darkly lit alleyways. Charles's face appeared ahead of her, urg-ing her forward, but just as she was about to reach out her hand for him, an animated mummy stepped in her way and began muttering and twitching. She had not been plagued by such ter-rible dreams since just after her mother had died.

She in no way relished the idea of attending a second séance, no matter what the great beyond might have to say about her literary career. She knew that Beryl might pooh-pooh her for her skittishness, so she made every effort to dress quietly and to descend the stairs without making them squeak underfoot. Not that she should have worried all that much. Beryl was never one for early rising if she did not have a particularly good excuse to do so. Nonetheless, Edwina quietly prepared a simple breakfast of tea and toast, and after leaving the washing up on the sideboard for Beddoes to attend to, she gestured for Crumpet to follow her down the hallway, where she collected a wide-brimmed straw hat and the little dog's leash. His toenails clattered on the hard floor as he pranced about her ankles, excitedly awaiting their walk.

The fresh air and the rambling walk lifted her spirits and improved her outlook, as they so often did. Perhaps the entire matter between Hazel and the vicar might be settled simply by talking to her. Edwina would give a great deal not to be required to attend a second séance, and she had always found Hazel to be a sensible woman. Surely, it would be possible to reason with her and bring the whole matter to a conclusion without requiring revisiting such a loathsome spectacle. Buoyed up by that notion, she quickened her pace as she headed for the small cottage Hazel called home on the outskirts of the village.

Hazel owned several properties throughout Walmsley Parva. She had inherited two from her parents upon their death and had somehow purchased an additional one on her own. She wisely rented out two of the three as a steady source of income. With the influx of outsiders to the village from places as far-flung as London, Hazel had managed to make a tidy living for herself, by all accounts. The Lintons were the latest in a steady stream of outsiders to take advantage of what Hazel had to offer. Perhaps that might be a way into the conversation, Edwina thought to herself as she approached Hawthorne Cottage.

She paused at the front gate and admired what Hazel had accomplished since taking over the property.

While the building was small, its roof was neatly thatched and in good repair. The paint on the window casements and the door looked fresh and vibrant. Window boxes filled with still-blooming petunias and lobelia hung on either side of the door. A crazy paving path, the gaps filled in with sweet alyssum and flowering thyme, led the eye from the gate to the front of the house. Edwina picked her way along the path and rapped sharply on the door using the large, apple-shaped knocker.

A curtain drawn across the glass in the door moved aside, and Hazel's face appeared in the gap. The knob turned, and the door flung open.

"Edwina, this is an unexpected pleasure. What brings you by?" Hazel asked as she smoothed the front of her housedress before patting her neat bun with a long-fingered hand.

"I do hope you won't mind me dropping in without an invitation, but I did wish to speak with you about your tenants," Edwina said.

"They haven't been giving you any trouble, have they?" Hazel said, opening the door even wider and beckoning Edwina inside. Some conversations were best not had on the front steps, no matter how far out of earshot one might be from the neighbors. After all, voices tended to float on the breeze in the village, and one could never be too careful when discussing matters of delicacy.

"No, nothing like that," Edwina said.

"Well, if you won't mind following me into the kitchen, I was just busy ladling out some stewed fruit. I might even be able to find a bit of joint for your little friend here," Hazel said, smiling down at Crumpet.

Edwina followed Hazel down a short, narrow corridor made all the more claustrophobic by an oversized hall table covered in framed photographs and bits of daily detritus. They entered the brightly lit, cheerful kitchen filled with the smell of simmering fruit. Edwina was put immediately in mind of Simpkins and his near-constant experimentation with new recipes for Colonel Kimberly's Condiment Company. From the smell of the contents of her stockpot, Hazel might have some suggestions to share with him.

"What's that you're making? It smells of honey and pears," Edwina asked.

"Almost right. It's quinces. I simply can't get enough of them. I've an enormous tree at the back of the garden and had a bumper crop of fruit this year. It takes a great deal of work to process them, but the results are worth it, I assure you."

Hazel lifted the teakettle from the hob and carried it to the sink, where she filled it with cold water before returning it to the flame. Busying herself with a covered dish she fetched from the larder, Hazel suddenly produced the promised bit of joint for Crumpet, chopping it into fine pieces before placing it on a plate on the floor before him. She retrieved a cake tin and produced two tea cakes and a pair of plates. In no time, she had settled again at the table, happily munching on a sample of her quince puree accompanied by a cup of tea.

"I'm sure Simpkins would be most interested in your recipe," Edwina said.

It wasn't just flattery. She was thoroughly enchanted by the flavor of the preserves. It seemed just the thing for Colonel Kimberly's company to add to its line of products.

A wide smile broke out across Hazel's face. "Do you really think so? It was my dear mother's recipe, after all, and I'm sure she will be most gratified to know it is being shared with so many, should he choose to use it for his company," Hazel said.

Edwina paused mid-bite. She knew for certain that Hazel's mother had been dead for several years, before her own mother, in fact. Discussing matters with her would prove difficult in the extreme. Although, perhaps, given her interest in spiritualism, Hazel did not feel that there was any problem in doing so. Her words, however, gave the perfect opening for the reason for Edwina's visit. Still, she wished to approach the topic obliquely.

"If it's all right with you, I will be sure to speak with him about it at the next opportunity," Edwina said.

"I'd be very pleased, you can be sure. But you aren't here to discuss recipes. Now, what is it you wanted to ask about the Lintons?" Hazel said, pouring a bit more tea into Edwina's cup.

"I've only just met Mrs. Linton, so that this perhaps seems a bit awkward and forward, which is why I'm here to speak with you," Edwina said. "And I must say it was not under the most pleasant of circumstances."

A flicker of concern passed over Hazel's face. "You'd best come out and say it."

"It's not a complaint. It's just that I was in the Woolery the other day, and Mrs. Linton broke down crying when Mrs. Dumbarton mentioned the passing of her dog. I wondered, as a follow pet lover, if you thought it might be appropriate for me to drop by with a cake or a bouquet of some sort. Or do you think such a thing might be too forward, given our limited acquaintance?"

Hazel sagged back against her chair with apparent relief. "I'm sure she would be most appreciative. It's been more than a week since the dear little thing passed over to the other side, and she bursts into floods of tears every time dogs are mentioned." Hazel stole a glance over at Crumpet, who lay on the floor in front of the empty plate as if willing more joint to appear. A lump grew in Edwina's throat. She did not wish to even imagine the day when the sound of scampering paws ceased to be heard throughout The Beeches.

"I shall include a condolence card as well. It's such a wrenching blow to have one's furry companions taken."

"That's just what Mrs. Linton said, despite my attempts to persuade her that she need not consider her dog completely beyond her reach."

"Are you saying you recommended she attend one of Maude's séances?" Edwina asked.

Hazel nodded vigorously. "As soon as I heard the news, I made a point to seek her out in order to invite her to one of the sessions."

Edwina carefully swallowed, her bite of food giving herself time to think about how best to proceed with her enquiries. She took a sip of tea before speaking once more.

"Was she receptive to your invitation? After all, not everyone is, I understand."

"No, they most certainly are not. In fact, some people are entirely unreasonable on the subject. I'm sorry to say Mrs. Linton was one of them. She seemed almost offended that I would suggest she might be able to contact her dear little doggy through Princess Rosanna and Maude." Hazel reached for the jar of quince preserves and spooned another dollop on top of her tea cake.

"I suppose not everyone feels that such pursuits align with their religious upbringing," Edwina said, keeping her eyes carefully trained on Hazel's face.

Hazel pursed her lips, then shrugged. "To each their own, I suppose. But if you ask me, it's rather narrow-minded, considering how closely aligned spiritualism is with more traditional Anglican beliefs. After all, if you believe in an afterlife, who's to say those in spirit are not eager to communicate with the rest of us?" Hazel asked.

Edwina had never really thought of it in those terms. She could see how someone inclined to a broad view might make that argument. Still, she doubted the vicar would be willing to change his opinion. Edwina had never thought of Wilfred Lowe-thorpe as a particularly flexible or visionary sort. He certainly was no iconoclast, with his sensible, oatmeal-colored cardigans and his unwavering adherence to the liturgical calendar. He also was a man incredibly disinclined to make waves. The fact that he had put his foot down about Hazel accompanying the séances was an indication of the vehemence of his feelings.

"If I had to guess, I would say that you had someone in mind when speaking of narrow-mindedness and traditional beliefs," Edwina said.

"I don't wish to speak ill of others, but the fact remains that the vicar and his wife have shown a shocking resistance to spiritualism." Hazel pried the lid off the cake tin and fetched out another tea cake for each of them. The vehemence with which she pressed the top back on to the container left Edwina in no doubt of her feelings on the matter.

"I certainly hope this difference of opinion will in no way impact your ability to serve as the church organist. After all, you have always been such a credit to our small parish. Not many churches the size of ours could boast such an accomplished musician," Edwina said, hoping she had not laid the flattery on as thickly as Hazel had the quince preserves.

"If only that were so. I suppose the news won't stay secret for long," Hazel said.

"Which news is that?" she asked.

"I'm afraid the vicar forced me to choose between serving as the church organist or the one for Maude's séances," she said.

Edwina hoped her face showed sufficient surprise. "What did you tell him?"

"What could I possibly say other than to tender my resignation, effective immediately." A grimace passed Hazel's face. Edwina felt sure there was real pain on Hazel's part about the entire affair.

"But that is simply dreadful news. How will we ever replace you?"

"How very kind of you to say. It pains me to mention that I had not yet left the church when Mrs. Corby piped up to insist she would take over my duties."

Even though Edwina had already been apprised of that bit of news, it still ran a shudder up between her bony shoulder blades. Mrs. Corby was not only an inept musician, but was also a thoroughly disagreeable soul. The notion of her having a position of prominence in the church did not bear thinking about.

"What a loss for us all. I don't suppose that you would reconsider your choice in the matter?"

"No, I would not. After the way the vicar berated me in front of the choir, I would not lower myself to do so. I am sorry, Edwina, but the church will just have to get along without me." Hazel reached for her teacup and took a noisy swallow.

"Are we to lose your talents at the cinema as well?" Edwina asked. "Surely, your duties to Maude can have no conflict there." The notion that Mrs. Corby might replace her at the Palais as well was a grievous one indeed. Edwina could make herself attend church services, no matter the quality of the organist. Entertainment was not the point of the church, at least not since medieval times. The cinema, however, was a different beast entirely. An amateur musician there would render the experience unsatisfactory and hardly worth the money, let alone the time spent in the darkened theater. She would be far more inclined to stay home for programs on the wireless instead.

"At present, there is no need for me to consider leaving Mr. Mumford's employ, but there is nothing to say that I will remain there in the future. After all, Maude may have more need of me if word of her abilities spreads."

Edwina did not quite like the tone of Hazel's voice. She sounded ever so slightly fanatical, and there was a gleam in her eyes that was more zealous than was ordinary for most of her neighbors. It was the kind of thing one associated with the type of religious extremists who left England for the American colonies in the seventeenth century, and look at the mess that had begotten.

"Do you think it likely that Maude will need you full-time?" Edwina asked.

"She may very well require me for as many hours a day as I can spare her. After all, Princess Rosanna is a superior guide."

"Has she provided you personally with valuable guidance?" Edwina asked. "She didn't seem to have been much help to poor Mrs. Watkins yesterday."

Hazel waved a hand in the air as if to bat away the criticism. "The spirits are not available at the instant behest of the living. They come when they wish and not a moment before."

"What about Charles and Rosanna's insistence that she had a message for him from someone he could not identify?" Edwina still could not shake how cruel that message had seemed to be in light of Mrs. Watkins's hope.

"All will be revealed in good time, I am convinced of it. As I said, Rosanna is superior." Hazel looked back over her shoulder to the cooker. Edwina took a final sip of her tea and pushed back her chair. She could certainly take a hint. What she could not do, apparently, was to convince Hazel to return to her position as church organist.

"Thank you for your time. I feel emboldened to send along a condolence to Mrs. Linton."

"I'll be sure to make a copy of my quince preserves recipe for you to give to Simpkins," she said. "Perhaps I can pass it to you at an upcoming séance, if you think you will join us again."

As much as she wished she could demur, Edwina knew there was no way to avoid going to another session with Maude and

Princess Rosanna. The case depended upon it, and she could not bring herself to even imagine letting Muriel down.

"I definitely intend to do so. When is the next one to be held?"

"At four o'clock this afternoon, as a matter of fact. Shall I tell Maude to expect you?"

"Please do. And Beryl too. We wouldn't miss it for the world."

Chapter 11

It was with some relief to Beryl that, when she returned, Edwina made no enquiries as to her absence. She remained remarkably reticent to mention her own activity, but Beryl did not feel she could pry, considering how little she wished to discuss anything to do with the airplane. They had just gotten back onto firm footing, and she was not eager to rock the boat.

When Edwina suggested they attend the séance that afternoon, Beryl readily agreed. Despite the warmth of the day, she even made certain to be prepared to go early enough that they were able to walk into the village rather than avail themselves of the motorcar. As they came in sight of the post office, Beryl couldn't help but notice that a crinkle appeared between Edwina's eyes as she glanced over at it. In fact, Edwina had seemed distracted and even a bit nervous during the entirety of their walk. She wondered if her friend was still thinking about Maude's comment concerning her literary career. It would be regrettable if the topic came up for a second time. After all, Edwina would hardly be as focused on catching Maude performing some sort of sleight of hand if her mind was distracted by comments about her closely guarded literary aspirations.

They paused in front of the tailor shop, and Beryl took a moment to look it over. The heavy drapes were once again drawn tightly together across the display windows facing the street, completely blotting out the view of the interior. Beryl thought it was a savvy business move as well. Shrouding the proceedings in mystery was sure to set tongues wagging anywhere, but in a place as small as Walmsley Parva, it would be a topic much discussed at the post office and the pub.

She gave Edwina a gentle pat on her back as they stepped up to the door. "I expect it will be much like it was last time."

Edwina turned toward her, the crinkle between her eyes deepened. "That's what I am afraid of." With that, she pressed down on the door latch and stepped inside.

Once again, Beryl felt momentarily blinded by the low light. A single lamp in the center of the table gave off a faint glimmer, leaving the sitters around the table bathed in shadow.

"How lovely that you could join us once more," Maude called out to them. Beryl wasn't sure, but she thought she heard a note of disingenuousness in the medium's voice. She thought it likely that a purported psychic might not encourage the attendance of professional investigators at her events. As her eyes grew accustomed to the gloom, she could make out the other attendees. Mrs. Watkins sat in the same spot she had occupied previously. Beryl wondered if she had convinced her husband not to complain about her attempts to contact their daughter or if she had slipped away without informing him. She hoped that there would not be a scene at the end again.

Minnie Mumford sat in the chair beside her. She shifted in her chair like a fidgety child. Beryl wondered if there was someone in particular that she wished to hear from or if she was simply curious. The only other participant, besides Maude's brother, was Chester White, the local bookie. Beryl knew him to be willing to accept tips on sporting events from almost any source. She thought it likely he was there in hopes of such information from the great beyond.

Beryl took a seat to the right of Chester, which happened to afford her a particularly good view of Maude. despite the gloom. She wanted to keep her attention directly on the performer rather than on any of the possible distractions Maude might have prepared. The sarcophagus sat behind her, its lid completely closed. No light emanated from it, green or otherwise. Edwina took the position beside her, with an angled view of the proceedings, and as soon as they were both seated, Maude spoke again.

"Please join hands, and I will entreat Princess Rosanna to guide me on your behalf."

Maude leaned against the back of her chair and closed her eyes. Her breathing slowed and deepened. For some reason, it seemed louder than it had the first time they attended. She started to twitch and moan before she leaned forward with a jerk. The lid of the sarcophagus creaked upright, a groaning, squeaking sound accompanying its movement. Beryl thought it likely that the force of Maude's sudden shift forward had triggered some sort of pulley system that lifted the lid of the coffin. Devices like that were amongst those Harry Houdini had mentioned to her on more than one occasion.

The phosphorescent glow that seeped from the opened container lent an eerie tinge to Maude's face. Little by little, the lid creaked open, and the light grew stronger. Beryl suddenly realized she had not noticed the sound of the lid lifting the first time they attended. It occurred to her that there was no musical accompaniment providing cover for any mechanical noises that might betray the underpinnings of the operation. Maybe Hazel had changed her mind about the position. Perhaps their services would not be required, after all. For Edwina's sake, she felt relief. For her own, she admitted disappointment. She would have dearly loved to have stories of her own to share with Harry the next time they met. Still, if Hazel had returned to her duties as the church organist, it would have to be considered a good result.

A sharp pain pulsed through her hand. While Edwina was a small woman with proportionally small hands, she had a remarkably strong grip, which she had employed without warning. Beryl was loath to shift her gaze from whatever Maude was up to, but Edwina gasped and squeezed even harder. Chester suddenly released her hand, scraped back his chair, and sprang to his feet. Wordlessly, he pointed to the fully opened sarcophagus. Beryl leaned to the side for a better view.

There, in place of Princess Rosanna's tightly wrapped mummy, lay the motionless figure of Hazel Moffat, the ornate ceremonial dagger protruding from her chest.

Chapter 12

Maude twisted around and then rose and motioned for her brother. Arthur bent his head toward hers and, after a moment of conference, gingerly lowered the lid of the sarcophagus. The green glow was immediately snuffed out, and the spell was broken. Maude turned to the sitters once more, and Edwina had to give credit where it was due. She did not seem rattled in the least, as befitted one who felt that death was not an end but rather a new beginning.

"Would you be so kind, Chester, as to fetch the constable?" she asked. The bookie nodded and rushed out of the room almost as quickly as one of the dogs at the races he took bets on from his customary table at the Dove and Duck.

Mrs. Watkins remained frozen in her chair, and Minnie had begun to weep quietly. She was almost as fond of gossiping as Prudence, but she was a kindly soul at heart, and the idea that someone as well liked and inoffensive as Hazel had met such a gruesome end surely would have distressed her. Maude spoke again.

"I think it would be best if you all moved into the anteroom to await Constable Gibbs," she said.

"Very sensible, sister dear," Arthur said.

He pulled open the door to the foyer and ushered the sitters out. Edwina noted that he pulled it closed behind him before his sister could exit the room herself. Surely, Constable Gibbs would not approve of her remaining unattended in the room with Hazel's body. What was her purpose in doing so? Was she merely hiding evidence of her chicanery connected to the séances, or had she something even more sinister to conceal? Beryl's gaze was also fixed on the door shielding Maude from view. She pushed past Arthur and pressed it open. Maude was nowhere to be seen. But before the constable arrived at the scene, Maude had appeared once more and had joined them in the crowded hallway.

The first thing Constable Doris Gibbs did, upon entering the shop, was to motion for Beryl and Edwina to follow her into the séance room. She closed the door behind them, then yanked open the draperies covering the front window. Although such a move exposed the crime scene to the prying eyes of most of the village, who had followed closely on her heels as she approached the crime scene, it still seemed a sensible move to Edwina. After all, it would be impossible to properly investigate in such darkness.

Next, she hoisted open the lid on the sarcophagus and peered into it. Seeing Hazel in the full light of day was even more gruesome than it had been in the gloom. Edwina shuddered as she took in the full horror of Hazel's demise. She wished she could still see her as she had looked when she had smiled as she accepted compliments about her quince preserves, but any other image of her was completely stamped out.

Constable Gibbs pulled out a police notebook, not unlike Edwina's own, and peered at them.

"I would have thought the two of you were more sensible than to believe a bunch of superstitious nonsense."

Edwina looked over her shoulder to be sure the door remained tightly closed, but still felt compelled to lower her voice. "We are actually here on a case."

The policewoman cocked an eyebrow. "Are you claiming to be psychic now too? How would you know to be here in time for Hazel's body to be discovered?"

"As helpful as it might be to add a certain psychic ability to our skill set, we were actually hired by Muriel to debunk Maude and her purported mediumship," Beryl said, her voice barely above a whisper.

"Now why would Muriel care about that?" the constable asked.

Edwina was momentarily taken aback. Constable Gibbs was generally well-informed concerning any public confrontations and even many private ones. The notion that the goings-on between the vicar and Hazel at something so visible as a choir practice was surprising indeed. Then Edwina remembered that the other woman had been away for a few days with her brass band for a prestigious competition. Edwina hadn't seen her since her return and regretted that it hardly seemed the moment to make enquiries after her success. Edwina had rather a soft spot for brass bands.

"The vicar did not feel Hazel's decision to serve as an accompanist for séances was compatible with her role as the church organist. When she chose to leave his employ, he took it hard," Edwina said.

Constable Gibbs nodded, as if it all made sense. "So Muriel stepped in, hoping to win Hazel back for her husband's sake, I assume."

"Precisely," Edwina said.

"I don't think Muriel felt any too warmly toward anyone claiming otherworldly talents herself. After all, it would be trying to serve as a vicar's wife for all those years if one didn't share at least a smidgeon of faith in the ideas and culture of the church," Beryl said.

"You don't mean to suggest that Muriel is responsible for this, do you?" the constable asked, scrawling Muriel's name and a question mark into her notebook.

The very notion! "Certainly not," Edwina said. "I only mentioned her to explain our presence here. I would be shocked if the vicar's wife could possibly be caught up in something like this." All three women turned once more to where Hazel's lifeless body lay.

"Not to mention that she wanted Hazel to stop playing for Maude, but not stop everything altogether," Beryl said.

Constable Gibbs tucked her notebook and pencil into her uniform jacket pocket and leaned over the sarcophagus. "The weapon seems unusual. It looks more like a stage prop than a knife meant for any sort of real damage."

"You'll have to ask Maude for details, but I do remember it sitting on the table in front of Princess Rosanna's sarcophagus when we attended the last time. It was right next to the chalice," Edwina said.

"Princess Rosanna?" The constable scowled. "She can't be a member of the royal family with a foreign name like that."

"Rosanna is the mummy that used to occupy the space where Hazel is now. According to Maude, she was an ancient Egyptian princess and now acts as her guide concerning all things metaphysical," Beryl said. Edwina detected the merest trace of scorn in Beryl's voice. It was unlike her to display derision toward others, and Edwina wondered if she was one of the rare people who found the unbridled taking of Egyptian antiquities to be an abhorrence. It would not surprise her in the least to discover that her friend had many valued acquaintances throughout that region and felt strongly that their cultural treasures were not for others to simply purloin, like so many seashells strewn along the shore.

"So there is a missing mummy in all this too?" Constable Gibbs asked.

Edwina had given no thought to the mummy's whereabouts. She looked around the room with growing unease. She had no desire to see it up close and certainly not outside of its proper resting place. Imagining it propped up somewhere, like in a chair at the Walmsley Parva Reading Room or stuffed into a closet at the Women's Institute, left her feeling queasy and light-headed.

"I shouldn't wonder if there was no mummy to be missed. If this operation is as much a fraud as I believe it to be, Princess Rosanna is nothing more than some old sheeting strips wrapped around artfully arranged fistfuls of hay or sacks of sawdust. Whoever did this to Hazel would have no trouble at all disposing of the purported princess in order to cover their tracks," Beryl said.

"So there is very little to go on so far," the constable said. "Neither of you have heard that Hazel had any ructions with anyone other than the vicar?"

Edwina had not mentioned her visit to Hazel's, but it seemed foolhardy and not public-spirited to keep it from the police. After all, she hadn't actually done anything immoral.

"I spoke with Hazel only a few hours ago, and she seemed just as usual, other than her unhappiness at the way the vicar had insisted on her making a choice between her jobs." Edwina could feel Beryl's eyes on her. "I had stopped in to try to persuade her to return to her duties as the church organist, as I felt it in the best interest of the village, but she would have none of it."

"She didn't seem agitated in any other way?" Constable Gibbs asked.

"Not in the slightest. We discussed how happy she was attending the séances, and she promised to send me a recipe for some preserves she thought Simpkins might wish to try at Colonel Kimberly's. She was normal in every way."

"I suppose I shall have to start with that lot out there, Lord help me," the constable said.

"You might try Mrs. Corby. If she knew that Edwina had tried to coax Hazel back into her role as the church organist, she might had decided to do away with her," Beryl said. Edwina could hear the teasing note in Beryl's voice, but Constable Gibbs's eyes gleamed at the suggestion. Mrs. Corby was a constant nuisance in the village, and Edwina would lay odds, if such a thing were not beneath her, that Constable Gibbs would be more than pleased to discover she was the one responsible for murder.

"Thanks very much for the suggestion. I will stop in to question her as soon as I am done here." With that, the constable pointed to the door. "I won't keep you any longer, but I do hope that if you run across anything I should know, you will pass it along."

"Does that mean we have your blessing to do a bit of poking around in the matter?" Beryl asked.

Constable Gibbs glanced at the body once more, then nodded. "I can use all the help I can get."

Chapter 13

"Well, that makes for a pleasant change, don't you think?" Edwina asked as they emerged onto the pavement and made their way along the High Street.

"You mean Constable Gibbs soliciting our assistance without cajolery?" Beryl asked.

"Exactly. Who would have thought she would come to value our help after her initial attitude toward our investigative abilities?"

Edwina had a point. The constable had made no bones about her hostility toward them when they first set themselves up as private-enquiry agents. It had taken a great deal of finesse to change her opinion of them and their skills. Beryl couldn't help but also think her antipathy toward them had much to do with the constable's own jealously guarded position as the village's only police officer, a position all the more remarkable considering her gender. It was easy to understand how she would not have wanted the endeavors of others to threaten her role. Beryl had similar experiences as the only woman in most of the areas in which she excelled. It was rare that she ever encountered other women on the airfield or the racetrack, and she was not entirely sure that she would not have found it ever so slightly unnerving if she did.

Edwina stopped dead in her tracks and faced her. "Seeing Hazel's body like that was simply appalling. I confess, despite how many cases we've worked, I still feel unsettled. She was the picture of health when I dropped by only hours ago."

Beryl laid a reassuring hand on her friend's arm. Sudden death was always distressing, and a murder especially so. "Anyone would be rattled by what we just witnessed. I hope we never become used to a life being violently taken."

Edwina looked up at her and nodded. Beryl tucked her arm through her friend's and led her gently up the street. Up ahead, Prudence Rathbone waved furiously at them. It would be impossible to pretend they had not seen her. Besides, Prudence was a font of information, and in regard to Hazel's murder, that was something in short supply. Beryl steered them toward the post office cum stationer cum sweet shop without undo haste. It wouldn't do to seem overly eager. Prudence revealed her best tidbits if her audience remained tantalizingly aloof.

Prudence held her hand to her eyes to shield them from the sun's warm glare and to better take in the goings-on at the former tailor's shop. A wagon used by the local undertaker had pulled up in front of the building and Prudence leaned forward as if magnetized to the scene. She shifted from foot to foot, as if struggling not to leave her shop unattended. They stopped in front of her and effectively blocked her view.

"Has Hazel taken ill?" Prudence asked.

"What makes you think that something has happened to her?" Beryl asked, following her policy of never giving Prudence any information if she could possibly help it.

"Considering the undertaker was called in, I should think there was something very wrong indeed at this afternoon's goings-on," Prudence said. Two bright spots of color appeared on her cheeks, as if the excitement of it all was making her feverish.

"But what caused you to believe that Hazel is the one affected?" Edwina asked. Beryl sent her an appreciative nod. Did Prudence know something through careful cultivation of the village grapevine, or was her knowledge firsthand?

"It has to be Hazel. The last time I saw her, she boasted that Maude never holds a séance without her to accompany it. All the sitters who entered the shop in time for the session, as well as Maude and Arthur, have exited on their own two feet," Prudence said. A note of exasperation rather than embarrassment tinged her voice.

Beryl could see no good reason not to tell Prudence what had occurred. After all, she was bound to find out shortly, and by being the first with the news, they might prompt a more forthcoming response from her than they could otherwise expect.

"There's a good reason you didn't see Hazel leaving the shop with the others. She was found dead inside the room after the séance had started," Beryl said.

Prudence's jaw unhinged like a snake about to swallow something very large indeed. Her eyes grew wide in her face, and the two feverish spots of color drained straightaway.

"Dead? But that's impossible. Hazel is the picture of health," she said, once she recovered her voice.

"I am afraid it's not impossible, but her state of health had nothing to do with it," Edwina said.

"You don't mean she was murdered, do you?" Prudence asked, regaining some of her usual zeal for the extraordinary.

Beryl lowered her voice as if to take Prudence into her confidence, knowing full well news about Hazel's murder would reach her through Minnie in only a few moments' time. Minnie and Prudence were both confirmed gossips and, as such, could be counted on to pass information back and forth between the two of them.

"Her body was found right there in the sarcophagus Maude uses as a prop in her séances."

Prudence gasped, and her hand shot to the base of her throat. If Beryl didn't suspect the worst of her on general principle, she would have said Prudence was genuinely shocked.

"But what has become of Princess Rosanna?" Prudence asked.

That explained it. Prudence must have a soft spot for the supernatural. "No one knows. Her mummy has disappeared, and Hazel was found in her place," she said.

"It really was quite horrid," Edwina said, abandoning her usual taciturn manner toward Prudence. "You're lucky you didn't witness the grisly scene."

From the look on Prudence's face, Beryl suspected she would have liked nothing more than to have borne witness to the grim discovery. She almost felt sorry for the postmistress as she kept gazing over Edwina's shoulder at the little group of sitters being questioned by Constable Gibbs. A slightly flinty gleam entered that same gaze as Constable Gibbs turned her attention to Minnie.

"How did she die?" Prudence asked.

Beryl and Edwina exchanged a glance. "It appears she was stabbed in the chest with a ceremonial dagger," Beryl said.

Prudence bobbed her head excitedly. "Does Constable Gibbs have a prime suspect?"

"I'm sure it would be inappropriate for us to speculate," Edwina said.

"Everyone knows the three of you are thick as thieves. I'm sure she must have given some sort of indication as to whom she thought the likely culprit," Prudence said, tapping a foot impatiently against the pavement.

"The whole situation is quite baffling. I don't believe there was anyone who had reason to dislike Hazel, and certainly not enough to wish her harm in any way," Edwina said.

Prudence's thin lips stretched back into a smile. "Well, that's where you're wrong. If I were in charge of the investigation, I'd start with one of the séance attendees."

Beryl arched an eyebrow, hoping to convey skepticism. Prudence never was one to divulge what she knew if she thought her audience was too eager to acquire her knowledge. It was far easier to feign a lack of interest than to attempt to pry it from her. As if reading her mind, Edwina gave voice to her disbelief.

"Surely, that can't be the case. Everyone in the room was utterly shocked by the discovery of her body, and all of them I would have counted as her friends or at least friendly acquaintances."

"That may have been true up to a few days ago, but Minnie Mumford has had a change of heart, that's for sure." She smiled triumphantly, and Beryl's stomach gave a bit of a lurch. She never did like to hear someone sounding so triumphant about another's potential downfall. Still, it was a lead they would need to follow up.

"But Minnie and Hazel were always on the best of terms, weren't they?" she asked, turning toward Edwina, who nodded vigorously.

"I should say that they were. In fact, I believe that Hazel might have even been intending to supply Minnie with some of her fabulous quince preserves for her tea room. She certainly wouldn't have done such a thing if they were not friendly indeed. After all, I happen to know those preserves were a labor of love," Edwina said.

Prudence let out a burst of laughter of the sort surely, during the days of her youth, her mother would have warned her against as unladylike. "After decades of ignorant bliss, the scales had finally fallen from Minnie's eyes concerning the antics of her husband, Clarence."

Beryl felt the news hit her stomach like a cup of Edwina's coffee. It was heavy and sour and gave her pain. Clarence Mumford was the sort of man who everyone in the village knew pursued women with legendary enthusiasm, despite his marital status. The only one who appeared not to realize what he was up to was his wife, Minnie. If she had finally been apprised of the news, she might well have been so humiliated as to take action. That said, Beryl had no idea what it had to do with Hazel. She looked over at Edwina, who gave the tiniest shake of her head as if she were equally in the dark.

"You can't be implying that Clarence and Hazel were romantically involved," Edwina said.

"They most certainly were. Clarence only hired her to play at the cinema in order to get his sticky paws all over her," Prudence said. There was something in her tone of voice that made Beryl wonder if what Prudence would have liked more than anything else in the world was for Clarence to attempt to put his paws on her.

"What makes you think that Minnie knew anything about it, even if it were true?" Beryl asked.

"Because Minnie told me so herself. She was in the post office just yesterday, looking as though she were about to burst into tears. When I asked her what was wrong, she confided in me that she had noticed Clarence exhibiting more of an interest in Hazel than she thought appropriate for an employer and employee."

Clarence had already lost the services of Eva Scott, the ticket salesgirl, due to his inappropriate behavior. Eva was just a young woman, with little experience of such matters, when he began a dogged campaign of harassment. It had gotten to be so uncomfortable that the girl's mother showed up at the cinema and told Clarence, in no uncertain terms, that her daughter would no longer be willing to work for him, despite the fact that jobs were not all that easy to come by, considering the economic situation. It seemed he had turned his lasciviousness on another of his employees, if Prudence were to be believed.

Minnie had broken away from the small group of séance attendees and was making her way toward the post office. Perhaps she had come to share her news with Prudence. Beryl did not want to stick around to listen to that, nor was she ready to question Minnie about the possibility that she was a murderer. She had taken the victim's death very much to heart, if her reaction to the body were anything to go by. As much as it seemed hard to believe that the mild-mannered tea-shop owner would resort to murder, Beryl had to admit it could happen. After all, it would have been utterly humiliating to discover that everyone in the village but her knew her husband's reputation. She could see from the way Minnie strained her gaze around the pair of them and toward Prudence that she was eager for a tête-à-tête, and it took no effort whatsoever to take their leave of her. As they moved out of earshot, Edwina turned toward her.

"You think she could have done it?"

"I'm rather afraid that she could," Beryl said.

Chapter 14

The courtroom was crowded; of course, it was. An inquest always created a great deal of interest, but the sensational nature of Hazel's death stoked the fire of local curiosity to a conflagration. The fact that Edwina was only filling in as the coroner only added to the appeal; the previous one had died just a few weeks before, and a new one hadn't been appointed.

Edwina cast her gaze about the room, her stomach aflutter with nerves as she realized every seat was filled and more people stood, pressed against the walls. She glanced up at the clock mounted high on a side wall. It was time to begin the proceedings, and Charles, not only her friend but also the local solicitor, who provided her with expertise during court sessions, was nowhere in sight. She was still new to the position and relied on his guidance in terms of the legal requirements. With no experience at all of inquests, she felt even more at sea than usual.

If she were to be completely honest with herself, she would also have to admit to the merest feeling of disappointment not only to be deprived of Charles's professional advice, but also of his company. Ever since Beryl had arrived in the village, she had persistently hinted that Charles was interested in her in a more than friendly way. Edwina had dismissed the suggestion out of hand at first, but over the last several weeks, she had softened to the idea. She had come to appreciate Charles's quiet support and unwavering devotion. Could it be that Beryl had been right all along?

Still, there was nothing to be done but to soldier on. It was an attitude that had helped the entire nation to make it through the war, after all. How many new experiences had people taken on with quiet determination, whether it was learning to grow vegetables or build armaments in a factory far from home. Surely, she could manage to conduct an inquest without a solicitor whispering advice in her ear.

She banged her gavel on the wooden desk and watched as the courtroom fell silent and all faces turned toward her. Never before had she felt so exposed. She took a steadying breath and addressed the crowd.

"These proceedings are an enquiry into the body found yesterday. We will be hearing testimony from a variety of witnesses and professionals in order to establish the victim's identity as well as the manner of death," she said.

She heard murmurs rumble through the crowd as well as Hazel's name bandied about. She brought the gavel down and called the first witness. Vicar Lowethorpe approached the bench and, in short order, gave evidence that established that the body found in the sarcophagus was indeed that of Hazel Moffat.

Next, Edwina called Dr. Nelson to the stand. He took his seat and positioned himself to easily view the courtroom as well as her. She thought fleetingly of his predecessor and how much she preferred him to the new doctor. It still stung to recall how Dr. Nelson had once dismissed her very real medical complaint because of his belief that women of a certain age were inclined to hypochondria. Still, he had performed Hazel's autopsy without delay and could be trusted to have done a careful job of it. After all, he had his professional reputation to consider. He faced the onlookers as he ran through the basic details of Hazel's physique. Edwina winced inwardly as the audience strained to hear such private details.

"The subject was a female, aged thirty-seven years, of medium build and well nourished. From the state of her organs, she gave every appearance of excellent health," he said.

Edwina thought an air of disappointment wafted from the crowd. How very dull it was to hear what one already knew to be true. Still, the doctor was not done giving his findings.

"Have you determined a cause of death?" Edwina asked.

He addressed the crowd, rather than her, once more. "She died of massive blood loss."

A rustle of whispers ripped through the room once more, and Edwina banged her gavel. "Quiet, please." She turned her gaze on the witness. "And do you have a cause for such trauma?"

"Her death was a result of some sort of sharpened instrument penetrating her chest cavity and piercing her heart," the doctor said.

"You say some sort of instrument. Is there some doubt as to the weapon found imbedded in her chest when her body was discovered?" Edwina asked.

The doctor turned to face her for the first time. "There is no doubt whatsoever. The blade found in her body could not possibly have been the one to kill her."

A collective gasp echoed throughout the room. Edwina felt the shock of it herself and, for a moment, forgot she was the one in charge of the proceedings. She wished once more for Charles's steadying presence. Thumping her gavel against the desk once more, she quieted the room and restored order.

"What convinced you that the blade found in the wound was not the murder weapon?" she asked.

"It was not long enough to have caused the totality of the injuries the victim sustained."

Edwina's stomach lurched. The injuries she had seen in clear view had appeared gruesome enough. She had not considered that there might be even more hidden from sight. Still, despite her qualms, she must do her duty and ask for an accounting of them.

"Would you elaborate?" she asked, discomfited all the more by the way every soul in the room strained forward to hang on every word.

"If you insist. The blade of the knife found protruding from her body was a mere two inches in length. If I had to hazard a guess, I would say it was more for show than for any sort of practical use." The doctor paused and allowed his gaze to wander around the room before continuing. "The weapon that killed her was far longer."

"And how do you know that to be true?" she asked.

"Because the weapon that ended her life not only entered her chest wall through the back, but also passed out through her front. Its blade would have measured at least three times that length."

Edwina's head felt light, and the room appeared out of focus. She took a deep breath.

"Do you have any idea what sort of instrument would have inflicted that type of injury?"

The doctor shook his head. "It could be anything from a long pair of shears to a farm implement. There was no evidence in the wound to either suggest or to eliminate anything in particular beyond length."

"Have you anything else to add?"

"Only that I fervently hope the perpetrator is caught. This was an appalling way to die."

*   *   *

Beryl made her way, along with so many others leaving the magistrate's court, to the Dove and Duck. It seemed to her a shame that Walmsley Parva no longer upheld the venerable tradition of holding inquests in pubs. She could not help but feel the proceedings would have gone down a bit easier with a pint of beer in her hand. From the looks on the faces of her fellow patrons, as they bellied up to the bar and tried to attract the barmaid's attention, most of them would have agreed with her.

All of the speculation that had been communicated in whispers during the proceedings was given full voice in the far more casual atmosphere of the pub. Beryl nodded to Jim, the pub's owner, as she gratefully accepted a tall glass of beer. She requested a double whiskey in addition, and once she received it, she carried both drinks to a table near the center of the room. There, seated at his customary place, was a man who rarely paid for his own.

Chester White, the local bookie, was not only a man who took bets on anything from horse races to cricket matches but was also a font of information about all things going on in the village as well as the surrounding towns. Chatting with him, especially after he had consumed a free double whiskey, would be a good starting point for the investigation. Unlike some others who were prone to mere idle gossip, edited and embroidered until it could not reasonably be considered useful, his was information to be trusted, as far as it went. She placed the glass on the table in front of him and waited for him to gesture toward the empty seat before lowering herself into it.

"Your friend did a credible job with the proceedings, I thought," Chester said, after taking a deep tug of his beverage and wiping his lips on the back of his hand.

"I thought so too. It would be hard to tell that conducting an inquest was not in her usual line of duties," Beryl said. "But I found that Edwina is good at almost anything she is willing to turn her hand to."

Chester drummed his knobby fingers on his leather-bound ledger, in which he made careful notes of bets placed by his customers. "I do believe you're right. Perhaps she will consider learning how to play the piano. The cinema just isn't going to be the same without Hazel to accompany the films."

Chester was certainly right about that. Beryl didn't like to imagine Mrs. Corby playing the accompaniment for the silent films whenever she wanted to attend a matinee. There must be someone else in town who could take Hazel's place, at least at the Palais. Perhaps she ought to make the suggestion to Edwina.

"It doesn't bear thinking about. Hazel is going to be sorely missed at the church as well as the cinema," Beryl said.

"She shall be missed in more places than that, from what I hear."

Now they were getting somewhere. Beryl waited for Chester to take another gulp of his whiskey before urging him along.

"Really? I thought her biggest claim to fame was her talent as a musician," she said.

Other voices were raising as the drinks continued to flow, and Beryl leaned a little closer to hear his answer.

"Well, she's gotten herself in cahoots with the Dinsdales, now hasn't she?"

That was an interesting turn of phrase. It was one she herself might have used but would not necessarily have said to anyone besides Edwina. In the time she had lived in the village, she had become much more conscientious about comments she made compared to when living in larger cities or while traveling. There was an enormous difference in the way one comported oneself if offense were not to be given and taken in such a tight-knit community. Grievances were hard to navigate when, everywhere one turned, the object of their discomfort appeared beside them. No, although keeping her cards close to her vest had never been a strong suit, Beryl had learned it was in her best interest to do so much of the time.

"It sounds as though you are a true believer," she said.

Chester snorted and thumped his hand down hard on top of a ledger. "I'll give you good odds of them being a pair of out-and-out frauds."

The bookie never gave odds on anything he didn't feel certain of. He was a sharp businessman, and while Beryl herself felt it unlikely that Maude and her spirit guide were, in fact, communicating with those beyond the veil, it cheered her to hear him say so.

"To tell the truth, I am quite a skeptic myself. But I didn't realize that Hazel might be in on the scam as well." She lifted her beer glass to her lips and gazed at him over the rim.

Chester leaned toward her slightly as the din increased. Snatches of conversation all around them were about Hazel and the missing mummy. She doubted anyone would notice any contribution Chester might have made to the conversation. Still, she wasn't about to tell him so. It might give him pause in his outpouring of a free flow of information.

"Now, that's something I wouldn't lay odds on. Part of me thinks that Hazel was the sort who was apt to believe in otherworldly mumbo jumbo. After all, she faithfully attended the church, and I can hardly see the difference between a séance and a sermon."

"But the other part of you?" Beryl prompted.

"Hazel was a very shrewd businesswoman. You don't end up with the kind of property ownership she did without having good sense on that score. It did cross my mind that she might be getting a percentage of the earnings in exchange for helping out with some of the special effects, if you get my meaning."

Now that was an angle Beryl had not considered. She

thought of Hazel as a benign sort of woman, likable but not likely to leave a huge impression on those she first met. She was just the sort of person who would fade into the background, hidden behind the piano, and left free to participate in whatever might aid in the overall success of the séances.

"Do you think that could be what led to her death?" she asked.

Chester shrugged. "I wouldn't lay odds on that either. At first glance, it doesn't seem likely that anyone would've had it out for her, but if someone felt that she was participating in fleecing them, who knows?" Chester drained his glass, then placed it back on the table with a bit of a thump.

Beryl shoved back her chair and made her way back to the bar to fetch him another drink. By the time she returned, she had decided to work the conversation around to a slightly different topic. She placed the glass before him once again and took her seat.

"Hazel wasn't one of your customers, was she?"

She didn't think that Chester would be the sort to murder one of his clients to get out of paying off a large winning, but one never knew. In her opinion, almost anyone might do almost anything under the right circumstances. So far, the bookie business seemed to be doing well, but she did not know that for sure. Although, if Hazel had been one of his clients, there was no reason for him to tell her the truth. After all, it wasn't as though he made a point of discussing such private business with those not directly involved in it.

"No, she wasn't. Like I said, she was a shrewd businesswoman. The only sort of gamble she took was on real estate. The closest she ever came to giving me money was renting to the Lintons. Mr. Linton has placed a bet a few times since he arrived in the village; the last time was quite a handsome flutter."

He cracked open the ledger and ran a blunt finger down a column of numbers before turning back a page or two. He seemed to find what he was looking for because he tapped up and down on an entry.

"Anthony Linton placed a large bet recently?" Beryl asked. "Does he play the horses?"

"Football match. One of the women's teams quarterfinals." He ran his finger to lines down the page and tapped on another entry. "The photographer made a similar bet on that match. They both did quite well out of it, from the looks of things."

One of the many surprises to emerge from the war years was the skyrocketing popularity of women's football leagues. As a means of exercise during breaks from factory work, droves of young women had taken enthusiastically to informal games played on the ground just outside at their workplaces. Before long, the factory owners began sponsoring the teams and helping them to organize formal matches. With so great a number of men serving overseas, the public's appetite for sport could not be met by attending games between male teams. The women ended up using their matches as fund-raisers for ambulances and for hospitals for returning soldiers. The matches turned out to be enormously successful both in terms of fan loyalty and in fund-raising.

The return of men after the war had done nothing to slow down the enthusiasm for these women's teams, and their ticket sales far outstripped those of their male counterparts. It was one place in sport where women were excelling and surpassing men. She had bet on many of those games herself, and it had always given her a feeling of pride to be able to do so. She could imagine a time in the future when most of the professional sports dominated by men would have equally popular women's teams. It might not happen in her lifetime, but she was sure it would come about eventually.

Still, she did wonder about the wherewithal for each of those men to place such a large bet. Most of Chester's customers were of far more modest means. For their bets to have stood out in his mind, they must have been outliers. Without appearing to do so, she glanced down at his ledger and attempted to read the exact amount for herself. As her eyes focused on the numbers just above Chester's finger, she barely managed to contain a gasp. Both of them had placed bets that amounted to several months' wages for the average workingman.

She had no real sense of the Lintons' economic status, but she would not have guessed that they were amongst the few who never needed to think anything whatsoever about their spending habits. The photographer seemed to be a solidly middle-class sort himself, although he was a business owner and without any family to support. If he chose to use his discretionary income on what could be considered foolhardiness, there was no one to tell him so. Still, although she was an enthusiastic gambler herself, she doubted she would have put so much on a single event.

"Had they both received some sort of hot tip about that match?" Beryl asked.

"You know I never discuss tips, hot or otherwise," Chester said.

Which was true. As many times as Beryl had tried to coax information out of him before laying her own money down, she had never known him to be forthcoming. He was, of course, happy to accept such information from others, and on occasion, she had provided it. After all, he had helped her out on more than one occasion with the information he had gleaned through his business, even though it had never been about horse races or football matches. It was the least she could do to pass along things she had heard and to stand him the odd drink now and again.

His eyes were focused over her shoulder, and she felt someone looming up behind her. She turned her head slightly and noticed that a line was starting to form behind her chair. It wouldn't do to take up any more of Chester's time. After all, paying customers awaited. She drained her glass and pushed back the chair.

"If you think of anything else I ought to know, you will tell me, won't you?" she asked.

"Now that is something you can bet on," Chester said.

Chapter 15

Edwina was of two minds about Charles's absence, but as she watched the last villager file out of the courtroom, she made up her mind. She picked up her handbag and adjusted her hat before heading out the door herself. No one seemed to notice her walking in the opposite direction of the pub, unlike most of the other inquest attendees. Perhaps that was to be expected. Unlike Beryl, Edwina was not someone known to frequent the pub.

The sun was shining brightly overhead as she left the village proper and turned down the lane that led to Charles's home. She wished that she had Crumpet at her side as she approached the front gate. Her dog always helped to alleviate any social awkwardness, especially with someone like Charles, who seemed to care for Crumpet almost as much as she did. She was torn between her disappointment at his absence, when she had counted on him, and genuine worry that something might have happened to him.

She told herself that she would feel better once she had spoken with him, no matter what he had to say. She had even thought of a legitimate reason to visit him in connection with the case that could not be seen as accusatory. Surely, Charles would know if Hazel had made a will, and it only made sense for her to ask about it as a part of the investigation.

She raised a gloved hand and grasped the brass door knocker. Although the sound of the knock rang loud and clear, she heard no footsteps approaching along the hall beyond the door. She waited a moment longer, then rapped the knocker with a will. She counted slowly to three hundred, then pressed her ear against the door, hoping no one would pass by and observe her in such an undignified position.

There was a faint sound of banging from within. She did the unthinkable and reached for the door handle. It turned easily in her hand, allowing her to creak the door open with ease. Tentatively, she stepped into the shadowy coolness of Charles's front hallway. In contrast to the habitual neatness she had encountered whenever she had dropped by in the past, the hallway was shockingly untidy. Shoes missing their mates littered the floor. The post had been scattered across the surface of the entryway table, as if someone had been looking for something. Upon a closer examination, she noticed that someone had scribbled all over the envelopes.

The sound of banging grew louder as she moved along the passageway and on toward Charles's kitchen. Could Charles had been the victim of a home invasion? Could the burglars be in the house even now, holding him against his will? She fervently wished that Beryl was with her, her alarming, but trusty pistol brandished firmly in her capable hand. Still, there was nothing for it. If Charles was in trouble, she was the only one available to assist him. She commanded her lungs to slow their breathing and crept forward as quietly as she could. Her only advantage was the element of surprise.

Whatever she had expected to find when she reached the

source of the sound was driven completely from her mind as she beheld the scene in front of her. Charles stood in the center of the room in his stocking feet, his jacket removed and his shirttail hanging down the back of his trousers. Tufts of his hair stood up at irregular angles from his head, completely at odds with his usual neatly slicked-back style. The floor was covered with an assortment of pots, pans, lids, and utensils. In the middle of it all was a child, gleefully beating on an upturned stockpot with a wooden spoon.

"Charles," she shouted, attempting to make her presence known. He turned and gave her a look of the most profound relief she thought she had ever seen. Her heart squeezed in her chest, and she took a few steps farther into the room. She laid her handbag on the kitchen table, then removed her hat and gloves. The child paused its banging as she knelt beside him on the floor.

"Hello there. Who might you be?"

The little boy, who she judged to be somewhere around two years old, gazed up at her with enormous blue eyes. He dropped the spoon and lifted his arms above his head. She got to her feet once more, scooped him up, and settled him on her hip. Instantly, he laid his head against her shoulder and popped a chubby little thumb into his mouth.

Keeping him carefully perched there, she moved to the cooker and retrieved the teakettle. She found it awkward to attempt to fill it using only one hand, but she managed it, nonetheless. Once she had placed it on the hob and switched on the gas, she turned her attention to Charles, who had sunk into a chair at the kitchen table.

"You never mentioned that you were expecting a houseguest," she said, as she took the seat opposite him and shifted the child into her lap. She glanced down and stroked the sandy curls at the nape of his neck.

Charles shook his head and exhaled deeply. "That's because I wasn't." He gestured toward the child. "This is Georgie, my cousin's son."

"I see. And how did he come to be here?" she asked.

"I fetched him late last night by train."

"How extraordinary. Will his visit be of long duration?"

Once again, Charles shook his head. "He isn't here for a visit. It seems I am to be his guardian."

Edwina could not believe her ears. How could such a thing have come to pass? She vaguely recollected Charles mentioning the few members of his extended family every now and again, but they lived at quite a distance, and contact between them was conducted via correspondence rather than in-person visits, for the most part.

"But what has become of his parents?"

Charles glanced down at the child, whose eyes were closed and whose breathing had slowed. He lowered his voice.

"His mother, my cousin, was involved in a motoring accident that, unfortunately, she did not survive."

A shudder ran through Edwina's body. Motoring accidents were one of her greatest fears. She felt certain she was bound to experience one every time she agreed to a ride in Beryl's motor-car. The idea that someone young enough to be Georgie's mother had been lost in one left her feeling faintly nauseated. She instinctively tightened her hold on the child, enough to cause him to stir in his sleep.

"What about his father?"

"He was lost on the front near the end of the war. He never even had the chance to meet the boy," Charles said. "My cousin had no siblings, nor do I, so I am his next of kin. I received a telephone call from the police alerting me to the terrible news, and I took the first train to collect him. We got back in the wee hours and have been at sixes and sevens ever since."

"You could have telephoned me, Charles. I would have been more than happy to assist you in any way that I could."

"I was too overwhelmed even to ask for help. I have no idea whatsoever how to take care of a child," he said.

"You seem to have been doing well enough, under the circumstances, although I can see how you would not have found time to attend Hazel's inquest," she said.

While she was in no way gladdened to hear the reason for Charles's absence from the courtroom, she was relieved that it was not because he did not care about her enough to bother to appear.

He leaned forward. "I am so very sorry to have left you to figure all that out on your own, although I am certain you managed with aplomb."

"It all turned out fine in the end, but you were sorely missed," she said.

Charles held her gaze, and, in his eyes, she saw a flicker of hope. The teakettle whistled, and she got to her feet, glad to have an excuse to look away. She passed the sleeping child to Charles without waking him, then busied herself adding tea leaves to the pot and fetching china cups from a cabinet.

"Were there any surprises from the witnesses?" he asked, as if he too wanted to steer the conversation to safer waters.

She carried the tea things to the table. "I should say so. Dr. Nelson announced that the dagger found lodged in her body was not the weapon that killed her."

"That is a surprise. Are there any suspects in the case thus far?" he asked.

"So far the only person mentioned is Minnie."

"Whyever would someone accuse her?"

"Apparently, she heard a rumor that her husband was showing an inappropriate interest in Hazel."

Charles snorted. "If Minnie had done away with all the

women Clarence pursued, the village would be almost exclusively populated by men. Why would Hazel provoke her to take action after all this time?"

"While his behavior has been common knowledge amongst most of the villagers, it has always seemed that Minnie remained blissfully unaware of it. Prudence claims that Minnie confided in her, the day before Hazel was murdered, that she had discovered what Clarence was up to and was devastated by it."

She poured the tea and slid a cup across to Charles, who thanked her before returning to Hazel's death.

"I still cannot believe she would harm anyone. She just doesn't seem the sort."

Edwina wasn't so sure. Humiliation was a powerful emotion and could lead to surprising action. Even someone as mild-mannered as Minnie might be driven to violence if she felt herself to have been played for a fool.

"Do you have an alternative suspect? An heir perhaps? After all, she had considerable property to leave to someone."

"If she did, I have no knowledge of them."

"She never had you draw up a will?"

"She brought it up from time to time and had expressed an interest in doing so, but like so many people, she never got around to it, at least not with me." Charles looked down at Georgie. "It was a good thing Polly had more sense."

A jolt passed through Edwina. "Polly?"

"Yes, Georgie's mother. Her name was Mary, but since there were several generations of Marys in the family, everyone called her Polly."

"But, at the séance, you said you didn't know anyone named Polly and that the message couldn't be for you."

Charles looked up at her, his eyes widened with surprise. "At the time of the séance, I didn't know anyone who had passed away named Polly. At least I didn't think that I did." He glanced back down at the sleeping child.

"You don't think Maude can actually speak with the dead, do you?"

"I don't know what to think."

Chapter 16

The pub was still filled to bursting when Beryl took her leave of Chester. The pavement outside the Dove and Duck was uncharacteristically empty other than a solitary ginger cat perched on the curb cleaning its paws.

As Beryl moved away from the pub, Maude and Arthur Dinsdale came into view. They had been conspicuously absent from the inquest, and Beryl wondered what that might mean. Had they simply been too distressed by what had happened to Hazel to hear the whole thing rehashed? She crossed the street and came alongside them, determined to do a bit of digging into their reasons for avoiding what so many others had seemed eager to embrace.

Arthur smiled at her as she lifted a hand in greeting, but Maude looked more reserved. She simply nodded her head solemnly as Beryl approached, and she fleetingly wondered if the other woman had heard that she was not actually a true believer. It would be too much to hope that such information would never make its way back to her. Besides, Beryl had made public commentaries when questioned by members of the press about her attendance at séances. It would be an easy enough thing to apprise herself of Beryl's true feelings.

"I noticed you didn't attend the inquest," she went ahead and said, sure it would do no good to beat around the bush.

"We saw no reason to just tread over the painful territory again by subjecting ourselves to the details of Dr. Nelson's findings," Maude said.

"Then you've heard what his findings were?" Beryl asked.

"No, I'm afraid we have not. We spent our morning shut away at home, avoiding news of the proceedings to the best of our ability." Arthur glanced down at his wristwatch before speaking again. "We thought it was finally safe to venture out and thought we might go ahead with some shopping we needed to do."

Maude lifted a wicker basket much like the one Edwina used for visiting the greengrocer and butcher shop, as if to support his claims. "Even those in the throes of grief must maintain the physical body. The cupboard is rather bare," she said.

"Then I suppose you did not hear about your ceremonial dagger," Beryl said, keeping her eyes carefully trained on Maude's face. She wished Edwina was here with her. She was much better at ferreting out lies than Beryl was. Besides, she couldn't very well keep an eye on both of them at the same time without help. She wondered where Edwina had gotten off to since the completion of the inquest. She had not seen her, although she would not have expected her to appear at the pub. It was something she was loath to do, and although Beryl could feel refreshed after visiting the Dove and Duck, she was certain it would have taken even more out of Edwina than the inquest had.

"What about it?" Arthur asked.

"It does not appear to have been the actual murder weapon. It seems someone simply placed it in Hazel's wound, for some sort of effect or to throw investigators off the scent. Or, I suppose, it could have been intended to implicate one or the other of you, if not both." She allowed her gaze to slip back and forth between the two siblings, eager to see how they took the news that someone might have targeted them for scrutiny.

"I know that people with my gifts are not always welcome in every quarter of society, but I would not have expected to hear that someone would go to those lengths to be rid of us," Maude said.

"It certainly isn't a very pleasant notion," Arthur said, reaching toward his sister and touching her arm in support. "I wouldn't take it to heart, my dear."

"I have no intention of allowing other people's opinions to dissuade me from my mission," Maude said.

"Do you have any idea who might have wished to point blame in your direction?" Beryl asked.

Arthur shrugged his broad shoulders and turned toward his sister once more, as if deferring to her greater understanding of the dynamics at work in Walmsley Parva.

"Although I am loath to implicate prominent and well-respected members of the community, it would not surprise me to hear that the vicar and his wife were not our biggest supporters. Hazel reported the considerable dust the vicar kicked up when she began serving as the accompanist for our séances. I can well imagine them being particularly interested in seeing the back of us," she said.

"I had heard something about an uproar over Hazel accepting employment from you as well as the church. But I should not have thought it would have led to murder. After all, she was a valued organist for the church, and murdering her certainly would not have brought her talents back to the weekly services."

"I didn't say that either the vicar or his wife was responsible for Hazel's death, just that they might take an opportunity to point blame in our direction, had they discovered the body."

Now that was a thought. Was it possible that whoever had actually killed Hazel was not the one who placed her body into Princess Rosanna's sarcophagus? Could there have been more than one party involved in what had happened to her? Maude had a clear expectation that the vicar and his wife had an ax to grind with them and a vested interest in seeing them leave the village. What better way to run them out of town than for them to be arrested for murder? That said, it did seem out of character for people as upright and God-fearing as the vicar and his wife to falsely accuse someone else of a crime. Shouldn't they be counted on to uphold truth and justice whenever possible?

"Do you have some reason to suspect they would have had access to the tailor shop?" Beryl asked.

"There's no reason to suspect that they had greater access than anyone else in the village. But it must be said they had no less access either. We simply don't lock it. Much like the church itself, we feel that there would be no reason for anyone to harm the places we gather or to take anything from them," Maude said.

"But someone did take Princess Rosanna, didn't they?" Beryl said.

The Dinsdales exchanged a glance. Beryl was not quite sure what to read in it, but it looked as though perhaps they had not entirely agreed on such a cavalier attitude toward their place of business.

"We have set up shop in towns and villages all across the country, and this is the first time anything like this has ever happened. It seems to us that there's a particularly criminal element here in Walmsley Parva for which we were not prepared," Arthur said.

Beryl could not disagree. For such a small village, there had certainly been a great deal of criminality since her arrival. Although, as Edwina had pointed out, there had been very little in that line before Beryl had appeared out of the blue almost a year previously. She had occasionally implied—although charitably, it must be said—that Beryl had brought something with her that altered the moral compass of the village. Beryl was more than happy to help set a new course in terms of outdated practices and shortsighted thinking, but she did not wish to be saddled with the responsibility for other people's poor decisions.

Still, it was interesting to consider that no one before had shown any inclination to purloin their precious mummy. Her gaze was drawn toward the bric-a-brac shop located halfway up the High Street. Although, even if the owner had been responsible for helping herself to Princess Rosanna, she would hardly be likely to try and sell it right there in the village under the Dinsdales' noses. It would be tantamount to admitting to murder.

She considered the fact that anyone at all could have entered the tailor shop in order to make the switch. But was their lack of security common knowledge? She herself had not realized they did not lock the building when they were not in attendance. Who else would have been likely to know such information?

"Did you make a point of telling people that you did not bother with securing the premises?" Beryl asked.

"I guess I would not say that we made a point to mention it, but we never bothered to hide the fact that the door was unlocked. After all, we often arrived at the shop later than some of those wishing to attend a session. Sitters are often extremely eager not to be late, we have found. Surely anyone standing there would have realized that they did not need a key to enter the building," Arthur said.

"Would you happen to remember who's attended sessions since you have arrived in town?" Beryl asked.

The siblings exchanged another glance before Maude turned to answer. "I would think that a good quarter of the village has turned out at one point or other. Considering what happened with Hazel, I would not be surprised for that number to double."

Although it left her feeling disappointed in humanity, Beryl thought it likely that Maude was correct in her assessment. There was nothing like a gruesome tragedy to inspire people to visit where it had unfolded. Who in the village would not wish to be able to say they'd for themselves seen the very spot where Hazel's body was found? It was the sort of story that would be told for at least another generation, if not longer. No one would wish to be left out of the opportunity to tell it. No, in terms of moneymaking, Hazel's death was one of the best things that could have happened for the Dinsdales' business. She tipped her head to one side and scrutinized them even more closely. Could that be the reason she had been killed?

"I think it's less likely that anyone who attended our séance would wish Hazel ill than those who were determinedly opposed to what we do," Arthur said. He nodded in the direction of a figure hurrying toward him from up the street. Mr. Watkins limped into view, his face set in a grim line of aggravation. Once again, his hand was raised skyward as he approached, and he shook his fist in their general direction.

"Do you believe that Mr. Watkins has something to do with Hazel's death?"

"From his attitude toward us, it wouldn't surprise me in the least," Maude said. She turned toward Mr. Watkins, a look of resignation stamped on her face.

"Are you speaking to us, sir?" she asked as the sound of his angry voice reached them.

He stopped on the curb beside them and shook his fist even more vigorously. "Of course, I'm talking to you. I told you to stop upsetting my wife, and you simply wouldn't listen. The poor woman has taken to her bed after what she saw at your last wicked gathering."

"I assure you, sir, we were in no way eager to put any of our attendees through what occurred. And we certainly would not have wished something like that upon Hazel. She was our friend and a valued member of our team," Arthur said.

"Hazel was just as much of a vulture as the pair of you. As far as I can see, you all deserve each other. It won't bother me none if the two of you meet a similarly bad end," he said.

Beryl didn't quite like the look in Mr. Watkins's eye. Nor did she think it prudent for him to say such things when no one knew who had murdered Hazel. He was making himself look like a likely suspect.

"Where were you when Hazel was killed?" Beryl asked. He turned to face her, as if he had forgotten she was there.

"Are you accusing me of something?" he asked.

"I'm only asking the same questions Constable Gibbs will, should she hear you making foolish remarks like that," Beryl said.

"I have no idea where I was since I don't know when she died," Mr. Watkins said, lowering his fist and crossing his arms over his chest.

"All right. Have you been anywhere near the tailor shop in the last day or two?" she asked.

"You know that I have. I cussed you out for flying your airplane too close to my livestock. We stood right here and discussed it. If you can't remember a thing like that you're no better than those two." He jerked his thumb toward the Dinsdales, then spun on his heel and stomped away. Beryl watched his retreating back, wondering if she had touched a nerve. Was he really simply distressed at the emotional state of his wife, or was he trying to frighten off the Dinsdales?

"Such a thoroughly unpleasant man. It's hard to believe that Mrs. Watkins is married to someone as abrasive as he," Maude said.

"Come now, my dear, you mustn't say such things. The

poor man has been through a great deal with the loss of his daughter. It's no wonder he's very protective of his wife, even if he is misguided about it all," Arthur said.

"That's a very generous attitude on your part," Beryl said. "Not everyone would be so tolerant of being insulted repeatedly."

"If there's one thing you learn very quickly in this line of work, it's that there will be people who are more than happy to insult you to your face, behind your back, and in the press. If we were to be upset every time such a thing occurred, we would have stopped offering these services long ago," Maude said.

"Had you never considered just that?" Beryl said.

"It's a calling. I have no more control over my willingness to serve as a channel than a bird has the ability to stop itself from singing."

"That said, perhaps it would be better if we finished up our errands and returned home." Arthur inclined his head toward the pub, where one or two stragglers had exited the building. "I'm not sure that we wish to subject ourselves to the idle chatter that surely will be flowing our way if we do not hurry."

They bid Beryl goodbye and made their way in the direction of the greengrocer. She watched as they strode off, wondering if they might have been involved somehow in either the murder or Hazel's body appearing in the tailor shop. After all, their suggestion that the vicar and his wife might have simply moved the body to discredit them could equally be said about the way it would affect their uptick in business. She decided to hurry back to The Beeches in order to mull it all over with Edwina, providing she had headed home.

Chapter 17

Edwina closed the door to Charles's house behind her and paused for a moment on the front step to collect her thoughts. The idea of his well-ordered bachelor existence being disarranged by the sudden appearance of a young child left her feeling unsettled. As much as she occasionally permitted herself to briefly grieve over the things in life that she regretted, that mercifully short list of might-have-beens, she did not allow herself to dwell on them, with one exception.

Edwina had always wished to become a mother. Lamentably, the opportunity to do so had not presented itself. Between the demands her mother had made before her death, precluding the possibility of her seriously entering the marriage market, and the dearth of available men after the war, she had found herself one of the million or so surplus women the country now counted as inhabitants. Without a husband, there could be no children, and it was an ache that kept her awake on many a night.

She had tried valiantly to fill the void with volunteerism in her beloved village and with Crumpet, as well as her garden.

The arrival of Beryl and Simpkins at The Beeches had done much to alleviate her deep feelings of loneliness, and the opening of the private-enquiry agency had gone a long way toward distracting her. She should even claim, without it being too fanciful a flight of imagination, that her novel was a child of sorts. After all, she was responsible for bringing it forth into the world.

But none of these things completely warded off or filled her underlying maternal drive. Edwina was not someone with even the smallest bit of confidence that life was fair, or even that it was intended to be. Surely, one could not have picked up a newspaper through the war and influenza years and retained that sort of foolish belief. That said, she marveled at the fact that Charles was to be so blessed by fate when he had never expressed any sort of interest in children. It was one of the things about him that had left her unmoved by his overtures of interest in her romantically. Not that she would have said so. And to give him his due, perhaps he would not have wanted to hint at such a delicate subject. After all, there was not a very great chance that she would be favored with a child of her own even if she were to marry so late in life.

The look of relief on Charles's face flooded back to her as she lifted Georgie into her arms and ceased the thunderous banging in his usually tranquil kitchen. A new notion flitted through her mind. Had Charles's interest in her sprung primarily from the belief that a life with her would not lead to the sort of toll a brood of young would bring? She supposed that might account for his inexplicable and persistent pursuit of her. And now here he was, entrusted with the care and raising of a small boy, with no wife to assist him. What was he going to do?

She descended to the lane and headed off without a clear sense of direction. She had promised Charles to ring him up in a few hours' time to check on how both he and Georgie were faring. She would have remained at his home longer, but she did not wish to intrude or to imply that Charles could not handle the situation without her assistance. Nor did she wish to make herself too much at home. After all, there was a shadowy line between herself and Charles that she had not felt inclined to cross, and the cozy feeling of sitting at his kitchen table holding a toddler made it seem as if she may have just passed over it.

She commanded herself to think of something else. Unbidden, the name of Georgie's mother, Polly, floated into her thoughts. While she had not felt convinced about Maude's psychic abilities, she could not deny that there was something eerie about Charles suddenly being in receipt of what sure must have been her greatest treasure. How would Beryl explain that once she knew about the child's unexpected arrival in Charles's life? Energized by the desire to talk it over with her friend, she turned back toward the village in search of her. Knowing Beryl, she had headed straight for the Dove and Duck as soon as the inquest had concluded.

Beryl had not ventured too far from the pub. Edwina came upon her near the millpond with a pensive look on her face. She stopped beside her, eager to share her news.

"You will never believe what has happened," she said.

"Is it about the case?" Beryl asked, turning her full attention to her friend.

"Indirectly, I suppose that it is," Edwina said. "I have just come from Charles's."

"Did he have a good reason for skipping out of the inquest?" Beryl asked.

"Indeed, he did. And a most surprising one too."

Beryl's forehead crinkled with concern. "He hasn't taken ill, has he?"

"That was my initial thought when he failed to appear in the courtroom, but it is nothing like that. He was called away to collect his cousin's child after she suffered a fatal accident."

Beryl's eyes widened. "What sort of accident?"

Edwina chided herself silently for mentioning the circumstances of the young mother's death. Conversations with Beryl on the subject of motoring safety often descended into terseness on her part and breezy dismissiveness on Beryl's. It was a topic best avoided whenever possible. Still there was no avoiding it now that she had brought it up.

"A motoring accident. I do not have the details, as I did not feel it appropriate to ask for them right in front of her orphaned son."

Beryl managed to nod in agreement. "How dreadful. How old is the child?"

"He appeared to be somewhere around two years of age. He is a very handsome little thing."

"You said orphaned. Has he no father?"

"He died serving in the war. Apparently, he never met his son." Edwina felt a lump rising in her throat as she considered how cruel such a thing seemed.

"Why has Charles been the one to swoop in and collect him?" Beryl asked.

"He was named in her will as Georgie's guardian."

Beryl's mouth dropped open. "Is this to be a permanent arrangement?"

"At present, that seems to be the situation. I think it has all been too great a shock for Charles to make any decisions about how to proceed other than bringing him home to Walmsley Parva. You should have seen the state of his kitchen when I arrived."

"I suppose that is a most compelling reason for missing the inquest. And it explains what became of you too. I thought perhaps you had headed straight home yourself after the rigors of the inquest."

Edwina hoped her nerves had not shown during the proceedings. "Was my unease that noticeable?"

"I am sure that it was not to anyone but me. You always are

a bit more formal and correct in attitude when you are not entirely sure of yourself in a situation, but that is not the sort of thing that makes most people question your competence. You pulled it all off like an old hand, despite Charles's absence."

Edwina felt a faint flush begin to rise at the nape of her neck. She still had not become entirely adept at receiving compliments, even though Beryl was generous at handing them out. Changing the subject was by far the easiest thing.

"You'll never believe Georgie's mother's name," she said.

"I wouldn't begin to guess."

"Her given name was Mary, but because there were so many others in her family, she was always called Polly. Don't you find that strange?"

"Do you mean because of Maude's comments at the séance?"

"Of course. You must admit, it is quite the coincidence."

Beryl shrugged. "Polly isn't the most unusual name. It could be attributed to a good guess, don't you think?"

"I don't know that I agree. I cannot help but wonder about Maude's abilities considering that she also mentioned Polly leaving Charles her greatest treasure."

"You think that was Georgie?"

"If he had been my son, he would have been mine," Edwina said, attempting to keep the tremor of longing from her voice. Beryl in no way shared her desire for a child. In fact, Edwina thought small humans represented one of the only things that her intrepid friend actually feared. Over the months that she had been in the village, she had developed some tolerance and possibly even a bit of affection for the younger generation of the Prentice family, but other than that, she kept children at arm's length.

"I am sure that you are right about her love for her son. I just am less convinced than ever that Maude has any sort of metaphysical ability."

Edwina could tell from the tone of Beryl's voice that there

was no profit in discussing the matter at length, at least not at the moment.

"You must have been as surprised as I when Dr. Nelson declared that the dagger was not the murder weapon," she said.

"I must admit, that did stir my imagination unpleasantly. To imagine someone running Hazel through with one sort of implement only to do it again with a second is frankly repellent."

"I felt the same. What kind of a person would do such a thing?"

"I was just discussing that with the Dinsdales. They suggested that the vicar and Muriel might be the ones responsible."

"Surely, they cannot think that they would have killed Hazel. After all, they wanted her back as the church organist in the worst way."

"That's what I said, but they suggested that perhaps the pair of them had found Hazel's body and had moved it into a place where the Dinsdales would be implicated and added their own dagger for good measure."

"They cannot really believe that, can they?"

Edwina was shocked. She could not imagine the vicar or his wife doing something so deliberately evil. Then again, it was difficult to fathom someone murdering Hazel either.

"I shouldn't have thought so, but you never know. The vicar's reaction to the séances was intense. But their suggestion did give me another idea. What if the Dinsdales were the ones who found her body and placed it in the sarcophagus?"

"Why would they have done that?"

"They pointed out themselves that there will be even more interest in attending their séances now, if only to view the gory site."

Edwina's sense of propriety felt assaulted. What sort of people would be so mercenary? Surely, the Dinsdales weren't so cavalier about death if they had dedicated their careers to exploring contact with those who had passed on.

"I find such a suggestion abhorrent. Do you think they actually did that? Would they have put their sitters through what we saw?"

"People have done far worse for money, as well you know. Think back on some of our previous cases."

Beryl had a point. They had seen a shocking amount of greed and other low emotions since opening their enquiry agency. Perhaps this was just the latest in a rash of distressing examples of inhumanity. Still, it wasn't the first line of enquiry she wished to pursue.

"Did you discover anything else while I was gone? Any tittle-tattle at the pub?"

"Not really. I spoke with Chester, but all he had to tell me was that he received a large bet from Hazel's tenant, Anthony Linton, and another from the local photographer recently. No one else has done anything the least bit odd that he has heard."

Chester wasn't a gossip like Prudence or Minnie, but Edwina had understood from both Beryl and Simpkins that the man was remarkably well informed about the goings-on in their village as well as the neighboring ones. If he had heard nothing, there was truly not a lot to go on. That left the lead from Prudence to explore.

"Shall we stop in at the Palais and ask Clarence about his interest in Hazel and whether or not his wife knew about it?" she asked.

"You read my mind, Ed."

Chapter 18

Clarence could be seen clearly through the large windows of the Palais cinema. Since Eva Scott had left his employ some weeks earlier, he had taken to staffing the ticket counter himself. He looked up expectantly as the two sleuths entered through the sparkling glass doors. His smile faded as he recognized the two women entering his place of business. Edwina, who had never been on the receiving end of his unwanted attention, had found it hard to believe when Beryl had first mentioned Clarence's enthusiasm for putting his hands where they did not belong. But even she had to admit that, with so many women in town complaining about his behavior, there had to be some truth to it. Clarence had been the subject of interrogation in the past in connection with crime, and Edwina thought his flickering smile reflected his concern that he might once again be on their suspect list. She did not feel remotely responsible for his discomfort. If he had not behaved in such a way that caused rumors about him to be bandied about the village, they would have no reason to pay him such a call.

"I don't suppose you're here to purchase tickets for the

matinee, are you?" Clarence asked, drumming his bony fingers against the countertop next to the brass till.

Beryl flashed him one of her dazzling smiles and shook her head, sending her blonde hair swishing slightly along her shoulders. She looked about the cinema lobby as if to ascertain that they were quite alone.

"I'm afraid it's rather more serious than that. But I don't suppose you're surprised to see us, now, are you?" she said.

"You're here about what happened to Hazel," he said as his shoulders slumped. He reached behind him and dragged a high metal stool forward and perched his rather bony backside upon it, as if he had lost the energy to stand.

"As a matter of fact, we are," Edwina said, stepping forward. She could hear that her voice had taken on a starchy sort of tone, but she simply could not help it. She took the bonds of matrimony quite seriously, despite her lack of experience with them, and felt aggrieved by those who did not. It bothered her to consider that, if Minnie were the one responsible for this heinous crime, she had vented her spleen on Hazel rather than on Clarence, who clearly was so unworthy of her esteem and long years of companionship.

"I'm telling you right now that I had absolutely nothing to do with what happened to her," Clarence said, his voice reaching up an octave higher than normal.

"That's not what we heard. You'd feel better if you got things off your chest," Beryl said.

Clarence crossed his long, slim arms across his chest. "I don't know what you've been hearing, but I had no hand in Hazel's unfortunate demise. Why would I have?" He lifted his chin defiantly.

Beryl and Edwina exchanged a glance, and Edwina gave a slight nod. Her friend was ever so much better at broaching the subject of infidelity.

"We have it on good authority that you were interested in Hazel romantically," Beryl said, raising a hand as Clarence began to sputter out a protest. "Don't bother to deny it. Everyone in town knows your proclivities."

"Most importantly, everyone now includes your poor, long-suffering wife, Minnie," Edwina said.

Clarence's arms fell away from his chest, and he sagged toward them, leaning heavily on the counter separating them from the rest of the lobby. "What do you mean Minnie knows?"

This was something Edwina had not expected. If Prudence Rathbone had heard it from Minnie herself, it seemed surprising that word had not gotten back to Clarence about the gossip. It was not as though Prudence was particularly tight-lipped when crowing about any morsels of news she happened to have gathered. Edwina could well imagine her delighting in watching Clarence's reaction to the news that his wife knew all about his extracurricular activities.

"That's what we've been told by a source who assured us it came straight from Minnie's own lips. You can't possibly expect us to believe that she did not confront you with it herself?" Beryl said.

Edwina wasn't so sure that Minnie would have confronted her husband. In fact, Edwina wondered how she would have managed to get the words out. As humiliating as it was to discover that her husband had been carrying on as he had, it still could be too much to ask him why he did it. Would she even want to hear the answer? Edwina was not so sure, had she been in Minnie's position, that she would have wished to know the truth. Somehow, it seemed beneath Minnie's dignity to have the conversation with Clarence. After all, what could the man possibly say to excuse himself for his actions? No, it was one thing to pour her heart out to her friend Prudence, however foolhardy that might have been. It was quite another to do so with the very person who had most harmed her.

"What passes between my wife and me has nothing whatsoever to do with anyone else," Clarence said, rallying to a surprising degree.

"Well, that might be true under other circumstances, but it holds absolutely no water during the course of a murder investigation. All dirty laundry one wished to keep pushed down into the bottom of the hamper, including yours, will surely be flapping about in the breeze for all the village to see," Beryl said.

Clarence's eyes widened, and he jumped to his feet, kicking a stool over in his haste. It crashed to the plushly carpeted floor with a clunk.

"My laundry, dirty or otherwise, has nothing to do with the pair of you. After all, you're not the police. You're simply poking your nose in where it doesn't belong, and I won't stand for it."

"If you won't speak to us on your own behalf, you might consider doing so for your poor wife. She's the one who seems the most likely suspect in all of this," Edwina said.

"Minnie would never hurt anyone. She can't possibly be a suspect," he said.

"Her name is being bandied about as someone who had good reason to kill Hazel. In fact, as far as Constable Gibbs has been able to ascertain, she's the only one with any real motive to do away with her," Edwina said.

It was almost the whole truth. Edwina had a terrible feeling that, whether or not she was guilty, poor Minnie looked for all the world like the only possible lead. And it wasn't as though Prudence was likely to keep her mouth shut about her claims concerning Minnie's distress over her husband's alleged infidelity. In fact, their visit to Clarence could be considered a favor of sorts. It would give him a chance to brace himself for whatever unpleasantness might unfold when Constable Gibbs came calling. That was, unless they could find a good reason to send her in another direction.

Clarence bent over and picked up the stool. He made quite a production of settling it firmly on its four spindly legs before perching on it once more. Edwina had the sense he was taking his time in order to concoct a story he felt would go down easily with the sleuths. She was so curious as to what he would come up with that she was not prepared for him to offer the truth.

"I truly had no idea Minnie suspected a thing." Clarence sighed deeply. Edwina could almost imagine he regretted what he had put his wife through. "It is true that I had a romantic interest in Hazel. I found her very attractive and even went so far as to turn on the charm whenever she worked a shift."

"Did she reciprocate your interest?" Beryl asked.

"At first, it seemed as though she did. She would laugh at my jokes, no matter how silly, and bat her eyelashes at me whenever I complimented her on something she was wearing or how well she played the accompaniment at any given film."

"Did something change?" Beryl asked.

"I'll say it did. She turned quite cold after a while. She had always seemed eager to meet my gaze or even to seek me out before or after her shift. Then it seemed as though her interest completely faded."

Edwina thought it likely that Hazel had simply come to her senses. After all, what sort of future could she have with a man who was purported to be a serial philanderer who never actually left his wife? It would have been a poor-enough bargain in a city like Manchester or London, but in a village like Walmsley Parva, it was societal suicide. Edwina could almost imagine that Hazel might have been so starved for attention that she let her emotions get the better of her when someone actually paid her any mind. But Hazel was a sensible woman, and it would be easy to picture her realizing the consequences of encouraging Clarence.

"Do you have any idea why she suddenly thought better of permitting your behavior?" Beryl asked.

Clarence pursed his lips as if peeved. "It was after the Dinsdales arrived in the village. Unless I miss my guess, Hazel thought Arthur Dinsdale offered greener pastures than did I. I saw them laughing and smiling together on several occasions since they first arrived in Walmsley Parva. Although what she saw in him, I can't imagine."

Edwina forced herself not to allow the gasp she felt bubbling up out of her mouth. She had never particularly warmed to Clarence, and she had found his character lacking in light of his womanizing reputation. But that level of arrogance was a bridge too far. What right had he to judge someone like Hazel who might have wanted to open her heart to someone eligible to marry her?

"Perhaps she saw someone who is actually available to have a legitimate relationship with her," Edwina said. "This conversation has provided us with one bit of solid information, however, that I am sure will bring you relief."

"What might that be?" Clarence asked.

"From your attitude toward Hazel's diminishing interest in you, I would have to say that you have shot to the top of the list of suspects. After all, your comments are exactly the sort of thing that a man who couldn't take no for an answer might make. We've seen situations like this from spurned lovers before, haven't we, Beryl?" Edwina asked, turning toward her friend.

"I should say so. Besides, I'm sure that the average resident of the village could see Clarence as a murderer much more easily than they could his wife. I'm sure you're very relieved to hear that, aren't you?" she asked, turning yet another bright smile on the shocked man sitting across the counter.

"We won't take up any more of your time. After all, we really ought to confer with Constable Gibbs," Edwina said. She spun on her low-heeled shoe and strode toward the door, feeling Beryl following closely behind her.

"Nice job, Ed," she said, patting her friend on the shoulder.

Chapter 19

"You know we are going to have to speak to Minnie about what happened, don't you?" Beryl asked. She knew that such conversations were difficult for Edwina. She never liked to think the worst of any of the other residents of her beloved village, especially not women who were as long-suffering as Minnie Mumford. After all, it would be very awkward to interrogate someone while sampling their delicious scones and thickly clotted cream. Even Beryl, who had a less refined taste for any sort of nourishment besides cocktails and coffee, could see how her friend would not be eager to have a rift with Minnie, considering the high regard for her edible offerings.

"Yes, I'm afraid that we are," Edwina said, slowing her pace as they came alongside Alma's House of Beauty. The proprietress knocked on the front window of her shop and beckoned them toward her. They entered, and Alma bustled toward them, locking the door behind them, and flipping the sign on the door to CLOSED.

She waved them over toward the row of seats placed below

the hair dryers and indicated they should make themselves at home.

"I've been waiting for a chance to speak to the two of you privately," Alma said.

"What is this about?" Edwina asked.

"Why, Hazel's murder, of course. I wondered if you had any suspects in the case," Alma said.

"There are one or two that have come up," Beryl said.

"I suppose you're questioning Minnie, and I thought I saw you coming out of the cinema, so that must mean that Clarence is also on the list," she said.

It wasn't that Alma was a gossip. She just happened to be in a position to hear a lot of goings-on from other women in the village. After all, the relationship between a hairdresser and her clientele was quite an intimate one. There was something about putting oneself in the hands of another that led to the sharing of confidences. Alma could be a useful source, in any case, but in one where there was so little to go on, she might prove especially valuable.

"I'm sure you understand that we cannot go into specifics, considering it's early in the investigation and we wouldn't want to cast aspersions on anyone who later turned out to be completely innocent," Beryl said.

It would never do to get on the bad side of the only hairdresser in town. While she was not opposed to the notion of taking the motorcar on a jaunt up to London, she did not want to have to do so every time she wished to have her hair washed and set. Nor was she eager for Edwina to feel she had to head out of the village in order to keep her modern bob neatly trimmed. She was so much happier since she had shed her long locks in favor of an up-to-date hairstyle.

"I understand completely. There are many things that I hear in the course of my workday that I don't share with anyone either. But I did think I might be able to offer some assistance, as it is my civic duty. I liked Hazel and would hate for whoever did this to get away with it," she said.

"We appreciate that," Edwina said. She pulled her trusty notebook from her pocket, along with her tiny pencil, and flipped open the cover, perching it on her leg, ready to take down whatever Alma had to share.

"I was thinking after the inquest that perhaps this whole investigation might run after false leads," Alma said.

"What would lead you to believe that?" Beryl asked.

"Well, I had just finished sweeping up hair trimmings after several different women had been at the shop. And it occurred to me how often women come in looking to change their appearance and that the last person to have requested something a bit different was Hazel."

"Go on," Beryl said.

"It was not long after the Dinsdales arrived in the village. Hazel brought in a magazine and asked me if I might be able to create a hairstyle for her that looked like the one on the woman on the front cover." Alma leaned back in her chair and drummed her fingers on the armrests. "The woman on the cover reminded me of someone, but it wasn't until after she had left my chair that it occurred to me who it was."

Edwina scribbled furiously in her notebook as Beryl continued taking a lead on the questioning. "And who was that?" she asked.

"Maude Dinsdale. Have either of you noticed how much the two of them looked alike?"

Beryl and Edwina exchanged a glance. Now that she came to think of it, Beryl would have to agree that, at least superficially, the two women could have been sisters.

"Do you think it was the hairstyle that made them look alike?" Beryl asked. She had used a similar guise many times during her work throughout the war years. A simple shift in the way she wore her hair or a quick dye job could utterly transform her appearance, at least superficially. Why couldn't the same be said for a church organist?

"I think the hairstyle was the icing on the cake. They were of a similar height and build, and their coloring was very much alike. Really, it was a matter of their hairstyle highlighting the fact that they could easily have been related."

"And why did you want to bring this up?" Edwina asked, pausing from her jottings.

"Well, it occurred to me that someone might have mistaken Hazel for Maude. Could it be that Hazel wasn't actually the intended victim at all?" Alma asked.

Beryl looked over at her friend, who wrote the question down quickly in her notebook before returning her gaze. Edwina raised an eyebrow as if the thought intrigued her.

"Are you suggesting that Maude had more enemies than Hazel? As though there were someone more likely to want to see her dead?" Edwina asked.

"I should think it is likely. After all, any psychic practitioner is bound to make enemies. It's not as though the position is not a controversial one. It certainly seems more likely that Maude Dinsdale had people who wished her ill than Hazel, the mild-mannered church organist who had lived peacefully amongst us her whole life," Alma said.

"Did you have anyone in particular in mind who you happen to know would hold such animosity toward Maude?" Edwina asked.

Alma shrugged. "That's far more your bailiwick than mine. I just thought you ought to know it occurred to me that Hazel's murder might be a case of mistaken identity. Who it was who mistook her—that is up to you to figure out."

*　*　*

Edwina and Beryl separated upon exiting Alma's House of Beauty. Edwina did not discourage Beryl when she expressed a desire to head back to The Beeches to write up a few thoughts about how the Dinsdales could have created the effects displayed at their séances. Not only would such musings likely prove helpful to the investigation, but they would leave Edwina on her own to question Minnie.

It was not that she thought Beryl insensitive, but rather that she felt certain Minnie would be more inclined to unburden herself to the smallest possible audience. Besides, as far as the village was concerned, Beryl was still a virtual stranger, and a matter as personal as the inconstancy of one's husband was only fit to be confided to friends of long standing. As Edwina had known Minnie for decades, she felt she passed muster on that front.

She paused outside the door to the Silver Spoon Tea Room, just as she had only days before when first she had encountered Maude. How long ago that seemed, as she recollected her anxiety about sending off her manuscript for scrutiny. Since Muriel had approached them about debunking the medium, she had given only a passing thought or two to her novel.

Minnie stood behind the counter cashing out Mrs. Dumbarton, proprietress of the Woolery, as Edwina entered the shop. She passed a few pleasant moments chatting with the yarn-store owner about her latest acquisition, a selection of lace-weight silk dyed in the most fashionable colors. Edwina promised to come by and purchase some for herself just as soon as she had completed the hat she had planned with her most recent purchase. She waited for Mrs. Dumbarton to leave before seating herself at a table with an excellent view of the door, just out of sight of the shop's largest window.

Minnie bustled over a moment later with an expectant smile on her face. She reminded Edwina distinctly of Clarence, and she wondered if a marriage of long standing truly did cause couples to begin to look alike. Although it must be said that while Clarence was long and thin, his wife was shorter and round, as could well be expected by a woman surrounded almost constantly by so many delicious treats. Edwina saw no reason not to avail herself of the day's specialties and requested a variety of tiny sandwiches and hot, buttered scones.

In the time it took Minnie to return with the tea tray covered with an assortment of baked goods, jams, and a pot of freshly brewed Earl Grey, Edwina's stomach began to rumble. It occurred to her that she had skipped breakfast on account of her nervous stomach, brought on by the ordeal of the inquest. As she eyed the cheese sandwiches, her mouth began to water.

"What a beautiful selection you've brought," she said. "But you've been far too generous. Won't you join me?"

Minnie looked around the shop, as if to reassure herself that they were on their own. While they had shared a meal in the shop on many occasions in the past, it had always been in the absence of other patrons. There is something ever so slightly unprofessional about being seen to be sitting down on the job. But as there were no other customers within sight nor were any approaching the doorway, she smiled and pulled out the chair opposite Edwina's. Edwina lifted the teapot and poured a generous serving in each of the cups, noting that Minnie had thought to include a second cup on the tea tray. Perhaps she was as eager to have a chat as Edwina was.

Edwina waited until they each had plates filled with a variety of Minnie's handiwork before broaching the subject of Hazel's murder.

"I don't believe I saw you at the inquest this morning," she said, keeping her eyes firmly on Minnie's face. Minnie kept her own attention on the cream scone in front of her. Was it Edwina's imagination, or did she seem unusually absorbed in the task of buttering each half straight to the edges? When she finally glanced up, her face was covered with red blotches, as if she were struggling with strong emotion.

"No, I had too much to do here at the shop this morning. Baking and the like. I'm sure you understand," she said.

"Have you had much custom this morning? I thought most of the village had turned out for the inquest. At least it looked that way from the size of the gathered crowd."

"No, not really. In fact, you're only my second customer of the day. It's a good thing you came in or all this will have gone to waste if business doesn't pick up before long." Minnie broke off a piece of the scone with her pudgy fingers and popped it into her mouth.

"I suppose it's not surprising. Beryl told me that most everyone who attended the inquest headed straight for the Dove and Duck as soon as it finished up. Apparently, there was much interest in discussing the goings-on."

"I'm sure it's no business of mine, whatever was being said," Minnie said.

Edwina was surprised at how determined Minnie seemed to be not to be drawn into conversation on such a popular subject. It seemed no one else in the village could stop talking about Hazel's murder. As much as she did not want Prudence to be correct, that Minnie might have good reason to do away with her romantic rival, she was not putting herself in a very good light by avoiding the topic so determinedly. Perhaps another tack might do the trick.

"Clarence didn't attend either, now that I come to think of it," Edwina said. "I'm rather surprised at that. Most of the other business owners in town were right up near the front of the courtroom. It was almost as though they thought that something as unsavory as a body turning up on the High Street was an affront to commerce."

At the mention of her husband's name, Minnie's face grew even more deeply flushed. Truly, Edwina felt sorry for the poor woman. To imagine oneself to be made miserable by the likes of Clarence Mumford was pitiable indeed.

"I don't know who you have been talking to, but Clarence would have no reason whatsoever to interest himself in Hazel Moffat, dead or alive," Minnie said.

She reached for the sugar bowl and dropped three lumps into her steaming cup before stirring it vigorously with one of her silver spoons. Edwina slid the dish of sliced lemons toward her companion. Minnie shook her head and busied herself with a crescent tomato sandwich sitting neatly in her plate. She disassembled and reassembled it four separate times before looking Edwina in the eye.

"Is there a reason you would expect I had been speaking with someone about your husband?" Edwina asked.

"That's what you do, isn't it? Don't you and Beryl flit about the village, asking impertinent questions every time misfortune occurs in the village? Really, I don't know what's gotten into you within the last few months," she said, before taking a large bite of her sandwich.

It was completely unlike Minnie to speak so harshly to anyone, let alone a repeat customer and longtime acquaintance. It was a measure of her distress that she would lash out in that way. That said, it did make it easier for Edwina to stop dancing around the questions floating through her mind. Perhaps the direct approach was more fitting under the circumstances.

"Since you brought it up, I suppose I do have a question for you, and I'm afraid that you won't appreciate it in the least," Edwina said.

Minnie crossed her arms over her chest and leaned against the back of her chair. "You'd best get on with it then."

"Where were you at the time Hazel was stabbed to death,

then stuffed into the sarcophagus in the tailor shop?" She shocked herself at her bluntness. Even Beryl would be unlikely to be so forthright when questioning a potential suspect.

"Are you accusing me of something?" Minnie's eyes had widened, and the high color had drained from her face.

Unless she were a very good actress, and Edwina had no reason to believe that she was, she was startled by the question. Whether that was because she really had nothing to do with the crime or because she had never expected to be caught, Edwina could not begin to guess.

"No. I'm not accusing you of anything exactly. I am, however, asking you to account for your whereabouts at the time when Hazel apparently was murdered," Edwina said.

"If you must know, I was doing a stock taking at the post office. You know how persnickety Prudence gets about her inventory, always thinking someone is filching things, even when they're not. She asked me to help out, as she often does, and I agreed to do so."

In fact, Edwina did know how persnickety Prudence could be when it came to her stock. Her gimlet gaze flitted from patron to patron as they moved about the post office cum sweet shop cum stationer, especially if those patrons happened to be children. She knew the count of her penny candies down to the last boiled sweet on any given day. Minnie's claim of assisting her was easy enough to believe. On more than one occasion, she had complained about being roped into the tedious task.

"You know, you're not the only one being questioned about an alibi," Edwina said, hoping her words would put things to rights with Minnie. She would hate to have to refrain from visiting the tea shop in the future. It would never do to feel unwelcome, as it was the only place to have a bite to eat in the village other than the Dove and Duck, a place whose door she rarely darkened.

Minnie harrumphed and reached for another sandwich. "And who else, might I ask, has been questioned?"

"Of course, you will recall that everyone who attended the séance was questioned by Constable Gibbs."

"Does that mean that Chester and the Dinsdales are also suspects?" Minnie asked, a note of hope creeping into her voice.

"I think it's safe to assume that anyone with such close ties to the séance room would fall under scrutiny. But I will tell you that Clarence has been questioned as well," Edwina said, hoping not to put Minnie's back up once more.

"But Clarence has never attended one of the Dinsdale's séances," she said.

"It seems that his working relationship with Hazel provoked some questions," Edwina said. She did not think it necessary to inform Minnie that the questions had come from Beryl and herself. She thought it unlikely Clarence would inform his wife of their visit, considering the topic of conversation. She doubted he would be eager to discuss such uncomfortable matters with his wife if he had not done so already.

"I see. Does that mean that the Lowethorpes are being questioned as well?"

"They certainly are on the list. After all, the vicar and his wife knew Hazel about as well as anyone else in the village. Perhaps they might have some insight as to why anyone would wish to see her harmed. You can't think of any reason now, can you?" Edwina asked.

Before she could answer, the bell on the door jangled loudly, and Minnie shot to her feet. Without a backward glance, she hurried toward a party of women whom Edwina did not recognize. She thought it likely they were a trio of motorists, the sort who found nothing so delightful as a jaunt out into the countryside for a bit of browsing in out-of-the-way shops, to be followed by a meal before returning to the city with tales of their adventures. She wouldn't get anything else out of Minnie with other patrons there to overhear their conversation. She took her time finishing up her food and even polished off the rest of the pot of tea before taking her leave of the tea room, lost in thought.

Chapter 20

Beryl hardly recognized the voice on the other end of the telephone line. Perhaps it was not just the fact that Charles sounded shrill and slightly panicked, but it was also that she was utterly unaccustomed to hearing so much ambient racket whenever he had called in the past. She could only guess that the noises emanated from his houseguest, Georgie. His telephone call had been in search of Edwina, and his attitude, when told she was not at home, was one of distress. Charles was the sort of person who weathered crises with aplomb. He was not, perhaps, the most daring of men, but she would be surprised if he were to lose his nerve in the face of adversity. That said, he sounded very close to the edge, and she assured him that she would pass his message on to Edwina as soon as was possible.

No sooner had she replaced the telephone receiver in its cradle than the subject of his enquiry appeared, looking tired and preoccupied. Crumpet raced down the hallway wagging his tail with ferocity as soon as his mistress stepped through the door. Before she could remove her hat, Beryl held up a restraining hand.

"Charles just telephoned, sounding as if he was on the verge of a breakdown," she said. "He was looking for you."

Edwina straightened her shoulders, and the faintest hint of a smile flitted across her face. Could it be that her diminutive friend was eager to assist with something as harrowing as a toddler? While Beryl prided herself on being the more adventurous of the two, daring and bold in the face of most challenges, she could not honestly admit to feeling remotely capable of handling a terror like that.

"Perhaps I should telephone him back straightaway," she said, striding toward the hall table, where the instrument sat, ready for use.

"You could do that, but I think it might be more useful if you were to head straight over in person. I'm not sure that the sort of assistance Charles requires can be offered from a distance," Beryl said.

"That's a very good idea. I think I shall invite them to come to dinner. It seems the very least I could do. I doubt very much that Charles will be up for preparing a meal for himself, let alone one that will nourish a child, if he is as frazzled as you make him out to be. Besides, I'm sure it will be great fun to have a small person at The Beeches, livening up the place a bit," Edwina said, retrieving her handbag from the floor, where she left it when she'd bent down to pet Crumpet on the head.

Beryl was not sure that The Beeches needed the sort of enlivening the presence of a child would provide. She thought herself quite lively enough for most situations and, truth be told, found the frantic, persistent pestering children seemed unable to refrain from to be exhausting beyond measure. What she had in mind had been much more along the lines of Edwina stopping in for an hour or two to put the child to sleep and provide Charles with a few words of wisdom. Surely, inviting them to dinner was above and beyond the call of duty. Still, she could hardly protest Edwina's offer of hospitality. After all, she had benefited from it so greatly herself, as had Simpkins, hob-nailed boots and all.

"You must do as you think is best," Beryl said, hoping that resignation did not sound in her voice. "I'm sure you'll have a great deal to tell me when you return."

Edwina shook her head. "I must insist that you accompany me. After all, we shall need your motorcar to bring the child back with us. His short little legs are certainly too small to walk the whole way from Charles's place."

Beryl staggered back. She placed a bracing hand on the wall behind her. The notion of a sticky small boy clambering up into her prized possession was unimaginable. It was one thing to get a bit of mud on the cherry red paint job or even a bit of grime on the chrome trim, but the idea of grubby fingers grasping at the leather upholstery left her reeling.

"Didn't he come with a pram or something?" she asked. In her experience, limited as it was, children always seem to be clustered about with quantities of gear. A trip to the grocer—or, God forbid, the village green—typically seemed laden with more equipment than she had ever trotted out for a six-month expedition into the bush.

"I have no idea what sort of worldly goods accompanied the poor little mite from his home to Charles's place. What I can say is I did not spot anything that looked remotely like a pram when I was there earlier today. I don't expect such a thing was a priority when Charles took possession of Georgie." She glared at Beryl as if she was an errant housemaid who had inadvertently spilled soup in a guest's lap at a dinner party.

But as she considered the tremendous loss little Georgie had suffered, she felt ashamed of her reluctance. What was the besmirching of her imported leather upholstery in comparison with the loss of a child's mother? And then there was Charles to consider. Truly, the man had sounded as though he were teetering on the brink of a breakdown when told that Edwina was nowhere to be found. Suddenly, her sense of adventure returned as she considered how little she knew about small humans. Perhaps she could treat it like any other unfamiliar territory. She pushed away from the wall and put on her bravest smile.

"Of course, we must collect them straightaway." She reached for a motoring cap from the hall tree and nestled it firmly against her head. Edwina lifted Crumpet's leash from its hook near the door and fastened it to his collar.

"That's the spirit. No one could possibly be so frightened of a little boy," she said.

Beryl hoped that Edwina was right.

Beryl drove the motorcar past the hedgerows lining the road at a leisurely enough pace for Edwina to spot small birds perched in their branches. While the experience was a novel one, she found it unnerving and stole sideways glances at her friend every few seconds. She was well aware that the prospect of spending time with a child was not something to which Beryl would eagerly look forward, but she had not realized it would fill her with quite so much reluctance.

At the crossroads, Beryl steered the vehicle toward the village proper rather than off in the direction of Charles's home.

"I believe you will find that Charles's house is in the opposite direction," Edwina said. "Have you changed your mind about collecting him?"

"I thought you knew me well enough to know I have an unfailing sense of direction. We are simply in need of petrol," Beryl said.

"I am glad to hear it. I would hate to think that you would be dissuaded from a course of action by a mere toddler."

Beryl jammed her foot down on the accelerator, and the vehicle shot forward. Edwina reached out for the dashboard to brace herself. She disliked traveling at high rates of speed, but she disliked seeing Beryl looking downhearted even more. There was nothing like a bit of a challenge to set her to rights. Only a moment or two later, Beryl slowed the motorcar to a stop in front of the petrol pump at the Blackburns' garage. Nora Blackburn stepped out of the building, wiping her hands on a pale blue rag that she then tucked into a pocket on the front of her coveralls. Her brother, Michael, followed on her heels and lifted his good arm in greeting.

"Could you fill it up please, Nora?" Beryl asked.

Nora nodded and proceeded to add petrol to the motorcar's tank. While she did so, Michael ambled up to the side of the vehicle, a warm smile on his handsome face.

"It's a beautiful afternoon for a ride out into the country," he said. "If we didn't have so much work stacked up, I'd have half a mind to ask if I could join you."

"I doubt very much you'd care to do something like that, even if you had the entire afternoon free," Beryl said.

"Is the vehicle playing up on you? We can find time to squeeze it in, if it is," Nora said.

She had proven to be a savvy businesswoman while her brother was off fighting at the front, keeping the operation going despite her lack of experience as a mechanic. She was a quick learner, however, and before long, her skill set had kept the few motorcars in the village on the road during those terrible years as well as becoming the expert for the maintenance of any tractors or pieces of farm machinery used to keep the local agricultural efforts on an even keel. When Michael returned, their business had flourished even more, with their reputation growing and spreading toward outlying communities. It was a measure of their esteem for Beryl that they would offer to squeeze her in if their docket was already so full.

"No, there is nothing wrong with my beauty," Beryl said,

patting the dashboard with one of her strong hands. "We're just not off on a jaunt into the countryside, at least not in the way that you mean."

"We are off to see Charles. Beryl is feeling a bit half-hearted about the visit," Edwina said.

Nora raised an eyebrow, but Michael was the one to speak. "You haven't had a falling out, have you?" he asked.

"No, it's nothing like that. It's just that he happens to have a small boy staying with him, and Beryl can think of other things she would prefer to use her time for than picking one up in her prize motorcar," Edwina said.

Michael nodded vigorously. "I can see why you wouldn't want to put a child in something as lovely as this. But why has Charles got a child visiting with him? That doesn't seem like his sort of thing, does it?"

Edwina was not entirely sure how much of Charles's news she should divulge. But it was not likely that word of Georgie's arrival would remain a secret for long. Besides, she didn't suppose Charles would mind her letting people know about the change in his household. It might even provoke more offers of assistance.

"Tragically, Charles's cousin was killed in an accident recently and, in her will, left the child in his care," Edwina said. "The whole thing was remarkably unexpected."

"How horrible for everyone involved," Nora said, returning to the petrol tank and wiping her hands on the rag once more. "Does Charles propose to care for the child himself?"

Edwina shrugged. "I'm sure I cannot say for certain what his plans are for the future. All I know is that it has come as quite a shock, and any assistance others could provide would be most welcome, I'm sure. After all, Charles has very little experience with children and is finding the situation a bit of a strain."

"That explains why Hazel came by to see us instead of heading to Charles's office or home to witness her will," Michael said.

Edwina's ears perked up. "When did she ask you to witness it?"

"The day before her body was discovered," Michael said. "Isn't that right?" He turned to his sister.

"Yes, it was. I remember thinking how surprised I was at the timing of it all. It was a good job she'd taken care of it just before someone decided to do away with her; otherwise, her estate would have been a right mess," Nora said.

Edwina wasn't sure that luck had had anything to do with it. Could it be that Hazel's will was what prompted someone to stab her to death? It seemed unlikely that the two events were not somehow connected. And was it possible that she did not want Charles to be aware of the contents of her will? Either way, it would be sensible to inform Constable Gibbs of its existence.

"I don't suppose you happened to see the contents of the will, did you?" Beryl asked. She looked over at Edwina, a bit of a gleam in her eye.

"Not at all. She had the body of the will covered over with a piece of paper. All we saw was the bottom statement that it was her last will and testament. She asked that we watch her sign it and that each of us sign it as witnesses to it in turn," Nora said.

"And she gave you no indication as to the beneficiaries?" Edwina asked.

"No, not at all. In fact, Michael made a bit of a joke about it, which put her back up a bit, didn't you?" Nora said.

"I asked if she was leaving it all to the church roof fund. She told me that all I needed to know was that it was none of my business. She was rather snippy about it," he said.

"The whole thing left a bad taste in our mouths. She interrupted us in the middle of a busy afternoon's worth of work to ask a favor and then took such an attitude with Michael. It really wasn't like her at all," Nora said.

"People can be quite touchy about such things. Not only do most of us dislike speaking about money, but the notion of our own passing is not something the average individual feels comfortable considering. I'm sure she didn't take much offense," Edwina said.

"Still, we would've thought she could've waited until Charles returned. What could have been so urgent about making it that very day anyway?" Michael asked.

"What indeed?" Beryl asked.

Chapter 21

By the time they had managed to stow Georgie in the back seat of the motorcar with Edwina and Crumpet, Beryl had broken a sweat. Charles sat limply beside her in the front seat, looking for all the world as though he had been in the trenches. The look on his face was uncannily similar to the ones she had seen so often on shell-shocked new recruits after their first few days near the front line. She thought it likely her own expression displayed similar emotion. She would have preferred to face down an entire line of German tanks than a similar number of small, sticky boys.

That said, as she peered into the rearview mirror and spotted Georgie resting his head, covered in blonde curls, against Edwina's chest, she couldn't help but feel conflicted. Edwina appeared more content than she had seen her in ages. It was true that Edwina had mentioned from time to time how she had always wished for a family of her own, but to see how patiently and tenderly she dealt with the uprooted child brought it home to Beryl in a way nothing had before. While she could not understand it herself, there was no disputing that Edwina found Georgie's company desirable.

Even Crumpet seemed to find the child's presence a source of happiness. While he sat on Edwina's other side, he placed his paws in her lap and covered the boy's face in kisses. Georgie giggled and squealed, a sound that sent a spasm of anguish across Charles. He looked as though he had reached his limit as far as childish glee was concerned. She stomped down on the accelerator, determined to reach The Beeches in record time. Charles was clearly in need of a stiff gin fizz, if not a double whiskey, or even two. Come to think of it, she could do with one of each herself.

From the delicious smell wafting down the hallway, Beryl could tell that Simpkins had been busy in their absence. By the time they had all clambered out of the motorcar and presented themselves in the parlor, he and Beddoes had managed to prepare a veritable feast. Perhaps it was his newly invented line of convenience foods for working women that accounted for the intrepidity with which the meal had been produced. If so, Beryl thought it likely the line of sauces, soups, and stews would prove popular with their intended market. Simpkins appeared in the doorway, wearing one of Edwina's frilly pinnies.

"This must be young Georgie then, I assume," he said, stepping across the polished floor with his customary heavy tread. Fortunately, he had traded his hobnailed boots for something less likely to injure the child should he step on him by accident. As far as Beryl knew, Simpkins had no more experience with children than did she or Charles. It surprised her when he dropped to the floor on the rug beside the toddler as if he were a far younger man. Georgie lunged toward him and threw himself into the elderly gardener's lap as if he had known him all his life. Crumpet squeezed himself into the remaining space on Simpkins's lap, and Beryl barely contained a gasp of surprise as Simpkins wrapped his arms around the pair of wiggling small creatures.

She looked over at Charles, who wore an expression of astonishment, quickly followed by one of enormous relief. He dropped into a nearby wingback chair and extended his legs as if he might drop off to sleep instantly. She wondered if he had gotten more than a few winks the night before or if he had tossed and turned in his bed either on account of the demands of his houseguest or preoccupation with his new situation. Either way, he looked as though he could do with a good night's rest.

"It is indeed. And a fine fellow he seems to be, would you not agree?" Edwina asked, crouching down beside the pair. Beryl thought it a good job that Beddoes had made such a thorough effort with the autumn cleaning if sprawling out across the floor was to become a regular occurrence.

"Certainly, he is. Crumpet is always an excellent judge of character, and he seems completely smitten by him," Simpkins said.

Once again, the little terrier passed his pink tongue across Georgie's cheeks in a frenzy of adoration. Or perhaps it had more to do with the fact that Charles had seemingly forgotten to wipe the child's face after his most recent meal. Beryl thought she detected smudges of jam on his chin and near his left ear.

Beddoes appeared in the doorway and entered with less standoffishness than usual. She was a proper, old-fashioned sort of a servant and, as Edwina had often reminded Beryl, one who respected herself enough to preserve what she perceived as the proper decorum between employer and employee in a household. But when her gaze landed on Georgie, she allowed herself an unprecedented smile. She went so far as to clap her hands together and, forgetting herself altogether, stepped across the room and bent over him, tussling his curly locks with her sturdy, strong fingers.

He looked up at her and raised his arms above his head. Beddoes glanced over at Edwina, who gave the slightest of nods. The housekeeper hoisted the child to her hip and jostled him up and down ever so gently. She didn't even flinch when he reached up with his sticky fingers to tug on her starched white collar.

"Now what do we have here?" she asked. "Could it be a little boy who would dearly love some supper?" Georgie nodded, sending his curls tumbling about his face. Beddoes smoothed the hair away from his eyes and looked at Edwina once more.

"I am sure that he is most anxious to tuck into one of Simpkins's delicious offerings. Would you like something to eat, Georgie?" Edwina asked.

Georgie nodded again and clapped his chubby hands together. Crumpet capered about at Beddoes's feet as if he were about to partake in the meal too.

"We thought it best to serve the meal in the kitchen this evening, if you don't mind, miss," Beddoes said, shifting Georgie to her other hip. "We thought the formality of the dining room might be asking a bit much of someone as young as him."

Simpkins got to his feet with less effort than Beryl would have thought possible. "And we thought you might wish to oversee his meal yourself," he said, turning to Edwina.

"How very sensible of you both. That was the perfect decision," Edwina said.

She turned toward Charles, as if to confer and gain his approval. But Charles was well past any such concerns. His head leaned back against the chair, his mouth slightly agape and a gentle snore emanating from his throat. His arms had fallen away from the armrests and his hands dangled toward the floor. Never had Beryl seen him in such a vulnerable state. Like most solicitors, he was a conservative and rather formal man in most aspects of his life. It was a reflection of his ordeal that he had collapsed so completely and unguardedly in front of others. Edwina lifted a finger toward her lips and motioned that all of them should slip quietly from the room without disturbing him.

The kitchen was as warm and cozy as ever. An extra chair had been brought in from another room, and someone had thoughtfully placed a stack of encyclopedias on it in order to create a sort of child chair for young Georgie. Beddoes placed him carefully atop the stack of books, and Simpkins slid him in tightly so that there would be little chance of him falling to the floor. Crumpet sensibly positioned himself on the floor beside him, gazing expectantly up at the table. Edwina sat beside him and tucked the kitchen toweling handed to her by Beddoes into the neck of his shirt, forming an ad hoc bib. Beryl placed herself on the opposite side of the table, where she could reasonably expect not to be roped into some sort of food-preparation duty like buttering bits of bread or cutting up the child's meat into tiny bites.

All throughout the meal, whenever his mouth was not completely stuffed with food, Georgie kept up a steady stream of childish prattle. Beddoes beamed down at him indulgently, even though more of his meal landed on her freshly scrubbed kitchen floor than it did in his mouth. Despite Edwina's valiant attempts to wipe smears of food from his cheeks and chin, he continued to look as though he had participated in a pie-eating contest with his hands tied behind his back.

Beryl excused herself momentarily and returned a few moments later with a tray holding a pitcher of gin fizzes and four crystal glasses. If she were going to make it all the way through to the end of the meal, she would require some fortification. In her absence, Georgie had managed to climb down from his seat and had commenced running circles around the kitchen table, Crumpet close on his heels. As she placed the tray of drinks on the table and offered them round, she was surprised and even gratified when, rather than spurning her offer, Beddoes cheerfully accepted one for herself. Was it possible that all it would take to thaw out the starchy, unimpeachable servant was an orphaned toddler?

She took her seat once more and stretched her legs out under the table, bumping into something unexpected. A small hand ran up and down her silk-clad trouser leg. It was not the first time she had experienced such forward behavior from a male dining partner, but it was the first time such a thing had been accompanied by a throaty giggle. She tipped her head and peered under the table, where Georgie's brilliant blue gaze met her own. He pulled himself up on the edge of her chair and leaned heavily against her. Before she realized what was happening, he had hauled himself into her lap and leaned into the crook of her arm. As quickly as had been the case with Charles, Georgie fell into a deep slumber. His small chest raised and fell rhythmically, and her heart gave a slight squeeze as his small thumb found its way between his two pink lips.

Astonished, she looked over at Edwina, who simply beamed. Simpkins raised a glass, as if to toast her on her success. Beddoes went so far as to nod at her approvingly. Edwina did the sensible thing, and slid Beryl's glass closer toward her hand. She took a fortifying sip and came to the only possible conclusion.

"I suppose there is nothing we can do but invite Charles to stay for as long as he needs our help, is there?" Beryl asked. She looked from Simpkins to Beddoes, then finally to Edwina. All three of them raised their glasses in a toast.

"It's the least we can do for the poor little fellow," Edwina said, utterly failing to keep the pleasure from her voice.

"Which poor little fellow is that? Georgie or Charles?" Simpkins asked.

"Both, I should think," Beddoes said, in a fit of boldness that seemed to surprise even herself. She quickly put her glass down on the table as if it was to blame for her forthrightness.

"That's right. Charles is at least as in need of our help as is this little man," she said, leaning toward Georgie. "If we are all in agreement, I shall ask Charles if he would like to stay for the time being."

Simpkins nodded. "It's the best idea you've had in ages."

Beryl was quite sure Edwina did not notice, but he gave Beddoes a wink.

"On your say-so, I'll make up two of the spare rooms," Beddoes said. "I think the yellow one would do nicely for Georgie."

Everyone turned expectantly toward Beryl, who looked down at Georgie, who had burrowed even more closely against her chest.

"Let me know when the room is ready, and I'll carry him upstairs," she said.

Chapter 22

It could not be said that the night had been restful or restorative. Although Georgie had slept so easily in Beryl's arms, he woke as soon as his head touched the freshly plumped pillow on the single bed in the yellow room. He slept fitfully throughout the night, despite Edwina's best efforts to comfort him, finally drifting off to sleep when Crumpet hopped up beside him and snuggled in close. She snatched a few hours rest sitting upright in a chair next to his bed, but when Georgie stirred as soon as the early morning sun streamed through the window, she woke feeling exhausted and wondering what a day with a child in the house might bring.

It transpired that the addition of a small human to the household brought a great deal of planning and effort. They had come away the evening before with no intention of ensconcing Charles and his young charge in the house for longer than a few hours, so naturally they had not brought any spare clothing for either of them. And so Georgie arrived at the breakfast table wearing the same clothing he had the day before, which was somewhat worse for having been through one meal with inexpert supervision. Simpkins had arisen early and prepared a full breakfast of porridge, toast soldiers, and softly boiled eggs for the lot of them, but Georgie was the only one with any appetite to speak of. Edwina toyed with a bit of toast and reluctantly sipped a cup of tea whilst wondering how she would manage the day on so little sleep.

Charles appeared at the table clad in a borrowed pair of Simpkins's pajamas, looking as haggard and gray as she felt. Beddoes hovered at the edges of the room, unsure of her role in the fray. Crumpet half-heartedly gobbled up bits of toast and dribbles of egg yolk that cascaded onto the floor around Georgie's chair. Beryl alone seemed unfazed by the night's disruptions, appearing earlier than was her habit in the kitchen, looking as fresh and energetic as ever.

Beryl had a legendary capacity for sleep, no matter the circumstances, and had not made a single appearance in the yellow room during the night claiming that she had been awakened. Edwina had never truly envied her friend until that very moment. Georgie giggled and waved his toast soldier in Beryl's direction, sending another shower of egg yolk about the kitchen.

"I've seen livelier-looking crowds at a funeral. What is the matter with all of you?" she asked, plopping into a chair next to Edwina and helping herself to a slice of toast.

"Don't tell me you managed to sleep through all the ruckus last night," Simpkins said, as he fetched a percolator from the hob to pour her a cup of coffee.

"What ruckus?" Beryl asked, not looking in the least as if she needed a jolt of caffeine.

"Georgie had trouble sleeping, which had a deleterious effect on most of us," Edwina said. She lowered her voice. "I expect he is missing his mum."

"Poor little tyke," Beryl said. Edwina was surprised at the warmth in her friend's voice. It seemed he was winning her over, one giggle at a time. "I wish there was something that I could do to help."

Edwina glanced over at Georgie. His face, as well as the entire front of his little shirt, was covered with his breakfast and his dinner, despite her best efforts to keep him clean. Charles's bony wrists poked out well past the cuffs of the borrowed pajama top, and a surprising quantity of stubble covered his cheeks and chin. Edwina had never before seen him looking so disheveled.

"As a matter of fact, there is. After breakfast, you could take the motorcar out to Charles's house to collect some clothing for them both, as well as a razor for Charles and what all else they might need," she said.

"I'd be happy to go, but I think someone should accompany me. I am not entirely sure what I ought to pack for either of them." Beryl looked expectantly at Charles, who shrank back in his chair, clutching his teacup to his chest like a talisman. He did not look in any fit state to leave the house.

"I think it would be best if Georgie and Charles were not separated, and I doubt that you would find it helpful if the child went along in the motorcar again," she said.

Beryl's eyes widened, and she shook her head. She might be warming to the boy, but there were limits.

"I suppose I could manage on my own if Charles doesn't mind putting up with my packing decisions," Beryl said.

Beryl considered herself to be an expert at packing, and by and large, Edwina admired her for her ability to be well equipped for any journey with the mere contents of a rucksack. However, Beryl never packed for anyone else, and Edwina suspected her method would not prove as successful when it came to a child's clothing needs. After all, Beryl, no matter the adventures she undertook, did not tend to dribble all of her food down the front of her. Edwina shifted in her chair to better include Beddoes in her line of sight.

"I think that you would benefit from some expert assistance," she said. "Beddoes, you haven't obliged with the packing at any of your other posts, by any chance?"

Edwina knew it was a risk. Beddoes and Beryl had not formed the warmest of connections during the housekeeper's tenure at The Beeches. Beryl had the insulting habit of attempting too much familiarity with domestic help. She couldn't be blamed for her lack of clarity on the traditional roles within a household between the servants and the served. She was an American, after all. But no matter how many times Edwina had tried to convince her that a well-trained servant would be offended by any offer of help with their duties, she remained unconvinced. It had made for weeks of difficulty when Beddoes had first arrived in the home, and even now Edwina feared Beddoes might hand in her notice in protest of Beryl's insensitive actions.

Still, needs must, and after her unprecedented behavior the night before in accepting a gin fizz from Beryl's own hand, Edwina thought the suggestion might be worth the risk. After all, while Beddoes did prefer to keep roles at The Beeches clearly defined, she also was a proud sort of woman who was not above mentioning the skills she possessed and the grandeur of the houses in which she'd served. Flattery might just win her over.

The housekeeper drew closer to the table. "Indeed, I have, miss, on many an occasion. I've served at more than my fair share of country-house parties and all that that entails."

"So would you be capable of advising Beryl on what would be correct to pack for our guests?"

"Certainly, miss. I can be prepared as soon as I am needed."

Beryl drained her cup before hopping to her feet like a mere girl. She turned to Beddoes.

"There's no time like the present. Shall we?"

Edwina was impressed that she managed not to smile at the housekeeper or to betray any enthusiasm for her company. She simply waved goodbye to Georgie and strode out of the room, with Beddoes hurrying along in her wake. Perhaps the two of them might finally have reached something that resembled a truce, possibly even a sort of understanding.

Edwina heard the crunch of gravel in the drive and was surprised to find that, in well under two hours, they had returned with enough clothing and personal items to set both Georgie and Charles up at The Beeches for the foreseeable future. She was more surprised to see the Dinsdales emerging from the back seat of the motorcar.

It was a relief to note that Beddoes did not seem any worse for wear from her outing with Beryl. Her face was as inscrutable as usual as she slid from the passenger front seat and carried to the house a large wicker basket filled with what appeared to be bits of clothing. Edwina held the door for the arriving party, lifting a questioning eyebrow toward Beryl, who bent toward her and whispered in her ear as she passed.

"They arrived at Charles's house looking to speak with him. When I told them he was at The Beeches, they insisted on accompanying us back here, but have yet state their business," she said, before striding along the back passage in search of Charles.

Edwina led the brother and sister to the parlor and settled them there before excusing herself to fetch their houseguest. In only a few moments' time, he had changed into a fresh set of clothing and had deftly applied his razor to his face. He looked remarkably unlike the man who had first appeared before her in his kitchen, Georgie banging away on a pot at his feet.

"Will I pass muster, do you think?" Charles asked as he descended the stairs and paused in the hallway. She looked him up and down, then nodded with approval.

"You always do," Edwina said, realizing as the words left her lips that that was indeed how she felt. She followed him into the parlor close on his heels. After all, it was her home, and even though she thought it likely the Dinsdales had come to call on Charles on some matter of legal business, she could not deny that she hoped they would not expect her to provide them with the same sort of privacy they should expect at his office. Beryl had seemingly had the same idea and had settled herself into her usual preferred seat with its excellent view of the door. She and Mr. Dinsdale were deep in conversation on the subject of an upcoming horse race upon which they both appeared to have placed considerable bets. Maude nodded as if she had received some sort of advance notice from the spirit realm as to the results of the race.

"Are you saying that you have a tipster on the other side of the veil?" Beryl asked, as Edwina closed the parlor door firmly behind her.

"Yes, I suppose that I am. You can't imagine I would encourage my brother to put his money on something that was not a sure bet, now would you?" Maude asked. The medium smiled, and Edwina was once again reminded of Alma's comment about how much she resembled Hazel, at least superficially.

"Well, I hope that your source is in error, as I have placed my money on a different horse altogether," Beryl said.

"I'm sure that our guests are not here to swap racing tips," Edwina said. "They would have gone to Chester for that, rather than Charles."

Charles took the cue and took a seat across from the Dinsdales. He templed his long fingers together on his lap and arranged his face in what Edwina thought of as his solicitor's expression.

"I hear you wanted to see me. How do you think that I may help you?" he asked.

The Dinsdales exchanged a glance, and Arthur gestured as if

to encourage his sister to be the one to speak on their behalf. Edwina had the distinct impression that she was the one to take the lead in anything the pair undertook.

"While it may seem a bit unseemly to ask after such a thing so quickly upon her passing, Arthur and I wanted to enquire as to the disposition of Hazel's will," Maude said.

Charles shifted slightly in his seat. "I'm afraid I don't understand your question."

"We were given to understand that Hazel left a considerable estate," Arthur said. Edwina did not quite like the predatory-looking gleam in his eye.

"While that may be, I have no knowledge either of the extent of Hazel's estate nor the disposition thereof," Charles said.

The Dinsdales looked at each other once more, this time a crackle of irritation passing between them.

"What do you mean you know nothing about Hazel's will?" Maude asked. She leaned forward, as if to intimidate Charles into revealing information he was withholding for some inexplicable purpose.

"I can only repeat that I do not know what you are talking about. I have never discussed Hazel's financial arrangements or holdings with her or anyone else. And I was never approached to prepare a will for her," he said.

"Now look here, it is your legal obligation to be forthcoming with such things, even if you do not approve of how someone wishes to dispose of their money," Arthur said, shaking a finger at Charles.

Charles drew himself up to his full height. Edwina could not recall a time when she had ever seen him look as though he were struggling to control his temper.

"I assure you I do not need you to school me on my own business."

"Arthur meant no offense, did you?" Maude said, reaching out and placing a restraining hand on his knee. It was an odd gesture, and one that Edwina found uncomfortable to witness. Had she concerns that her brother might lose his own temper and lay his hands on Charles? Nothing like that had ever occurred in her parlor during her lifetime, and she did not wish to witness a scene of violence, especially with the child in the house to think of.

"No, of course not," he said. "It's just that sometimes it puts my back up thinking about how people try to withhold what we are due because of prejudice concerning your profession, my dear."

Beryl looked Arthur up and down before inserting herself into the conversation. "I believe the only one exhibiting prejudice here today is you, sir. You are impugning Charles's professional reputation by suggesting he would permit his feelings on any subject to impact the carrying out of his duties. And unless I'm misunderstanding you, you are implying that he is lying when he says he knows nothing of Hazel's estate."

Arthur began to sputter, and Charles held up a hand as if to quell the disagreement.

"I'm sure that Mr. Dinsdale spoke without thinking things through. It often happens where money is involved. But tell me, what made you believe that I had drawn up the will for Hazel?" he said.

"Because she told us that she was going to ask you to do so," Maude said.

"When was this?" Edwina asked.

"The day before she died. She had generously announced, after a private session with her in which we were able to make contact with her dearly departed father, that she had been moved to leave her estate to us for the continuation of our work," Maude said.

Beryl snorted, then tried to cover up the sound with a cough. Arthur looked at her with undisguised venom. "That's right. And she wouldn't be the first to have felt moved to do so.

Maude's gift is a considerable one, and any number of people are extremely grateful for her help. If they wish to display that through monetary means, we feel it our duty to accept their generosity. After all, it helps us to continue to assist other souls who are yearning to connect with their loved ones who have passed over."

"Well, regardless of what she told you, I assure you she never came to see me."

"You were out of town that day, weren't you, Charles?" Edwina reminded him.

"Yes, I was. It's possible that Hazel had every intention of visiting me to draw up a will but found me absent from my home and office."

"You expect us to believe that, do you?" Arthur asked. His face was turning a deep shade of vermilion, and Edwina wondered fleetingly if they would have cause to telephone for the doctor.

Just then, she heard a knock upon the parlor door, and Beddoes entered the room with a freshly washed and dressed Georgie perched on her hip.

"Excuse me for interrupting, miss," Beddoes said. "But Master Georgie insisted on playing with the doggy."

Crumpet emerged from his basket near Edwina's feet. As much as he seemed to have enjoyed playing with the small child, the effort in doing so had thoroughly worn him out, and he had fallen deeply asleep, despite the presence of visitors. He sprang from his basket, apparently refreshed from his nap, and raced to the doorway, where he sat up on his hind feet, batting at Georgie's toes with his front paws. Beddoes withdrew from the parlor, Crumpet racing along behind her. Charles waited until the door was closed before answering this question. He got to his feet and towered over the rest of the group.

"It matters to me very little what you believe, Mr. Dinsdale. Georgie is my cousin Polly's son. She was unfortunately killed in a motoring accident. I was out of the village collecting Georgie, someone I believe your sister described as Polly's greatest treasure. If that's not proof enough for you, I don't know what would be."

Maude got to her feet and tugged at her brother's arm. "We can't keep you any longer. Please accept my apologies for my brother's rude behavior. The best of luck to you and poor little Georgie."

Edwina watched as they exited the room, Arthur looking more disgruntled with each step he took.

"Well, what do you think of that?" Beryl asked.

"I think the Dinsdales just jumped to the head of my list of suspects in Hazel's murder," Charles said.

Edwina was not sure that she agreed. Would they have been so foolish as to appear eager to collect on her estate if they had something to do with her murder?

"I noticed you didn't tell them about what the Blackburns mentioned," Beryl said.

"The Blackburns?" Charles asked.

Edwina nodded. "We stopped in for some petrol at the Blackburns' garage before we collected you and Georgie yesterday. They told us that Hazel had stopped by and interrupted their day of work asking them to witness her last will and testament."

"I wonder if she ever did really try to find me or if she decided to go ahead and write one herself. Oftentimes people do that, especially if they think that they will be judged on the disposition they wish for their estate," Charles said.

"It also means that the will is not safely tucked away in your office," Edwina said. "I expect it must be at her home—and you?"

"That would be my best guess," Charles said. "Often people keep them in a safe or even in a locked drawer in a desk at their home. It's not the most advisable thing, considering the possibility of fire or even inadvertent loss of the document, but it is popular with the average person who does not rely upon a so-licitor."

"We ought to tell Constable Gibbs about the will the Black-burns said they witnessed, as well as the fact that the Dinsdales claim she left all of her property to them," Edwina said.

"You know, if the Dinsdales were as good at connecting with people on the other side as they claim to be, they really ought to just ask Hazel about the whole thing," Beryl said.

"Better yet, they could ask her to tell them who killed her," Charles said.

Chapter 23

Beryl was relieved to see that it did not take too much coaxing to convince Edwina to leave Georgie in Beddoes's capable care, at least for long enough to drop in on Constable Gibbs. She refrained from suggesting that they take the motorcar in order to prolong their outing, despite the look of concern on Charles's face when he learned that they were leaving. While she still believed that inviting Charles to stay had been the right thing to do, she had no intention of shirking their professional responsibilities because of it.

Besides, as much as it was evident that Edwina adored Georgie, it was also clear that having a child around was something that would take some getting used to, even for the most enthusiastic of caretakers. No, Edwina definitely needed a bit of a break, and there was nothing like pursuing an investigation to provide a thorough distraction from anything else going on in one's life.

Constable Gibbs was seated at the small table at the rear of the police station. She looked up expectantly as they entered and beckoned them into the inner sanctum beyond the long counter designed to keep the public on the other side of the room. Beryl still could not quite believe that Doris Gibbs had come to look upon them as helpful colleagues rather than a general nuisance. So much had changed in only a few short months, most of it extremely gratifying.

"I hope you're here to tell me that you have some sort of a lead to contribute. I'm not sure that I'm making much headway on my end," she said.

Edwina pulled out her trusty pocket notebook and tiny pencil and laid them on the table before her. "We have come into some information that might be worth considering."

Constable Gibbs leaned forward. "I'll be interested in anything you've got."

Beryl stretched her legs out under the table and leaned back in her seat. "Have you heard the rumors about Clarence Mumford and Hazel?" she asked.

The policewoman arched an eyebrow. "Not Hazel specifically, although with Clarence's reputation, I suppose it shouldn't surprise me. Where did you hear a thing like that?"

"Where else? Prudence told us about it," Beryl said.

"And, unfortunately, what she really wanted us to know was that his wife, Minnie, knew all about it," Edwina said, glancing up from her notebook.

"Is that so?" asked the constable. "And here I was thinking that Minnie was entirely oblivious to her husband's carrying on."

"That's what we thought at first, especially considering it was Prudence who told us about it," Beryl said.

"She does like to stir things up whenever possible," Constable Gibbs said. "But you said at first. Did something occur to change your mind?"

Edwina turned a few pages back in her notebook. She tapped her finger on a line of neat handwriting. "Minnie didn't come right out and say that she believed it, but when I questioned her about Clarence and Hazel, she appeared to be aware of the rumors."

"Did she now? I can't see Minnie taking something like that well at all," the constable said.

"She was very defensive. She denied that Clarence could have been involved with Hazel, no matter what anyone had to say about it." Edwina ran her finger down the page. "Which I suppose doesn't get Clarence entirely off the hook for Hazel's murder either. If Minnie finally caught on to what he was up to, he might have been inclined toward violence."

Constable Gibbs reached for an apple from the bowl of fruit placed in the middle of the table and rubbed it against her uniform jacket before taking a bite. She nodded thoughtfully while she chewed, as if mulling over the notion that Clarence might have taken his bad behavior into a new realm.

"Did you speak with Clarence about the rumors?" she asked.

"We did. He admits that he actively pursued her and even thought that he was making some headway," Beryl said. "But he claimed that she suddenly turned cold on him and directed her interest elsewhere."

"Let me guess. The new object of her affections was Arthur Dinsdale," Constable Gibbs said.

"That was what he said," Edwina said, consulting her notebook once more. "How did you know?"

The constable smiled. "You're not the only one who knows how to conduct an investigation or who has access to people in the village. More than one person had things to say about Arthur Dinsdale turning on the charm whenever Hazel was in his vicinity."

"That brings up another possibility," Beryl said. "In fact, it's the reason that we came by here to speak with you."

The constable sat up a bit straighter and placed her apple on the table. "I'm all ears."

"Arthur and Maude Dinsdale stopped by The Beeches to speak with Charles about Hazel's will," Beryl said.

Constable Gibbs tipped her head to one side, as if not quite sure what she was hearing. "Why would they be looking for Charles at The Beeches instead of his own house?" she asked.

Beryl looked over at Edwina, who gave a slight bob to her head. How much her friend had changed of late. To think that when she had first moved in, Edwina was mortified by the idea of a few unpaid bills at the local shops. Now she was willing to move the man widely reported to be interested in her romantically into her home without feeling the need to hide it. Beryl's heart swelled with pride.

"Charles has recently been entrusted with the care of his cousin's young son. Since he has little to no experience with children, we decided it would be in both his and the child's best interest to come to stay for the time being," Beryl said.

Constable Gibbs lifted the apple once more and took a large bite. Once again, she chewed it slowly, with a thoughtful look plastered across her face. One of the things that Beryl admired about Doris Gibbs was the fact that she rarely spoke without considering the impact of her words. Perhaps that really was the secret to her managing to maintain her position as the village constable throughout the war years and even after the men returned from the front. Although they had had their differences in the past, Beryl respected her and the job she did as well as the way she went about it.

"I'm very surprised to hear that Charles has been thrust into the role of caregiver. Most men would be happy to leave that job to someone else, after all," she said. "That said, I'm not surprised to hear that he turned to Edwina for help nor that you were willing to give it." The constable turned toward Edwina and smiled.

From Beryl's vantage point, she could see a deep red flush rising up the back of Edwina's neck, as it always did when her friend was embarrassed. She had still not acquired the skill of accepting compliments with grace. Nor had she become accustomed to the suggestion that she might have a romantic interest in Charles. Perhaps it would be best to steer the conversation back toward the investigation instead of their personal lives.

"Regardless of his reason for being there, the Dinsdales tracked him down because they seem to think that they were the beneficiaries of Hazel's will," Beryl said.

"And are they?" the constable asked.

Beryl shrugged. "Charles didn't actually draw up her will, so he had no way of knowing its contents. To tell you the truth, the Dinsdales were very surprised to hear that he had not done so and even went so far as to suggest that he was lying about the whole thing."

The constable's eyes widened in surprise. "How ridiculous. Charles is as straight an arrow as ever there was."

"We were all very startled by the accusation," Edwina said. "He finally did manage to convince them that he had no idea as to the disposition of her estate. They were quite put out about the whole thing."

"Are you convinced that they thought she had made a will out in their favor?" the constable asked.

"It appeared so. They seemed very sure of themselves when they posed the question to Charles and extremely frustrated when they received no satisfaction," Edwina said.

"So they might've had a reason to do away with her themselves," Constable Gibbs said.

"They may have. And there is more," Beryl said.

She looked over at Edwina, encouraging her to take up the story. "We didn't tell the Dinsdales this, but Beryl and I heard from Nora and Michael Blackburn that Hazel asked them to witness her will the day before she died."

"Why would they have done that instead of going to Charles?"

"It could have been for a couple of reasons. One was that Charles was out of town fetching Georgie. But the second possibility is that she had no intention of discussing it with him regardless. Charles mentioned that oftentimes people who feel that they will be criticized for the way they dispose of their estate will write up a will on their own instead of asking a solicitor to do so," Edwina said.

"I suppose that makes sense. After all, one doesn't necessarily want to feel chastised for their last will and testament," the constable said. "Did Nora and Michael happen to see how she left her property and money?"

"No. They said that she had the important bits of the document covered over with a blank sheet of paper and simply had them witness her signing it," Beryl said.

"It would be helpful to get a look at the will. I suppose that the first place to start would be Hazel's own home," Constable Gibbs said. "I'll head over there after we finish speaking."

"Did you run into any information you'd like to share with us?" Edwina asked.

"As matter of fact, my line of enquiry was focused on Mr. Watkins. After the way he acted following that first séance the two of you attended, he jumped straight to the top of my list."

"He threatened the Dinsdales a second time in my presence too," Beryl said.

"That's the first I've heard of that. He doesn't have much of an alibi either," Constable Gibbs said.

"Not much of one, or not one at all?" Beryl asked.

"It's not one that's verifiable. He claimed to have been working on a broken tractor but had to stop to ask the Blackburns for a part. He said that, when he arrived, the garage was closed, so no one saw him there," she said.

"And no one spotted him around the garage at that time?" Edwina asked.

"Not that I've been able to discover. If he did, in fact, approach the garage at approximately the time of Hazel's murder, there is no one who can vouch for him. And of all the people on the suspect list, he's the one who has shown the most tendency toward violence, what with the way he has been acting out in public ever since the Dinsdales arrived."

As much as she felt sorry for Mr. Watkins and all that he had suffered since the tragic death of his daughter, Polly, she could not disagree with the constable about his apparent proclivity for violence. He had been thoroughly unpleasant after the séance, and although Beryl felt that she could handle herself in a confrontation, she had been slightly unnerved by the way he had shoved his fist in her face and shouted about the way her plane had disrupted his livestock. If he lost his temper over something as insignificant as that, what would he do in private to someone like Hazel, who he felt was manipulating his fragile and grief-stricken wife? As they took their leave of the constable, she couldn't help but feel as though Mr. Watkins might be in for another wave of difficulties, but this time one of his own making.

Chapter 24

Even though the case was uppermost in her mind, Beryl still had repairs to do on her new airplane. She took her leave of Edwina and, upon exiting the police station, headed toward the outbuilding where she had housed their latest acquisition. Although she felt a bit guilty about it, she did not tell Edwina the purpose of her visit to the plane. She had mumbled something about giving it a bit of a buff and polish, which she decided was as close to the truth as was prudent to share. After all, if she ever hoped to get Edwina up in the plane, it would not do for her to know that it had ever been damaged at all. And then there was the small matter of Beryl's nagging suspicion that perhaps Edwina had been involved in the sabotage in the first place. Either way, she had no desire to discuss with her dear friend what had become of the airplane until it was but a faint memory.

The outbuilding held not only the airplane but also a box of tools and a pair of coveralls, which she availed herself of immediately upon entry. Beryl was not averse to getting her hands dirty, but she was proud of her wardrobe and had no intention of besmirching her trousers and blouse with grease. As she shrugged into the coverall, she considered the case. Even though they had gotten to the bottom of several previous crimes, she found this one to be particularly baffling. Although the Dinsdales made decent suspects because of the claims they were named in Hazel's will, she was not convinced they placed her body in Princess Rosanna's sarcophagus. Although the argument could easily be made that they leaned toward the spectacular during their séances and that her death would draw paying crowds, she doubted that either of them would be so naïve as to ask after Hazel's estate so quickly if they were involved in her death. Besides, what had become of Princess Rosanna?

She did think it was possible that what appeared to be a well-wrapped mummy was nothing more than some sort of stuffing wound up in strips of cloth. It was not as though the Dinsdales encouraged their sitters to view the interior of the sarcophagus with any real scrutiny. The low lighting during séances surely was meant to obscure much of what was actually going on, including the lack of authenticity with their centerpiece prop. Beryl had seen her fair share of mummies in museums and even, on occasion, at dig sites in Egypt, and she could not say that the purported princess seemed to correspond with her memory of those occasions. If she had to put her finger on exactly what was different about the Dinsdales' mummy, it would be that she seemed to be a bit more robust in size than the others Beryl had seen. It was almost as though they had modeled their bit of theater on the proportions of a live woman rather than one who would be as reduced in size as an ancient Egyptian princess would be.

But who did that leave? She wished she felt as though Clarence were the one at fault, as she found him to be a blight on the village. His reputation as a man who took liberties where women were concerned was well deserved, and after his unwanted advances toward a young woman in his employ several weeks earlier, Beryl found she could barely tolerate the sight of him. While she would feel grieved indeed if the only cinema in town were to be closed because its owner had been arrested for murder, it would be a small price to pay for being rid of someone like him. Perhaps Simpkins could be persuaded to purchase the property, if it came to that, and maybe even Eva Scott, the young woman who had been so treacherously accosted by her employer, would consent to return under new management.

Beryl supposed it was possible that Clarence could have been the one to murder Hazel in order to keep his wife from finding out about his bad behavior, but it was not, in her opinion, the most likely scenario. After all, he had gotten away with the behavior for years. What would cause him to snap and take action so late into his marriage? No, the sad fact was that it seemed far more likely that his wife, the long-suffering Minnie, was the culprit. There was something particularly disturbing about realizing one was the last to know about something so humiliating. Beryl had been in that position once or twice herself, and while she could well understand the impulse to violence upon the scales falling from her eyes, she had prudently decided to break off the relationship and head out on an adventure instead. In fact, relationships going awry had been the fuel behind many of her exploits. The dissolution of at least two of her marriages had led to her breaking land-speed records, resulting in international fame.

But Minnie wasn't the sort to call attention to herself by taking off in a fast motorcar or to the skies in the airplane. Beryl could well imagine her lashing out when so utterly humiliated and then quietly going about her business as if nothing had ever happened. She did not wish to believe the mild-mannered tea-shop owner was to blame, but unlike Edwina, she could absolutely imagine it to be the case.

It was one of the things that made their partnership such a

strong one, she thought. Edwina held such a depth of understanding concerning her fellow villagers and such a wealth of history to draw on that she often made connections where Beryl simply did not. On the other hand, that same long-standing relationship with the locals could color Edwina's view and leave her convinced that someone could not possibly lash out in an unexpected way. In a village where so little had changed until the war, it was easy to understand why Edwina might feel that life there was remarkably predictable and characters fixed. Beryl had the sense that perhaps this case was not quite like the others in that it was going to take something new and extraordinary to get to the bottom of it.

She bent down and pulled an adjustable spanner from her toolbox. She carried it to the plane and climbed up onto a stack of crates that served as a sort of scaffolding. Light from a window tucked up high into the side of the building provided plenty of illumination on the task at hand. From her increased height atop the fruit crates, she was able to look through that same window, where a bit of motion caught her eye. Arthur Dinsdale was making his way through the door of Bernard Stevens's photography studio. She couldn't help but note that he glanced over his shoulder furtively before entering the back door of the studio.

She stood watching the door, wondering why he had entered through the rear. To her knowledge, customers always entered through the front door and into the showroom, where Mr. Stevens was happy to sell them on the idea of a studio portrait. As far as Beryl knew, the back room was an area that was off-limits to customers. She had the sense that that was where he kept his dark room. If he was like most photographers she had met, he would be too paranoid about someone inadvertently exposing his film and ruining his work to encourage members of the public to enter that space. She had not heard anything about Mr. Dinsdale being on terms of any great intimacy with Mr.

Stevens, nor had any rumors been bandied about that they shared an interest in photography.

She bent over the engine and began diagnosing the difficulty therein. As she tightened hoses and adjusted belts, she began to hum under her breath. Although she did not appreciate someone sabotaging her plane, she had forgotten how much she enjoyed sorting out problems like this one. Perhaps that was one of the reasons she so enjoyed getting to the bottom of criminality as well. There was something quite similar between the two types of activities. They both relied on seeing a situation in disarray and putting it to rights.

Before she had made any substantial progress on her part, she noticed Mr. Dinsdale slinking back out of the studio once more. This time, he was tucking a thick envelope into his jacket pocket. Once again, he looked about, as if assuring himself that he was unobserved. While Beryl did not enjoy the photographer's company particularly, she could not see why Arthur would be so wary of anybody connecting him to the photography studio. As far as she had been able to tell, the enterprise was entirely on the up-and-up. Someone had put about a rumor that Bernard was known to take unauthorized photographs, through their open windows, of women in varying states of undress without their knowledge, but it had not been substantiated. The worst that could be said of him was that he was a bit of a bore and overly fond of dull subject matter for his photographs.

Beryl found his obsession with the ducks at the millpond tedious in the extreme, but she could not see how there was any harm in it. Besides, the rumors concerning Bernard had floated about before the Dinsdales had arrived in the village, and she could not see how they would have heard them. Everyone had been in a hurry to forget all the unpleasantness that had surrounded that case of poison-pen letters. She turned back to the airplane but found her attention was just not on it. She climbed

down and pulled off her coverall, determined to head back to
The Beeches.

No sooner had Edwina parted from Beryl and headed down
the High Street than Prudence stepped out onto the pavement
and waved her over. Edwina did not care for the eagerness on
the postmistress's face, always a harbinger of unpleasantness to
come. She stifled her disquiet and crossed the street to enter the
post office. After all, perhaps Prudence had some information
regarding the case that she was itching to share.

She entered the shop, her sense of unease growing as Prudence hurried to the counter where she managed the postal
business. She tugged a parcel from a wooden cubby mounted
on the wall behind the counter and made a show of scrutinizing
the address before sliding it toward Edwina.

Edwina's heart thudded violently in her chest. It was clear
that the parcel was the same size and shape as the one she had
sent off to the publishing house only a few days prior. Surely a
careful consideration of her manuscript could not have been
conducted if it had been so quickly returned.

"Edwina, what a woman of mystery you have turned out to
be," Prudence said, tapping the return label on the parcel with a
bony, knuckled finger. "Have you and Beryl expanded your
business to include cases in London now? I should have
thought that you had enough mischief here in Walmsley Parva
to keep you occupied."

Edwina did her best not to let her relief show. Perhaps Prudence had not realized that the parcel was from a publishing
house and was only interested in the fact that it had come from
London. With a little luck, she might be able to keep her di-
verted from her secret. She knew that the best way to draw
Prudence's attention was to make her work for the bits of information she so desperately desired.

"While Beryl and I will always put the majority of our business focus on Walmsley Parva and the surrounding area, we would be unwise not to consider further opportunities should they present themselves," Edwina said. "I'm sure that, as a businesswoman yourself, you must agree that it is unwise not to take advantage of possible expansion."

Prudence bobbed her head up and down. She was quite a successful businesswoman, despite her feverish dedication to gossip, which from time to time ruffled the feathers of her customers. But, as the only post office, sweet shop, and stationery shop in the village, she was able to get away with a great deal more than she might have, should any competition have presented itself. Still, she had taken a business left to her by her parents and increased its value year after year. She seemed to have a knack for hunting down novel offerings that her customers could not resist. As much as Edwina did not enjoy the postmistress's company, she did admire her business savvy.

"I often thought the same thing myself." Prudence leaned her elbows on the glass counter in front of her and cupped her chin in her hands.

It was an almost girlish posture, and Edwina felt her heart soften slightly toward the usually irksome character before her. Perhaps Prudence was a woman ahead of her time who found solace in gossip about the lives of others, since her own had not turned out exactly the way she might have liked. Prudence was another one of those women who likely would have married, had things turned out differently. Her parents had needed her assistance in the shop from the time she was quite a young girl, and although customers floated in and out of the shop every hour they were open, it did not provide her with much of an opportunity to go out and socialize with any available young men.

And with her sharp mind and sharper tongue, she would have been the sort of woman who had an even shorter list of interested suitors than had her manner been more compliant.

Add to that the fact that the number of eligible men after the war and the flu epidemic was severely decreased, and it was almost a given that Prudence would never have a family of her own. In a way, Prudence's business was her life's sole focus, if one did not include her meddling in the affairs of others. A surge of gratitude for her own situation welled up within Edwina.

"I can well imagine that you would have, considering how much you've expanded your own business here. Why, I remember years ago, when your parents were making the decisions, how the sweet-shop portion of your business had not yet come into being."

The faintest bit of a blush colored Prudence's usually pale cheeks. Edwina guessed that she was no more accustomed to receiving compliments than Edwina herself had been before Beryl had arrived and bolstered her confidence. She felt slightly guilty at never having made any effort to see Prudence as someone who had her own trials to bear. Nor had she given her credit for the way she had been innovating, despite the difficulties being a woman in business brought.

"I suppose it all came out of the fact that I wasn't able to find any sweets in the village that I preferred. I decided that if I was interested in a wider variety of choices, others would be too."

"Well, I know that I've always appreciated the selection you provided. It's such a luxury not to have to go out of the village for so many options. It's almost like you brought the big city to the village with all this," Edwina said, gesturing toward the glass case filled with boiled sweets and chocolates of countless varieties.

"That's very kind of you to say. It has been a great deal of work to keep track of all the different sorts of items I offer here, but I think it's worth it," Prudence said.

Edwina glanced around the shop. Between the stationery, the stamps, and the candy, there was a great deal to manage. So many of the items available were small in size and numerous in quantity. Which put her in mind of something else Prudence might help her with.

"I have always marveled that you are able to know just where any item in the shop might be found and whether or not you actually had it in stock. I should think it would be a challenge to hold so many bits of information in your head."

Prudence straightened up, as if deciding whether or not she should feel complimented or insulted. The temptation to bristle got the better of her.

"I should think that I would be able to keep it all in mind, considering it's my responsibility to do so. Being postmistress is a sacred duty, as I'm sure you must realize," Prudence said.

"I meant no disrespect to your capabilities, Prudence. I only meant you must have some sort of rigorous methodology for keeping account of all of these disparate items. I'm sure that the Royal Mail requires you to keep an accurate list of all of your postage stamps, at the very least," Edwina said.

Prudence's shoulders lowered away from her ears slightly. She sniffed loudly. "Well, that's true. Not everyone gives real thought to how stamps could be considered legal tender. It is absolutely imperative not to let them go astray any more than one would money from the till."

"It's a responsible position indeed," Edwina said. "I remember, during the war years, keeping ledgers of items for the Women's Land Army. It must be at least as complicated as that, if not much more so."

"I'll say it is. Day in and day out, I run up my figures and track them. I reconcile the books at the end of every week and send in my reports on a monthly basis."

"Do you not find it all very tedious?" Edwina asked. She knew that she had felt that way about the recordkeeping for the Women's Land Army. She hadn't minded anything to do with settling the staff or helping them to work out any difficulties. But keeping track of all of the hours they worked and the quantities of food they produced was her least favorite part of the job.

"I don't find that I mind all that much," Prudence said. "In fact, I find it rather satisfying when the numbers all match up."

That was something that Edwina could understand from her knitting. It was one of life's small pleasures to get to the end of a row and realize that a complicated pattern had come out with the correct number of stitches in the end.

"It must be nice to have some help with it all once in a while, though, I would imagine," she said.

"It can be good to have a bit of company, as long as the person doesn't end up speaking to me when I'm in the middle of counting a drawer of stamps or a box of note cards," Prudence said.

"Minnie happened to mention that she occasionally helped you out with all that. I suppose that, with her own shop to tend, she has a better sense of when to keep quiet," Edwina said, working the conversation around to Minnie's alibi.

"Yes, she was very helpful in that way. I would have thought, with her talkative nature, she might be more hindrance than help, but it turns out she's very sensible and has a good eye for detail," Prudence said.

"Does she help you with it often?"

"She does actually. Since Minnie does her own inventory, I invite her to give me a hand, and generally she agrees. Of course, I pay her with a box of chocolates by way of a thank-you."

Edwina stepped toward a display of bottled inks, some of which were labeled as imported from France. She plucked from the rack one filled with deep green ink and held it up toward the light streaming through the window. Out of the corner of her eye, she could see Prudence leaning slightly toward her. The price displayed on the rack was several pence higher for this particular bottle than for the average ink. Edwina usually used such bottles to fill her pens. If Prudence's mind were focused on making a sale, she might not notice she was being questioned about Minnie rather too closely. Edwina tipped the bottle back and forth, as if examining it closely.

"I think Minnie mentioned something about inventorying quite recently. She said yesterday or the day before, I think," Edwina said.

Prudence took a step toward the rack of inks and plucked the warm russet shade from the rack. She handed it to Edwina for consideration before answering.

"No, I think you must be mistaken. Minnie was here earlier in the week. It was before all the excitement with Hazel broke out."

"Now, I thought for sure that Minnie mentioned having had a good chat with you about possible suspects in the murder while the two of you were conducting inventory," Edwina said. She surprised herself at how easily the lie tripped off her tongue. While Beryl had been a very good influence in so many ways, her elasticity with the truth was not her most admirable quality, at least as far as normal polite society was concerned, although Edwina had to admit that it had served them both in good stead as private-enquiry agents.

Prudence turned to face her. There was nothing she could stand less than being contradicted about what she felt she knew for sure.

"You are certainly mistaken. In fact, Hazel tried to come into the shop as we were doing inventory, and I had to turn her away. You can't have an accurate count if customers are in here buying things in the midst of it."

"Minnie must be thinking of some other occasion then, I suppose," Edwina said, handing the russet-colored ink back to Prudence. There would be enough autumn colors surrounding them soon. She did not wish to look at them while conducting her correspondence.

Prudence sniffed again. "We all get a bit muddled up some-times, I suppose." She looked pointedly at the bottle of ink, and Edwina took the hint.

"If you'd be so kind as to wrap this up for me and put it on

my account, I would appreciate it." Edwina handed her a bottle
of green ink.

Prudence hummed under her breath as she wrapped the bottle in layers of tissue paper and cotton string for safe transport,
and Edwina felt her heart sinking in her chest. Was Minnie simply muddled in her thinking, as Prudence suggested, or had she
deliberately lied about her whereabouts at the time of Hazel's
death?

Chapter 25

Beddoes let Constable Gibbs in through the front door just as Edwina was descending the front staircase, after having put Georgie down for an afternoon nap. While she had enjoyed playing with him that morning, it was a relief to once again have some time to herself, and she had been planning on puttering about in the garden, trimming back some of the plants, and pondering which things to add the following year. Instead, the look on Constable Gibbs's face left her in no doubt that her plans for the afternoon had suddenly changed. Beryl had arrived back at The Beeches just after Edwina had herself and was ensconced in the parlor, with her feet propped up on the ottoman, sipping on a tumbler of amber liquid. Edwina thought it a bit early for her friend to be indulging in spirits, but she kept her comments to herself.

Once the constable had been given a seat and had accepted a drink of her own, Edwina plucked her knitting from the basket next to her favorite chair. She found that not only did her own nerves calm as she added row after row to a project, it seemed to be soothing to those around her as well. Perhaps there was something mesmerizing about the rhythmic motion of her two hands moving back and forth steadily. Whatever the reason, she found it was a good tactic to employ when others appeared the least bit frazzled. Not that Constable Gibbs could be considered anything less than a consummate professional. However, the events of the past few days had been a lot for anyone to have to deal with.

"I can't imagine you're here just for chat and a drink," Beryl said, shifting in her seat and looking at the policewoman.

Constable Gibbs took a long sip of her beverage before letting out a deep sigh. "I came by to tell the two of you that I think I've cracked the case."

Edwina arched an eyebrow at Beryl. Earlier, they had discussed when they ought to let the constable know about Minnie's lack of an alibi. The constable had beaten them to it by appearing at The Beeches without warning. Edwina's stomach clenched at the thought of the mild-mannered shopkeeper being hauled before the magistrate's court, before being bound over to the assizes.

"So, who do you feel is the culprit?" Beryl asked.

"Arthur Dinsdale. And you won't believe the reason why," she said.

Beryl looked over at Edwina and nodded. If anyone were to be found guilty, an outsider was preferable to someone like Minnie.

"What have you discovered?" Edwina asked. She laid her knitting in her lap, too focused on what the constable had to say to continue doing anything else.

"From the very beginning of this case, I felt as though we needed to have more information about those newcomers. So I set about conducting a background check on them. It seems that they are not brother and sister at all," she said.

Beryl had thought that the two did not look much alike, but having met families all over the world, she had come to realize that such was not always the case. Besides, in the case of many families, it would not do to ask a lot of questions. Between infidelities, deaths, and adoptions within a family to protect the reputation of some poor unfortunate young girl, it was far more polite to keep one's observations to oneself. Still, it did make for an interesting tidbit of information.

"Are they related?" she asked.

The constable nodded and took another sip before continuing. "Oh yes, they are. As a matter of fact, they're each other's next of kin."

"They're married?" Beryl asked. She must be losing her edge. Beryl prided herself on being highly attuned to romantic connections between those around her. In fact, she had noticed Charles's interest in Edwina from the very first time she spotted the two of them together. It was a skill that had served her in good stead throughout her life, and she could not believe she had missed something like that with the Dinsdales. Theirs must be an unusual marriage indeed.

"For years, in fact," the constable said.

"So why have they presented themselves to the general public as brother and sister?" Edwina asked. "Aren't people much more likely to pass themselves off as a married couple when they aren't?"

Edwina had a good point. While social norms were loosening all the time, especially since so many people had moved far from home during the war years, there was still a great deal of stigma attached to unmarried persons cohabitating. People lied about their marital status all the time, but not in the way that the Dinsdales had. If someone were to point out that the newly arrived Lintons were, in fact, not actually a married couple, that would have been much easier to believe.

"Money," the constable said, smacking one hand against her thigh for emphasis. "Arthur Dinsdale was cozying up to unmarried women in order to bilk them out of their money."

"Is that what you think happened to Hazel?" Edwina asked.

"It's exactly what I think. Which is why I've arrested Arthur Dinsdale for her murder," she said.

"Are you quite sure about that?" Beryl asked. "Do you think he murdered her because she made her will over to them?"

"It certainly doesn't make the case weaker that they're going about telling people that they stand to inherit her property. But no, I don't think that is the reason. I think that she found out that he had been courting her under the false pretense that he was free to do so. When she discovered that he wasn't, not only did she revoke her will, but she was in a position to expose them and prevent them from being able to exploit anyone else here in the village," the constable said.

As much as it had not been her line of thinking, Beryl had to agree that the theory had real merit. Hazel certainly would have been a plum prize to have plucked, but if she came to realize the truth about the Dinsdales, she was in a position to make them miserable indeed. There were certainly other women in the village with financial resources whom he could have wished to take advantage of. If he was able to murder Hazel before she could make a new will, not only would that have saved his reputation, but he would have stood to inherit her money as well.

"It seems as though perhaps you solved it then," Beryl said.

"I believe so."

"What about Maude? You don't think that Arthur would have been the only one responsible, do you?" Edwina asked.

"I am still not sure about her. I didn't feel as though I had enough evidence to hold them both, and he seemed the more likely of the two to have committed the actual crime. After all, running someone through is not such an easy thing to accomplish," Constable Gibbs said.

A grim memory of bayonets and the sound of muffled grunts popped up in Beryl's mind. For a terrible moment, the room before her faded and was replaced by a scene best forgotten.

She got to her feet and refilled her glass from the cart on the far side of the room.

"Will you continue to look for evidence of a conspiracy between them?" Edwina asked.

"I will certainly keep an open mind about Maude as I gather all the evidence needed to pursue the case against her husband. After all, none of us want anyone connected with Hazel's death to go unpunished."

Beryl returned to her seat, glad of the distraction from her own thoughts that Edwina's question provided.

Edwina still did not look convinced. "Who would have been so foolish, though, as to let everyone know that Hazel had named them in her will if they were the ones who killed her?"

Constable Gibbs shrugged and got to her feet. "Not every murderer is a genius. Besides, maybe they thought that by making that sort of announcement, that was exactly the sort of thing the authorities would think and discount them because of it. A double bluff, so to speak." The constable settled her uniform cap back on her head. "I just wanted to update you so that you would stop putting out effort about the case. I hate you to waste your time. Thank you for all you've done so far."

Beryl walked the constable to the door. She couldn't help but feel disappointed that she and Edwina were not the ones to get to the bottom of the case. While she respected the constable and enjoyed working with her, she could not deny the fact that she had a somewhat competitive attitude toward the arrangement. After all, she did like to win at any endeavor in which she involved herself. There was something of a hollow feeling in the pit of her stomach as she returned to the parlor and took her seat once more.

"So, what do you think of that?" she asked Edwina, who had begun knitting once more.

"I think that if Arthur is guilty, Maude must also be involved somehow."

"I agree. The constable has made a good case for his guilt, though, hasn't she?"

"Indeed, she has. Did you have any idea that the two of them weren't actually siblings?"

"No, I am sorry to say that I didn't. I was too concerned about the fraud they were perpetrating at their séances to consider what else they might be lying about."

"I hate to admit it, but I feel rather relieved to think it was them. After all, it does get Minnie off the hook, now, doesn't it?" she asked.

"It certainly does do that, and rather neatly too. So you're not upset that the constable solved the crime before we could?" Beryl asked.

Edwina looked and her eyes widened in surprise. "Of course not. The only thing that matters is that justice is done for Hazel," she said. But despite her friend's protestations, Beryl thought she could detect a bit of regret in Edwina's voice.

When Beddoes escorted the Lintons into her library, Edwina's first thought was that Charles would need a place of his own in the house to receive clients. She sought him out in the kitchen, where he was making a valiant attempt at spooning porridge into Georgie's tiny mouth, without the appearance of success. The child squealed as Edwina entered the room and clapped his chubby hands together with excitement. Her heart lifted at the notion that, in such a short amount of time, Georgie had come to care for her.

Charles gave her a look of relief as Edwina informed him that he had visitors. Beddoes followed closely on Edwina's heels and, with an attitude that brooked no resistance, took over with the feeding. Edwina wondered at the protocol in the circumstances. She had been busy at work in the library on some correspondence for the private-enquiry business and was loath to leave it unfinished. She also was not sure as to her role.

After all, she was the mistress of the house, despite the fact that the callers had asked for Charles. Charles seemed to sense her discomfort as they started back down the hallway.

"Would you be willing to keep the Lintons company while I slip upstairs quickly to change into something more suitable for receiving visitors?" he asked. Charles gestured toward the streaks of porridge and something that looked like jam covering his shirtfront.

She was happy to agree and made her way to the library, where she found Anthony Linton perusing a shelf of gardening books. Phyllis sat in a chair opposite Edwina's wide desk. Crumpet stood on his hind legs, his front paws on her knees.

"I hope that Crumpet is not making a nuisance of himself," Edwina said.

"Not at all. I miss my own dog terribly, and I am delighted to have his company," Phyllis said. Edwina thought she detected tears shimmering in Phyllis's eyes. While she did not encourage her dog to push himself onto visitors, she was glad he was providing comfort to a fellow dog lover. Anthony seemed eager to change the subject from his wife's grief.

"I see that you are an avid gardener," Anthony said.

"There are few things I love to do more than puttering about in my garden. Are you interested in horticulture too?" she asked.

"I am new to the pastime, but I am eager to learn and have enjoyed getting my hands dirty at The Swallows' Nest. The garden there is a bit overgrown, but I think it could be returned to its former glory with some devoted attention," he said.

"Anthony has become quite passionate about his new hobby," Phyllis said.

"Do you share your husband's interest?" Edwina asked.

"I prefer reading and knitting, but I am more than happy to have bunches of fresh flowers to arrange for the house, thanks to his efforts," she said.

Charles stepped through the door, looking nothing like a man who had just been feeding porridge to a moving target. He had even donned a tie, neatly knotted and held together with a diamond-studded clasp. He reached out and shook hands with Anthony and nodded at Phyllis.

"I understand that you wished to speak with me. How may I help you?" he asked, taking a seat behind Edwina's desk. She brushed aside a small ripple of annoyance and arched an eyebrow at him, as if to ask should she leave. He gestured his head toward a chair nearby and she lowered herself into it as unobtrusively as possible.

"As you are the only solicitor in the village, we thought you would be the one to ask about the disposition of Hazel Moffat's estate," Anthony said.

A flutter of excitement filled Edwina's chest. Here was yet another party expressing interest in Hazel's will. Had the Lintons some expectation of inheriting as well? If so, what sort of relationship had they had with their landlady?

"I am afraid that, although I am the only solicitor here in Walmsley Parva, I am in no way knowledgeable about Hazel's will, as I did not draw one up for her," he said.

"Oh dear. Now what are we to do?" Phyllis asked, lifting her hand off of Crumpet's head and looking up at her husband.

"I'm sure everything will be fine when all is said and done, my love," Anthony said, taking the seat beside her and reaching for her hand.

"Is there some sort of problem that you thought the will would resolve?" Charles asked.

Edwina had the sense he was leading the conversation in a direction that would probe into Hazel's death. Perhaps he was no more convinced of Arthur Dinsdale's guilt than was she.

"We don't wish to seem unfeeling, but we've become very attached to The Swallows' Nest and had hoped that we might be able to negotiate with whoever had inherited the property," Phyllis said.

"I see. That does present a bit of a gray area," Charles said.

"It certainly does. We're entirely uncertain about whether or not we will be able to remain at the property," Anthony said. "My wife is quite a sentimental sort, and I don't wish for her to become even more attached to the place if we're just going to be chucked out by whoever inherits it in the end."

Phyllis snapped open her small handbag and withdrew a handkerchief. She dabbed her eyes as her shoulders started to shake.

"May I get you a glass of water?" Edwina asked, leaning forward.

Phyllis shook her head. "No, please forgive my outburst. It's just that we had to bury our beloved dog there at the property, and I simply cannot stand the idea of not having put down roots there, now that it is his final resting place."

A lump rose in Edwina's throat. She could well imagine how wrenching such a thing could be. It didn't bear thinking about as she glanced over at Crumpet. She couldn't imagine the day when he was no longer there. How much worse would it be if she also had to vacate the place where he was buried? She glanced over at Charles, who gave her a small smile of encouragement, as if he read her mind.

"I'm sorry I cannot give you any real assurance as to what will happen in the future, but I can say that, as no will has been produced thus far, it may be some time before any sort of change needs to be made by anyone, including you," he said.

The Lintons exchanged a glance. "So, you think that we will not need to vacate in the near future?" Anthony asked.

"I cannot make any promises. What I can tell you is that, in cases like these, tenants do have some rights, and until her will is found, no one can ask you to leave the premises," Charles said.

"See, my dear, I told you things would be all right in the end," Anthony said. He got to his feet and tugged gently on his wife's hand, drawing her upward as well.

"Will you let us know if you hear that an heir is named?" Phyllis asked. "The more time we have to make peace with whatever will happen, the better."

"Of course, Charles will let you know if he hears anything regarding your situation," Edwina said. "Won't you?" She turned toward her friend, who nodded.

"I'll pass along any information within my ability to do so. Wait and see; things will turn out just fine in the end, I'm sure."

Crumpet followed along next to Edwina as she walked the Lintons to the door and saw them out. She dropped to her knees in the hallway and rubbed Crumpet's ears with both of her hands. Truly, she felt enormously sorrowful for Mrs. Linton. She returned to the library, where Charles had removed himself from her desk chair.

"I am terribly sorry to have imposed on your space. I just thought that, if you were off to the side a bit, you could remain in the room without either of us calling attention to your presence. It was dreadfully high-handed of me, I know, but I wondered if they might have something useful to say about your case."

Edwina had already forgotten her annoyance over being displaced, and Charles's reasoning was sound. How like him to have come up with a tidy solution to a potentially awkward situation. And it was like him, as well, to consider her professional interests. He really was a most remarkable man, despite his rather ordinary appearance.

"There is no need to apologize," she said.

"What do you think of their visit?" he asked.

"I confess I was hopeful that their interest in Hazel's will might provide another avenue in the case to explore, since I am not convinced that Arthur Dinsdale is the culprit," she said.

"But you no longer think there was anything nefarious in their question?"

"It seemed to me that I would be eager to know what the future might hold if I were in their shoes. It is dreadful to contemplate." Edwina bent down to stroke Crumpet once more. When she straightened, Charles was looking at her with an expression she could not quite decipher.

"I too am eager to know what the future might hold," he said. "But for now, I'll leave you to your work."

Edwina watched his back as he passed out through the door and closed it softly behind him.

Chapter 26

Edwina needed to clear her head. Between the sorrow she felt for Phyllis Linton and the agitation she felt after Charles mentioned the future, she could not settle down to work at her desk. She decided to go looking for Beryl and found her in the summerhouse stretched out in a chaise longue, her eyes closed. Beryl's eyes creaked open as a stray twig snapped under Edwina's small foot.

"What is it, Ed? You look a bit peaky," she asked, sitting up and swinging her feet to the floor.

"The Lintons were just here asking after Hazel's estate," Edwina said.

"What's got you so riled up about that? Do you think they are suspects?"

"I just can't shake the feeling that this case isn't really solved. As soon as they came asking about Hazel's will, I wondered if they might be involved in her death. If I'm still asking that sort of question, it tells me I'm not convinced that Constable Gibbs has arrested the real culprit."

Beryl got to her feet. "If you're not satisfied, I'm not satisfied. What do you propose we do about it?"

"I think we should speak with Minnie. After all, she did lie about her whereabouts at the time of Hazel's death. I'd like to ask her where she really was," Edwina said.

"Fine by me. I had no plans for the rest of the day other than to take a bit of a nap and perhaps wander down to the Dove and Duck this evening for a bit of excitement."

She followed Edwina back into the house, where her friend whistled for Crumpet; after snapping his lead to his collar, she reached for her third-best hat before heading out the door. Beryl couldn't shake the feeling that her friend had not told her everything that was troubling her. While she was not as good at detecting untruths as Edwina, she did know when something was wrong with her friend. Still, it never did to press her about such things. She would unburden herself when she was ready, and not a moment before.

The weather was warm, and even though she preferred to take the motorcar out for a jaunt whenever the smallest excuse presented itself, she had to admit that the walk felt good. Even though the temperatures had been unusually warm, she knew that the colder weather would arrive before long and the number of fine days would be coming to a close for months to come. She wondered what the future might hold as she considered the notion of being trapped inside with a small child in the house. Would it make things more or less tolerable as the days grew shorter and the village became even sleepier, as it invariably did when no one felt much like being outside? Before she had met Jack, the newsboy, and his family, she would never have considered it possible that children might help to pass the time pleasantly. But having spent time with him and his younger siblings, she had come to realize that she might be better at connecting with small persons than she had ever believed possible. Perhaps things with Georgie might turn out the same way.

She and Edwina walked the entire way into the village, each lost in her own thoughts. Neither of them was in a particular hurry, and Edwina gave Crumpet his head to sniff luxuriously at whatever scents caught his fancy. Edwina tended to be indulgent where Crumpet was concerned, but even for her, this seemed an extravagant display of patience. Beryl wondered briefly if something had happened with the dog during the Lintons' visit, but she did not wish to pry. Edwina was terribly sensitive where her little dog was concerned.

They arrived at the Silver Spoon Tea Room just as Minnie was carrying a tray of freshly baked buns to a glass case on the front counter. She looked up at them, and in place of her usual warm smile of greeting, a wrinkle of concern furrowed her brow. No other patrons sat at the tables in the eatery, and so Edwina confidently stepped up to the counter with Beryl close on her heels.

"I'm so glad we caught you on your own, Minnie. We have a few questions for you," Edwina said. Minnie looked as though she might burst into tears as she kept her eyes focused on filling the case with replenished baked goods.

"I'm very busy this afternoon, as you can well see," she said.

Beryl looked pointedly around the room. "I do think you could spare us a moment or two of your time. You're not exactly overrun with customers, now, are you?"

"Besides, I'm sure you would prefer to have this conversation out of the earshot of anyone else. If you will simply answer our questions quickly, we will be on our way," Edwina said.

Minnie placed the last bun in the case and lowered the lid. "Since you put it that way, I guess you'd best get on with it," she said.

She crossed her arms over her ample chest and stood there, with the long counter between them. Beryl could see this was not going to be a cozy chat over a pot of tea and some tiny sandwiches. Edwina must truly have a bee in her bonnet about the case if she were taking such a direct approach. Generally, she eased her way around to a topic of conversation that might be considered discomforting, rather than the head-on approach

Beryl favored. Perhaps she had been too much of an influence on her friend. Or maybe whatever was bothering her had brought out her assertive side. Either way, it was expeditious. At least it would be if they managed to get to the truth of Minnie's whereabouts at the time of the murder.

"Do you remember telling me that you were taking inventory with Prudence at her shop at the time Hazel was killed?" Edwina said.

Two red spots of color flushed Minnie's cheeks as she nodded her head. "That's right, I did."

"But it's not right at all, is it?" Edwina asked.

"Are you accusing me of lying?" Minnie asked, the splotches on her cheeks growing larger.

"Let's just say that Prudence does not confirm your story. She claims that you assisted her with the inventory the day before Hazel died. In fact, she remembers Hazel attempting to come into the shop during the stocktaking."

Minnie cast her gaze to the floor, as if she could not make eye contact with Edwina. She let out a deep sigh and emerged from behind the counter. They followed her to a table at the back of the tea shop and watched as she sank into a chair with her back to the wall.

"That's right, I wasn't with Prudence. I'm sorry that I told you a fib," she said. "It's just that the truth was so embarrassing."

"Does this have something to do with Clarence?" Beryl asked. She had seen that look before on women's faces when they had come to suspect that their husbands were up to no good with another woman.

Minnie nodded. "How did you know?" she asked.

Beryl leaned across the table and patted Minnie on the hand. "It's something I've had to deal with myself on occasion," she said. And that was the honest truth. As much as Beryl prided herself on being the sort of woman that many men found interesting, she was not immune to those same men having their heads turned in other directions as well. She knew the sting of one's pride being wounded by infidelity, and her heart went out to Minnie, who had not had any prior experience with the pain of it.

"Surely not," Minnie said, her mouth falling open in surprise. "But you're so beautiful and accomplished."

Beryl squeezed her hand. "That has very little to do with such things, I'm afraid. Just as your husband's behavior has nothing whatsoever to do with you either, as I hope you are aware."

Beryl felt Edwina's glance, and out of the corner of her eye, she noticed her friend nodding approvingly. Generally, in such situations, Edwina was the one to bring the kindly words. But in this case, Beryl had far more experience of the sort of thing Minnie was enduring, and she was surprised at how proud she felt at being able to assist in this way.

Minnie started to sob. Edwina fished a clean handkerchief from her handbag and passed it across to the poor woman. "I think you would feel better if you told us all about it."

Once Minnie had dabbed her eyes and gently blown her nose, she nodded.

"Once I heard the rumors about Clarence and Hazel, I couldn't believe it. And then I got to thinking that perhaps there was some truth in it, and although I'm embarrassed by the whole thing, I have to admit that I went to spy on him at the cinema. I thought I might catch him red-handed."

"And did you see him with Hazel?" Edwina asked.

"No, I didn't. I snuck in the back way and crept toward the office, where I assumed they might be cavorting, if the rumors were true," she said. "But when I arrived, there was nothing to see."

Beryl and Edwina exchanged a glance.

"Did you see Clarence there on his own?" Beryl asked.

"I didn't see anyone at all. The cinema wasn't open at the

time, and I let myself in with the key at the back. There was really no reason why anyone would have been there, after all, but I figured it was just the sort of place Clarence would have privacy to conduct himself as he pleased," Minnie said.

"Did you hear anyone in the building?" Beryl asked.

"No, I can't say that I did. It's a large place, and sometimes it is subject to the sort of creaks and groans that all large old buildings are. But the truth is that I didn't stay for very long. In fact, I decided I didn't really want to catch him, even if he were behaving so deceitfully. It would be incredibly awkward to catch them in the act, now, wouldn't it?" Minnie asked.

Beryl would have to agree with that sentiment. She vividly recalled the small number of times she had caught an object of her affection cavorting with another woman. It had taken all of her considerable poise to navigate such awkwardness, and she did not blame Minnie for losing her nerve in the end.

"That's completely understandable. Did you ask your husband where he was when you did not find him there?" Beryl asked.

"No, of course not. If I had done so, it would have raised questions about why I was asking in the first place. Clarence would have been extremely suspicious if I were to interrogate him in the least," Minnie said.

"Thank you for your honesty," Edwina said.

"What's this all about anyway?" Minnie asked. "I thought that Arthur Dinsdale had been arrested for Hazel's murder. You aren't still looking into the case, are you?"

Edwina pushed back her chair and stood. "We always feel it is the best policy to tie up any loose ends, even when a case seems as though it's coming to a close," she said.

"I see. You won't tell Clarence what I said to you, will you?" Minnie asked.

"I see no reason to do so," Beryl said.

"Good. Because now that Hazel is no longer a threat to our

marriage, I prefer to pretend none of this ever happened," Minnie said.

Mrs. Dumbarton pushed open the door and entered the shop just then, and Minnie got to her feet to greet her. Beryl noticed the mild-mannered shopkeeper had done a remarkably good job of appearing cheerful as she welcomed the newcomer. She wondered if Minnie were an adept actress and if they ought to believe a thing she had to say. As they exited the building and Edwina untied Crumpet from a lamppost next to the shop, Beryl voiced her concerns.

"She recovered herself quite nicely there at the end, didn't she?" Beryl asked.

"She did seem to plaster a smile on her face with ease. But that could just be the English penchant for a stiff upper lip. I did think about one thing, however," Edwina said.

"Let me guess. Neither Minnie nor Clarence seems to have an alibi for the time of Hazel's death," Beryl said.

"Exactly."

Chapter 27

No sooner had they returned to The Beeches than Simpkins clattered down the long hallway and popped his head into the parlor. Beryl was fixing a pitcher of her justifiably famous gin fizzes, and Edwina thought Simpkins had simply shown his usual knack for appearing whenever alcohol was on offer. But directly behind him, Maude Dinsdale's face peeked over his shoulder.

"We have a visitor," Simpkins announced, as he crossed the room and made straight for the drinks tray.

"I hope I'm not intruding by appearing without warning, but I felt I had to see you," Maude said, not looking the least as if she were embarrassed by any potential rudeness.

"Not at all. May I offer you a drink?" Beryl said, holding the pitcher aloft.

"That would be most welcome," Maude said, as she sank into the sofa without being invited to do so. Edwina could not very well admonish her for making herself at home without appearing rude herself, but she had been hoping for a few minutes' respite from responsibility. Georgie had gone down for a nap while they were out visiting the tea shop and had managed to stay asleep after their return. She had wanted nothing more than to sit and contemplate how she would construct the hat she was planning while sipping on one of Beryl's concoctions.

Instead, it was clear Maude wished to beg some sort of assistance from them. She let out a sigh and hoped it didn't show as she accepted a drink of her own from Simpkins's gnarled hand. He took a seat beside her and gave her a look that told her he understood her frustration. Edwina could hardly credit the change in her relationship with Simpkins over the last several months. To have gone from a contentious employer and employee situation to one that could only truly be called family was a miracle indeed.

In fact, if she were to be entirely honest, she would have to admit that Simpkins probably knew her as well as anyone else in the world. While she and Beryl shared a particularly warm friendship, Simpkins had known her from the time she was born and had been at her side during the long years Beryl was gallivanting around the world. She gave him an uncharacteristic wink before turning to the task at hand.

"What is it that you think we can do for you?" she asked, as Beryl sat down beside the purported medium.

From the look on Beryl's face, Edwina had to wonder if her friend were assessing the other woman for cards hidden up her sleeve or other trappings of chicanery.

"I hate to admit it, but I'm frightened," Maude said.

Edwina thought that was nothing less than the honest truth. Maude did indeed look frightened, and Edwina felt she was wise to feel that way. After all, it was certainly Constable Gibbs's intention to find proof that she was also involved in Hazel's murder, whether as an actual wielder of weaponry or simply someone who helped to plot the crime. But it would not do to admit as much. Constable Gibbs could use all the advantage possible, considering how scant the proof of the Dinsdales' guilt seemed to be. Tipping her hand and revealing the police-woman's intention would not be helpful in the least.

"I'm surprised to hear that someone so comfortable convers-ing in the realm of the dead would find anything earthly fright-ening in the least," Beryl said. Edwina thought her friend had not done a particularly good job of hiding her disdain. Usually, Edwina was the far more judgmental of the two of them. She didn't think it was the fact that Maude was possibly a charlatan that bothered her friend. It was more that she did not respect anyone who did not make a more professional stab at whatever she tried her hand to. After all, Beryl was someone who threw herself into her many ventures.

"I have nothing to fear from the dead. It's the living who worry me," Maude said.

"Anyone amongst living in particular that you have in mind?" Beryl asked.

"If I knew that, I would do something about it."

"You may be the only one in the village who's feeling that way. I believe most other residents are feeling a sense of relief, now that your husband has been arrested for the crime," Beryl said.

Maude shifted in her seat and stared at her. "Arthur being ar-rested has only increased my agitation. Not only am I certain he's not the one who carried out this heinous crime, but now I'm all on my own and afraid for my life," Maude said.

"Why should you be worried about being targeted?" Ed-wina asked.

"Surely you must have noticed how much Hazel and I re-semble each other," she said.

"Your husband does seem to have a type, now, doesn't he?" Beryl asked.

"I see you've heard about our relationship then," Maude said, taking a long sip of her drink.

"I'm afraid that, in a village this size, everyone has heard about it," Edwina said. "You didn't really hope to keep it under wraps once the constable had discovered the truth, now did you?"

"One could hope. Although I suppose it was entirely unrealistic of me," Maude said.

"So you believe that you were the intended target of the murder?" Edwina asked.

Maude nodded. "Not everyone is as open to the idea of the spirit realm as I might like. I must confess that there have been people in the past who have been angered by the messages I delivered, and it seems much more likely that I would have stirred such passion than that Hazel would have done so," she said.

Edwina had to agree that Maude had a point. Until the Dinsdales had arrived in the village, Hazel had never had any trouble with anyone whatsoever. She had been well liked and respected and had a role to play within the village. Edwina could not recall her even having the sort of tussles about church fetes or Women's Institute committees that so many of her fellow villagers indulged in. Maude certainly seemed more likely to have courted difficulty than Hazel ever had done.

"Do you have anyone in particular in mind who you think would have been angry enough to attempt to kill you?" Beryl asked.

"Well, Mr. Watkins certainly is not my biggest supporter. He has accosted me on more than one occasion and has threatened me loudly and often," Maude said.

"He did make rather a scene in front of the séance the first time we attended," Edwina said.

"And it wasn't the only time. But, besides him, I wouldn't put it past the vicar and his wife. They both had plenty of choice things to say about Hazel deciding to continue her employment with me rather than at the church," Maude said.

"You really can't believe that either of the Lowethorpes would have committed violence, can you?" Edwina asked. There was something quite shocking about the notion of the vicar or his wife taking such steps. What was the world coming to?

"Well, I don't know, now do I?" Maude said. "They both have had harsh things to say to me and cross the street to avoid me whenever possible."

"I should think the fact they are trying to physically avoid you might indicate that they weren't the sort to be confrontational," Beryl said.

"They've only stopped shouting at me since Hazel died. It could be guilt that's making them keep their distance," Maude said. "Or the fact that they are concerned that I can sense their culpability if they get too close."

"Is that one of your skills?" Simpkins asked.

Maude shrugged. "I do get that feeling now and again when someone is telling me an untruth. I suppose you must be rather good at that yourself, considering your profession," she said, turning to include both Beryl and Edwina in her gaze.

"It does come in rather handy. And, I can tell you, I haven't sensed any such thing from either of the Lowethorpes," Edwina said. She could feel her voice becoming prim. The very idea of such upstanding citizens being involved in something so ugly rubbed her entirely the wrong way.

"Speaking of dishonesty, why did you decide to pose as siblings instead of the married couple you are?" Beryl asked.

Maude took a deep breath and paused for a moment before answering. "There are certain advantages to traveling as unmarried people. Arthur has always been quite a charmer, and it never hurts, when setting up in a new place, for the local women to be eager to make his acquaintance," Maude said.

"I should think that it would be a great advantage in your line of work. After all, aren't the majority of your clients women?" Beryl asked.

"Yes, they are. I find that women are far more spiritual-minded than men."

Edwina thought that it might also have a great deal to do with the fact that women outnumbered men by so many all across the country since the war.

"That bit of deception doesn't make you seem all that trustworthy with your business, though, does it?" Beryl asked. "After all, if you would lie about being married, what's to say that you are not the sort of person who would make up all sorts of other things as well."

"I see that you're not much of a believer. I would've thought that a woman with your vast experience of the world would be far more open-minded," Maude said. "Or have the papers entirely misrepresented you?"

Beryl got to her feet and went to fetch the pitcher of drinks. She topped off everyone else's before refilling her own glass.

"I don't think the newspapers have particularly misrepresented me over the years. And I don't think of myself as closeminded. After all, I've seen a great deal of the world, as you say, and have had any number of experiences that I could not quite explain. It's just that I've also seen innumerable charlatans and have had the very great pleasure of attending séances on more than one occasion with Harry Houdini, who kindly pointed out the way that they perform their tricks," Beryl said.

"And have you found me to be performing any of them myself?" Maude asked.

"It would be tedious to go into all that now, but I will say that I would have thought the phosphorescent paint to be beneath you or any medium at this point, since it's been so overused," Beryl said.

Maude smiled and rattled the ice in her class. "Just because one does this and that to enhance the experience for the sitters does not negate the fact that spirits are real and eager to be in touch."

Edwina felt her stomach gathering into a knot. She hated scenes of any sort and felt that Beryl might be unwilling to back off before this visit turned into one. She wished she had some sort of psychic powers herself that could allow Beryl to read her mind. Instead, she had to content herself with trying to change the subject slightly.

"Was Hazel in on your secret?" she asked.

"Certainly not. We needed a policy never to let anyone in on that bit of information. After all, who could we be sure to trust with it?"

"Is there any way she could have discovered it for herself?" Beryl asked.

"Are you accusing me of having a reason to do away with her?" Maude asked.

"The constable certainly seems to think at least your husband is involved. Why not you as well?" Beryl asked.

Edwina's heart sank. Constable Gibbs's advantage seemed to be lessening by the moment.

"You've described how your 'brother' being unmarried was helpful to your business, but what about your part in it all?" Edwina asked.

Maude smiled at her and leaned forward slightly. She shrugged her broad shoulders. "Spinsters are always allowed to be more eccentric than other women. In fact, it's almost expected of them. Haven't you found that to be so?"

A flush sprang to Edwina's pale cheeks. Although she had reconciled herself to her role as a spinster years before, she did not care to consider that others might find her position eccentric. With so many other women remaining unmarried, it wasn't even particularly unusual. Edwina had always equated eccentricity with impropriety, and she had taken great pains to uphold the social contract whenever possible. Although, she had to admit that, over the last few months, she had thrown off the traces more and more often. From starting the private-enquiry agency with Beryl, to moving Simpkins into the house, to agreeing to take on the role of magistrate, one might accuse her of being eccentric. Still, she thought it a far cry from offering her services as a psychic medium.

Fortunately, the sound of Georgie crying lustily from the second floor filtered into the room before she had to reply. She hastily placed her drink on the table beside her and got to her feet.

"I'm sorry, I have important matters to attend to. I'm sure that Simpkins would be happy to show you out," she said.

Beryl thought that Edwina had been rather a good sport about the whole spinster comment from Maude. She had taken great delight in seeing the backside of the purported medium after Edwina swept out of the room. It made her blood boil to think of someone insulting her friend. While Beryl would consider being called an eccentric the highest of compliments, she knew that Edwina did not feel the same way. Beryl had come very close to losing her temper, which was not something she was much inclined to do. In order to work off some pent-up energy, she excused herself from The Beeches and hopped into her motorcar for a drive, as she so often did when feeling restless or overcome by unpleasant emotion.

Thinking about a case also helped her to find emotional equilibrium. As she rolled along, she considered what Maude had to say about her own fears. Although she was more than happy to consider that the Dinsdales could be responsible for any number of crimes, she had to admit that Maude made a compelling point. And she had seemed genuinely frightened. Mr. Watkins had been ferocious in his response to his wife attending the séances. Was it possible he had mistaken Hazel for Maude and had killed her?

She had to admit that it was a possibility. After all, he was not as young as he used to be, and perhaps his eyesight had failed him. And it was true that the two women looked a great deal alike, especially from behind. She supposed it was possible that whoever had run Hazel through had done so without realizing they had picked the wrong victim until it was too late. And since no one was sure where Hazel's murder had been committed, it was possible that it could have been in a place where Maude had been expected to be at least as easily as Hazel. If Hazel had been found in her own home, they could have ruled out that possibility, but as they had no location, they truly could not.

With Mr. Watkins on her mind, she turned toward the village and, in a few moments' time, pulled to a stop in front of the Blackburns' garage. Nora stepped out of the large doors dressed in her usual coveralls. She tucked a greasy rag into her back pocket and greeted Beryl with her usual warmth.

"There's nothing wrong with your motorcar, I hope," Nora said.

Beryl pushed open the door of the vehicle and stepped out. "I'm happy to say that it's running just fine. Actually, I'm here on an entirely different matter," she said.

"You're not still working on the murder, are you?" Nora asked, a flicker of worry crossing her face. Beryl knew that Nora's brother, Michael, had been a suspect in previous crimes and that his mental health was not all that one might wish. She suspected that the younger woman worried constantly about him being accused of anything because of his unpredictable reaction to stress.

"I'm afraid that I am, but it's nothing for you to worry about. I just had a question for you that I hoped you might be able to answer," she said.

"It's not about Michael, is it?" Nora asked.

"Not in the least. I actually wanted to know if you saw Mr. Watkins at approximately the time that Hazel was killed?" Beryl asked.

"Why, did he say that he was here?" Nora asked.

"He mentioned that he came by for a part to fix his tractor that is broken down," Beryl said.

"He may have done, but I cannot verify it if he did," Nora

said. "I closed early that day and took Michael over to a dance in Pershing Magna."

"That timing is fortunate," Beryl said.

Nora wiped her hands on the front of her coveralls. Beryl wondered if her palms were sweating from nerves or if they were simply dirty.

"To tell you the truth, he was a little bit worked up about the murder. You know how he gets," Nora said.

Indeed, Beryl did. Her heart had gone out to the young man when she had first met him. He had had what was euphemistically called a bad war and had come home robbed of his senses for some time. It had taken the consistent and innovative efforts of more than one person to return him to his life as well as could be expected. The damage to his arm was nothing in comparison with that of his spirit, after all that he had seen. If Michael had been her brother, she would have wanted to keep his mind from turning toward the subject of death by any means possible too.

"I completely understand. Did the two of you have a good time?"

"You know, we really did. Michael is quite a hit whenever he goes out dancing, and it wouldn't surprise me if, before long, he ends up finding a nice girl to settle down with," Nora said.

Beryl's thoughts returned to Edwina and that dreaded word *spinster*. She thought it likely that label would remain fixed to Nora as well, although it did not seem as though the young woman was particularly troubled by her life. She seemed to thrive in her role as business owner and mechanic. In fact, women like Nora gave Beryl hope for the future. She preferred the notion that it was possible for someone of either gender to make their life into what they most preferred rather than what society told them it ought to be.

"I'm sure that, should that day ever come, the two of you will still rub along just fine," Beryl said.

"I hope so. After all, we've got a good thing going here. If we didn't, I wouldn't be able to do things like close early to take off to go dancing," she said with a smile.

Out of the corner of Beryl's eye, she caught sight of a familiar figure. Maude Dinsdale came into sight and pushed open the door of the tailor shop. Beryl had not realized quite how close it was to the garage. It would not have taken much time at all for Mr. Watkins to leave the garage and enter the building where the séances were held. It also would have been easy for him to see if Hazel had been coming or going and to have followed her somewhere in order to kill her. If his eyesight was not particularly sharp, he could easily have mistaken Hazel for Maude. In fact, even with Beryl's eyesight being as good as it was, she had to admit the two looked remarkably alike from this distance. As much as she wished she were convinced of the Dinsdales' guilt, she would be remiss not to consider that Mr. Watkins could easily have been the one to carry out the crime.

Chapter 28

From the moment Georgie had arrived, Crumpet had grasped the positives in the situation. Never before had so much food cascaded to the floor, ripe for the gobbling. Georgie's face generally rewarded canine kisses with additional flavorful treats. And certainly, it had to be said that Georgie was more often up for playful activity than anyone else in the house. But for all that, it was clear to Edwina, when Georgie grasped the little dog's ears with both hands and gave them a firm tug, that Crumpet, most assuredly, would benefit from some time apart from the toddler.

She did not even need to whistle for him in order to coax him down the hallway toward the front door. He was almost outside before she could snap on his lead and avail herself of her hat. She looked down at him with some sympathy as they made their way swiftly down the drive, gravel crunching beneath their feet. If she had been the sort of woman to whistle under her breath, she would have done so.

Although she was delighted by Georgie's presence, it had to be said that it took some getting used to. Each night that she tucked him into bed in the yellow room on the second floor, she heaved a sigh of exhaustion and not a small amount of relief. She was coming to understand why very small children were almost exclusively the purview of the young rather than the middle-aged. All she wanted to do after ensuring that the boy had fallen asleep was to sit in her favorite chair and stare out the window. She had not managed to summon the energy at the end of the day to knit or even to read.

They took their time meandering into the village. Edwina thought the very least she could do was to allow Crumpet to sniff luxuriantly at every little thing that caught his fancy. By the time they reached the village proper, she was feeling somewhat restored and noticed that Crumpet seemed more like himself as well. In fact, he seemed perfectly willing to be tied to the railing in front of the reading room in order for his mistress to see if there might be some sort of light reading material to avail herself of, no matter her level of exhaustion. If the situation with Charles and Georgie were to persist for any great length of time, she would have to figure out how not to allow all of her hobbies to fall by the wayside. She had no intention of entirely forgetting herself simply because the household had increased in size.

Edwina pushed open the door of the reading room and stepped inside. As always, she found herself immediately soothed by the familiar smell of old books and dust. While her perfect paragon of a housekeeper would find the state of the reading room utterly appalling, Edwina found it comforting in the extreme. During the long years of her mother's feigned illnesses, one of the only reprieves she had found from constantly tending to her was to offer to change out their borrowed books twice a week. Edwina had always been an avid reader, but had become even more so during those difficult years.

After her mother died, she found it comforting to continue the practice of her twice-weekly jaunts into the small but amply stocked building. When her mother had been alive, she had availed herself of one of the overstuffed and threadbare chairs in an alcove at the back of the building for a half hour's peace before returning to perform her duties as an unnecessary nurse-maid. Once she had the house entirely to herself after her mother's death, she had not bothered to remain in the building beyond the time she spent selecting new reading material.

With Georgie in the house, however, once again she could understand the value in spending a few stolen moments some-where quiet. Crumpet would be just fine tied to the railing out-side, given that the heat of the day had passed, and she would not stay for too long. She made her way to the back of the room and ran her finger along the spines of her favorite section, a well-thumbed collection of Western novels. Her heart lurched in her chest as she suddenly thought of her manuscript and the fact that a stranger might, at that very moment, be reading through it and making a decision as to its merits.

She forced herself to breathe slowly into her nose and out through her mouth. She was not a published author now. She had nothing to lose by being rejected and had thoroughly en-joyed the experience of completing a novel. No matter what happened, it could be considered a positive experience. After all, the authors with books on the shelf had taken the very same risk she had. She gave her head a shake and pulled two thick volumes by Zane Gray from the shelf.

She carried the books to the table at the front of the room and opened the ledger intended for borrowers to jot down the information about the volumes they had selected, as well as their own names. While Edwina did not like to consider herself to be a gossip, she could not refute the fact that she took an in-terest in her neighbors. She was pleased to note that the last person to record their loans was Phyllis Linton, whose tastes ran to local history. In fact, she had borrowed a half dozen vol-umes on prominent local families as well as local fauna and maps of property boundaries.

It seemed the Lintons were indeed interested in the village and all its goings-on. Perhaps they would be able to purchase the property after all. It would do the village good to have such interested young people put down roots there. They were young enough that she could imagine that, one day, children might be part of their family, a thing any village was glad to see.

A movement just outside on the pavement caught her eye through the window. Constable Gibbs had stopped directly in front of the building to greet Crumpet. She looked up and lifted a hand toward Edwina before mounting the stairs and opening the door. Edwina thought the constable must have something important to share with her. Constable Gibbs was known to have hobbies outside of work, but reading was not amongst them.

"I'm glad I caught you in the village. It saved me a trip out to The Beeches," the constable said.

Edwina capped her pen and slipped it back into her handbag in order to give the constable her full attention.

"Have you discovered something new?" she asked.

The constable shook her head. "It's more what I haven't discovered. No matter how thoroughly I searched Hazel's home, I have not been able to turn up her will," she said.

"How strange. I would've thought her home was the only place for it, considering she did not have Charles draw it up," Edwina said.

"That's what I thought too. It just doesn't make any sense that it would go missing. After all, why would anyone benefit from making it disappear?" Constable Gibbs asked.

"Do you think it's possible that Hazel destroyed it after having the Blackburns witness it? Could she have had something come to her attention that made her reconsider how she wanted to dispose of the property?" Edwina asked.

The constable raised one eyebrow. "Do you think she caught wind of some sort of tomfoolery on the part of the Dinsdales?"

"I suppose that that's entirely possible. After all, who had a better chance at seeing the inner workings of their séances than the accompanist?" Edwina asked.

"She would have been the one in the best position to spot something underhanded, I suppose."

Another thought occurred to Edwina. "You know, they came to Charles to ask if he had the will. They claimed that it had been made out in their favor."

"Do you think that they genuinely believe that he had it?"

"That's one possibility. But I think it's just as likely that Hazel might have told them she destroyed her will. With her dead and the will destroyed, the Dinsdales could've planted the seed in Charles's mind that they were the beneficiaries without revealing that Hazel had changed her mind," Edwina said.

"But how could they possibly benefit from something like that?"

"I suppose that, given enough time, they might produce a credible forgery. They would need, of course, to get hold of Hazel's signature somehow, but I suppose anyone might do that if they were able to sneak into her house for a good look around," she said. "After all, everyone has things they have signed in their homes, don't they? Canceled checks they have endorsed, contracts, birthday cards they intend to send, that sort of thing."

The constable drummed her fingers on the countertop beside her. "I wonder if I ought to conduct a search of the Dinsdales' residence, looking for just such a thing."

"You also might wait to see if perhaps Maude simply produces one. According to Nora, she and Michael witnessed Hazel's will. I don't know if that's common knowledge. If Maude were to produce a will that did not include their signatures, you could be quite certain it was false and save yourself the trouble of an exhaustive search."

Constable Gibbs looked at her with widened eyes. "You know, Edwina, for such an upstanding citizen, you have quite a criminal bent to your imagination. Perhaps that is what makes you such a good investigator."

Edwina's cheeks pinked with pleasure. It was not like Constable Gibbs to come out and simply state that she valued Edwina's prowess when it came to detecting. As she thought about how much had changed since she and Beryl had opened the private-enquiry agency, she felt a swelling of pride in her thin chest.

"That's quite a compliment coming from someone such as yourself, Doris."

"Just don't tell Beryl that I said so. She tends to behave a bit too high-handedly without any encouragement." With that, the constable touched her hat. "You'll let me know if you hear any more about the will, won't you?"

"You'll be the first one that I contact, rest assured."

Edwina left the reading room directly on the constable's heels. Beryl was moving down the street with a bulky parcel clamped under her arm. It bore a disconcerting resemblance to her manuscript, and she wondered if, by chance, Prudence had given it to her friend to bring back to The Beeches. She untied Crumpet's leash from the iron railing outside the reading room and hurried toward her friend.

The sun beat down on her shoulders as she hastened her footsteps. Crumpet seemed less than pleased at her pace. In fact, he attempted to slow her down by inspecting a clump of purslane emerging through a crack in the pavement. She felt the tiniest bit guilty about hurrying him along, but considered he had had a leisurely enough walk on the way into the village to sustain him. Beryl was too good of an investigator not to suspect what the package held if she kept it in her possession for long. And while Edwina did not think that her friend would be anything but supportive of her attempt at publication, she was not ready to divulge it just yet.

As she drew alongside Beryl, her friend came to a stop and lifted her hand in a wave.

"Hello, Ed. It looks like you've been hiding out in the reading room. Have you had enough of our young guest yet?" she asked with a smile.

Edwina bristled at being found out. She wanted to be the far more tolerant of the two when it came to the sorts of behaviors young children displayed. She eyed the package narrowly and decided to dare to change the subject.

"I just found myself in need of a bit of light reading material. What's that you've got there?" she asked.

Beryl tapped the package with her free hand. "It's the parts I've been waiting for to improve the airplane. I was just over at the garage to collect it. I had an interesting conversation with Nora about Mr. Watkins's alibis while I was at it," she said.

Edwina leaned toward her eagerly. "Was he there when he said he was?"

"That's just the thing. The garage was closed, so there was no way to confirm where he was. As far as I'm concerned, he still makes a decent suspect, despite my preference for the culprits being the Dinsdales."

Just as the words left Beryl's lips, Mrs. Watkins came into view. She spotted the two sleuths and made a beeline for them right there in the middle of the street.

"Are you two responsible for what's happened to Arthur Dinsdale?" she asked, her voice carrying all up and down the street. Edwina could tell that it had done so by the way that other passersby stopped in their tracks and looked over their shoulders while attempting to appear not to do so. In fact, Mrs. Scott stuck her head out of the greengrocer's door, and Alma Poole suddenly busied herself sweeping the stoop in front of the beauty shop.

"What do you mean 'happened to'?" Beryl asked.

"His arrest, of course. What's to become of the séances? Be-

tween Hazel's murder and his arrest, there's no way that
Maude can be expected to go on conducting any sort of com-
munion with the departed," Mrs. Watkins said, her voice becoming shrill.

"Don't forget the disappearance of Princess Rosanna," Beryl
said, winking at Edwina. Fortunately, Mrs. Watkins did not
notice that bit of cheek. She was far too busy being outraged by
the situation Maude faced.

"Certainly, that's had a deleterious effect as well. If you wish
to go about investigating something, perhaps you ought to
poke your nose into the disappearance of the princess rather
than seeking to discredit a man as honorable as Mr. Dinsdale,"
Mrs. Watkins said. She raised her fist and shook it right under
Beryl's nose, in a disconcerting reenactment of her husband's
earlier behavior.

Edwina could not help but think that this had something to
do with much more than a wrongly accused new neighbor. She
put her hand through Mrs. Watkins's arm, the one not raised
up in a threatening manner, and gently drew her toward a
bench next to the millpond. As they walked along, she could
feel the older woman's body trembling, as if overcome by
strong emotion. She had never known Mrs. Watkins to be the
sort to create a scene in public or otherwise. Even when her
daughter had died, she had comported herself with decorum.
Edwina doubted she would have managed as well herself had
she been in the other woman's shoes. When they reached the
bench, she and Beryl sat on either side of her and gave each
other worried glances.

"Now, Mrs. Watkins, surely you know that we do not have
the power to arrest anyone, no matter what we might think of
the situation. If Constable Gibbs has done so, it is because she
believes a good case can be made for Arthur's culpability," Edwina said.

"But it just doesn't make any sense. How would a man so

devoted to such goodness do a thing like that? Especially to Hazel, who was such an important part of the spiritual circle?" Mrs. Watkins asked.

"Just because someone claims a strong connection with the otherworldly, it does not necessarily mean that they have a faultless character," Edwina said, willing Beryl to keep her comments to herself.

Mrs. Watkins sagged against the back of the bench. "I suppose you're right. There are such terrible reports in the newspapers about the goings-on of politicians and vicars and the like. I don't know what the world is coming to."

Edwina patted her hand. "I'm sorry that you have been so distressed by all of this," she said.

"You know I wouldn't be ordinarily, but I am just so convinced of Maude's ability to contact the spirit world, and I'm desperate to speak with my Polly," she said, a tear running down her cheek.

"Why are you so convinced that they would be able to assist you in speaking with your daughter?" Beryl asked.

Mrs. Watkins shifted and looked her in the face. "You saw it with your own eyes, didn't you?"

"Saw what?" Beryl asked.

"It's all over the village about Charles's cousin. I thought that Maude was mistaken in insisting that a message from a woman named Polly was for him, and I thought she was a fraud or simply not very good at her job. But then when I heard about the child, I knew she truly had the gift," Mrs. Watkins said.

Edwina did not quite like the tone of Mrs. Watkins's voice. Not only was it shrill, but her words were coming out so quickly that she sounded almost manic. She glanced over at Beryl once more.

"It is possible that she simply got lucky with her pronouncements, isn't it?" Edwina asked.

Mrs. Watkins turned to face her. The gleam in her eye was feverish. "Luck, was it? I can't see how you could possibly believe a thing like that. Her specifics were so clear. And it's not the only time she's had something spot-on to tell someone, I'll have you know."

"Really? Can you give us another example?" Beryl asked.

Edwina fervently hoped that Mrs. Watkins had not heard something about her novel. She would hate to be one of the examples bandied about the village.

Mrs. Watkins held up one finger. "She told Mrs. Linton that her dog was unwell before it died." She held up a second finger. "She mentioned to Minnie that she ought to keep an eye on her husband's shenanigans." She held up a third finger. "And she told Hazel that her mother wanted her to be sure to go ahead and make a will. If that's not proof, I don't know what is."

Edwina had not heard about all of those predictions. And while she did not necessarily believe that Maude had any type of spiritual gifts, it could not be denied that those bits of knowledge could prove important. After all, it could be claimed that Maude mentioning Clarence's behavior could have given Minnie a motive for Hazel's murder. And it could be argued that her encouraging Hazel to make a will pointed to her guilt. It seemed that no matter what they uncovered in this case, nothing became any clearer.

"I can see why you might feel convinced by those bits of information. From whom did you hear them?" Beryl asked.

"Straight from the horse's mouth, so to speak. No matter what my husband has to say about such things, I have been in regular attendance at the séances. I heard them with my own two ears. And I can tell you, they had a powerful effect on the sitters."

"I do hope that your attendance is not putting a wedge between you and your husband. After all, the two of you have been through so much already," Edwina said. She worried that her remarks could be construed as prying into someone else's private business, but she could not help herself.

Mrs. Watkins got to her feet. "I would ask you to mind your own business about the state of my marriage. It doesn't matter what you or my husband or anyone else has to say about it. It doesn't matter what it will cost. There is nothing that will stop me from trying to get in touch with our Polly." With that, she stomped off across the village green. Beryl waited for her to be safely out of earshot before speaking. "She sounds a bit crazed, doesn't she?"

"I'm afraid so. Still, I don't think that she would've done anything to harm anyone involved in the séances, considering how vehemently she feels about it all."

"She may not have done anything about it, but considering her behavior, I can absolutely see her husband being desperate to put a stop to it. He must be worried sick about her."

Edwina nodded slowly, but was not entirely sure Beryl was correct in her assessment of Mr. Watkins's motives.

"I'm sure he is concerned about her, but he might be concerned about something else even more."

"His bank account?" Beryl asked.

"Exactly."

Chapter 29

Beryl tightened the last bolt into place and leaned away from the airplane. With a sense of satisfaction, she wiped her hands on a well-used rag before climbing down from the stack of wooden crates she had used as an improvised ladder for the repairs. Hopefully, there would be no more sabotage, and she would be able to take the plane up very soon. Her palms practically itched to lift open the cockpit door and grasp the controls. But she had promised Ed that she would be back in time for luncheon. She knew if she headed out in the airplane now, she would be tempted to fly straight across the English Channel and spend the afternoon in Paris rather than Walmsley Parva.

As much as she loved her life at The Beeches and all of the many comforts associated with so much domesticity, she did from time to time miss her footloose lifestyle. Ed had always been more than understanding of her desire to take off at a moment's notice, but somehow, with the arrival of Georgie in the household, she did not feel as though she could leave her friend shouldering so much new responsibility without her support.

Beryl wondered how long Charles and the child would remain in residence at The Beeches. Not that she was trying to hurry them out in any way, but she was curious about what the future might hold. For a fleeting moment, she entertained the notion of how comforting it would be if someone like Maude really could tell what lay ahead. Then a shiver ran up her spine. She had seen a great many things it had been best not to be prepared for ahead of time.

She replaced the wrench in her toolbox and fastened its latch firmly shut. She draped the rag atop the box before sliding open the heavy door and stepping outside. Although it grieved her to do so, considering how tranquil and respectable she had always found the village to be, Beryl snapped a padlock through the hasp on the door and gave it a firm tug, to be sure it was properly latched. She glanced down at her wristwatch and noted she still had some time before she had agreed to return to The Beeches. As she turned her head toward the pub, wondering if she might meet up with someone interesting over a pint, her gaze fell upon Mr. Stevens's photography studio. Perhaps it might be more interesting to check in with him about the package she had seen Mr. Dinsdale sneaking into the back of the building on her last visit to repair her airplane. She had a sneaking suspicion about why he might have been paying a surreptitious call on the photographer.

As she expected, Bernard Stevens was nowhere to be seen as she entered through the front door of the studio. His voice called out from the back room, where she assumed he was busy with developing films or enlarging prints. He called out to assure her he would be with her in a moment, so she made herself at home, wandering slowly around the perimeter of the room, eyeing the gallery of portraits and landscapes he had pinned up for customers to peruse. He was a wholly adequate photographer, but not one she felt was overflowing with either artistic talent or imagination. Most of his landscapes were of the predictable sort, picturesque and bland. His portraits were even less inspiring, as they generally featured sulky children or self-conscious women.

The only photographs that seemed to strike an emotional chord were those Bernard had taken of the flock of ducks who made the millpond on the village green their home. Bernard had an inexplicable interest in the birds and had documented the lives of many from their days as mere hatchlings up through adulthood. Odd as it might seem, Beryl found his peculiar interest rather moving. She was leaning forward and inspecting one photograph of a duck with an outstretched wing when she heard Bernard clearing his throat behind her.

"How lovely to see you again, Miss Helliwell. Is there something particular I can assist you with?" he asked.

She needed a believable excuse and, as making up things on the fly was one of her specialties, had no trouble doing so.

"I suppose you heard the news that I have recently come into possession of an airplane," Beryl said.

"Everyone in the village has heard that news. After all, you did make quite a dramatic entrance with it, I seem to recall," Bernard said.

Beryl was pleased to think she still had the capacity to cause something of a sensation, even if it was only in the village.

"I wondered if you might have any camera equipment suited for taking aerial photographs on hand," she said. "Edwina is somewhat reluctant to try out the pleasures of flying, and I thought, with her interest in photography, she might be persuaded, given the right incentive."

Bernard's craggy face split into a wide smile. After all, what small businessperson would not be delighted at the prospect of selling specialty equipment, and most likely at a premium price? Besides, as an avid photographer himself, the notion of aerial photography might appeal to him particularly, considering his love of animals who took to the skies.

"I have just the thing. Wait right here while I fetch it for you," he said, hurrying to the back room once more.

Beryl inspected the remaining duck portraits as she waited for him and considered how she might move the topic of conversation round to Mr. Dinsdale. Fortunately, Bernard required a few moments to locate the camera he had in mind. When he returned, his arms filled with a large carton, he had a look of triumph on his face.

"That's a lot of kit you have there," Beryl said.

"I thought it best to provide you with a range of choices. Although I would recommend this particular model as by far the most useful for your purposes," he said as he held out a black, sleek camera with a rugged strap she could see Edwina fastening sturdily around her neck.

She held it in her hands and turned it over carefully, noticing its heft and gleaming chrome fittings. Discreetly, she noted the price on the tag and decided right then and there to make a present of it for Edwina. It was the least she could do after suspecting her of sabotaging the airplane. Besides, she needed something to take her mind off of young Georgie.

"This seems like exactly the sort of thing I had in mind," she said. "I hope that you won't take offense, but frankly, I am a bit surprised that you would have this piece of specialty gear on site rather than needing to write away and order it for me."

Bernard made a slight bow. "I pride myself in providing the same sorts of sophisticated equipment and services my customers might find in a far larger city. I feel it my duty to provide the opportunities of the wider world to my fellow villagers."

"What other sorts of specialty photography do you provide? I should have thought that aerial photography might be by far the most exotic," she said.

"Well, of course, it is highly specialized, but there are other sorts of photographs one might wish to take that are not the run-of-the-mill," he said.

"Like what?" she asked.

Bernard looked around, as though he did not wish to be overheard by passersby. He took a step closer and lowered his voice slightly. "Something you and Miss Davenport might be interested in, now that I come to think of it. Have you heard of spy cameras?"

Beryl certainly had heard of spy cameras, having been in possession of one at many points during the war. She would be happy never to be in possession of one of the horrid things again. That said, she need not mention her thoughts on the subject to Bernard now that he was becoming loquacious.

"I know a little about them, certainly. I suppose you think that such a thing might be useful for us in terms of our business," she said.

"That's exactly what I was thinking. You could easily have a handbag or a hat or even a bit of jewelry fitted out with one. Although it must be said the jewelry would have to be quite a large piece. The technology is simply not yet what I expect it will become in the future," he said.

"I shall have to discuss that with Edwina. It might come in very handy on a surveillance mission of some sort one day," she said. "Speaking of seeing things in connection with the case, I do have a question for you."

Bernard took a step backward and crossed his arms over his chest. All signs of the affable salesman were gone.

"I'll answer it if I'm able," he said.

"It's just that I wondered if perhaps some of your specialty camera equipment and techniques might be being used to assist the Dinsdales with the atmosphere, shall we say, at their séances."

Suddenly, Bernard found the tips of his shoes engrossing. "I'm sure I don't know what you mean."

"I mean that I saw Mr. Dinsdale exiting through the back door of your studio, unlike a typical customer. As he left the building, I saw him tucking a bulging envelope into his jacket pocket. My best guess is that you are involved in the production of the sort of photographs no nice man would wish to be associated with. I should very much hate to have to ask the constable her thoughts on that sort of thing going on right beneath her nose," Beryl said.

She hated to sound like such a prude but needs must. Only a few weeks earlier, a poison-pen letter had accused him of the very same thing, and although he had denied it then, there was no way for him to entirely clear the cloud from his name. Bernard swallowed rapidly several times, sending his large Adam's apple bobbing wildly in his throat. He looked up, and Beryl noticed that a slight sheen of perspiration had appeared across his brow.

"I most certainly would prefer you not to insinuate such a thing to Constable Gibbs. I assure you, I am in no way the sort of man who creates the type of photographs you might be implying," he said.

Beryl looked him up and down and wished once more she had Edwina's innate ability to uncover untruths. Certainly, Bernard was rattled, and she suspected there was something else he was not telling her, although she wasn't certain exactly what that might be.

"I don't feel convinced. I do believe that you are still withholding something for me on this subject. Now why might that be? You didn't have something to do with Hazel's death, did you?" she asked.

Bernard stumbled backward and careened into one of his display counters. He grasped the edge of it behind him as if to keep himself from sinking to the floor.

"I most assuredly did not." He heaved an enormous sigh. "If I tell you what I was really up to, will you promise not to carry tales about smutty images to the constable?"

Beryl drew an X across her chest with her finger. "Cross my heart. So, what was it that he was doing here?"

"He was having me assist him with some spirit photographs."
That made a great deal more sense than the idea of Bernard
sneaking about in the night, snapping photographs of women
through their windows. In her opinion, it was an equally repellent thing that he had participated in, but it made much more
sense in light of Arthur Dinsdale being involved.

"So you mean the sort of thing where the image of a loved
one who has died appears in another sort of photograph altogether?"

Bernard nodded his head. "That's exactly what I mean.
Arthur told me it was really a kind of public service for the bereaved."

Beryl snorted. "I understand the money for such things is
pretty good too. How many of them did you create for him?"

"Two or three dozen so far," he said.

Beryl's blood began to boil. Not only was she outraged by
the way charlatans took advantage of the grieving during
séances, but the notion that they would go so far as to produce
photographic evidence of their chicanery made her see red.
After all, for so many, a photographic image of their loved one
was all they had left of them. Considering that bodies were not
even brought back from the front in order to be given a final
resting place near their families, the desperation to connect
with them was greater than it might have been under normal
circumstances. The outrage of taking advantage of such people
made her feel faintly nauseated.

"And how was such a thing first arranged?"

"Arthur came by a few days ago with a list of names he
wished for me to produce images of. He knew I would have
negatives of many of the villagers who have passed on within
the last several years and made me a business proposition about
creating images for Maude's clients," he said.

"When exactly did this occur? How quickly can you turn
out three dozen spurious images?" Beryl asked.

"Actually, it doesn't take so very long at all. I had to find the images he requested, but that also doesn't take very long, considering the fact that I keep impeccable records of all my transactions. After that, it is a bit of fuss to actually produce something that is a credible ghostly image, but it wasn't beyond my skill," he said, a note of pride creeping into his voice. "In fact, it was only three nights ago that he came to me with the suggestion."

"What time exactly?"

"Does it matter?"

"Yes, it might."

"It was the afternoon of my half day. I wanted to be sure we were not interrupted, which I'm sure you can imagine."

"So it was during the very time that Hazel was killed?" Beryl asked.

A look of comprehension flashed across Bernard's face. "Yes, I suppose that it was. Arthur was with me from just past closing until approximately half seven. Does this mean that he could not have been involved in Hazel's murder after all?" he asked.

"It very much looks that way," Beryl said. "I need to speak with the constable straightaway."

"Are you going to tell her about my part in all this?"

"No, but, as a matter of fact, you are going to tell her yourself," she said. She grasped him by the arm and pulled him toward the door. "And before I forget, please make sure that you put the cost of the camera on my account and have it and any necessary accessories sent to The Beeches at your earliest convenience. That is, providing you aren't stuck at the police station indefinitely."

She swept out of the shop, banging the door shut behind her.

Chapter 30

Edwina could hardly believe the news when Beryl returned home for lunch, only a few moments late and only slightly grubby. Surely, Arthur Dinsdale could not have felt it more serious to be exposed as a fraud than to be accused of murder. All throughout the meal, she, Simpkins, Charles, and Beryl discussed the matter at hand. If Arthur Dinsdale could not be held accountable for Hazel's murder, did that not get his wife off the hook as well? And since it was clear the two of them were, at least to some degree, involved in fraud, how had they managed?

Edwina lowered her fork and rested it against the side of her china plate. Georgie sat next to her, banging his chubby hands against the dining room table. She had made the executive decision to include him in the meal, as it seemed clear to her that Beddoes was desperately in need of a break. As much as that paragon of housekeeping had outperformed all expectations for her duties, Edwina knew it was asking a great deal to add nanny to her job description without warning. The child had brought an exuberance to the meal rarely seen at The Beeches since the time of Edwina's own extreme youth.

She thought of her own lunches taken in the nursery with her own nanny and then later a governess. As she looked around at the haggard faces of her dear friends, an idea occurred to her. It was something she should've thought of immediately upon hearing of Charles's situation. She tucked the thought away for the present and determined to act on it as soon as possible. In fact, she scraped back her chair to excuse herself.

"Charles, if you and Simpkins could keep an eye on Georgie for the next hour or so, Beryl and I have business in the village," she said, eyeing her friend purposefully. Beryl was always one to take a hint and nodded in agreement.

"I'll just fetch my handbag, and we will be off," she said.

Edwina felt ever so slightly guilty, given the bereft look on Charles's face. While he seemed very affectionate with the child and willing to do his part, it could not be said that he took to parenting tasks with anything resembling confidence. In fact, Simpkins was far more at ease with Georgie than with his own family members. Edwina gave Simpkins a grateful smile as he waved her off with a snaggle-toothed grin. Just having a little boy around had put a spring in the old man's step that she had not seen since before his wife had died. She met Beryl in the drive and, given her impatience to arrive in the village, actually suggested the two of them take the motorcar. Beryl had the good grace not to comment but simply sprang into the driver's seat with every appearance of pleasure.

"Where to?" Beryl asked, as she pointed the nose of the cherry-red vehicle down the gravel driveway.

"The post office. I wish to place an advertisement," she said.

"That sounds very mysterious," Beryl said.

"All will be revealed in time," Edwina said.

Beryl stomped down on the accelerator and, in what seemed an impossibly short amount of time, drew to a stop directly in front of the post office. Anyone could see Prudence in the plate-glass window feigning busyness with a feather duster. Although it was obvious she was standing at the best vantage point of the police station, she could not fault her this time for her curiosity. She doubted she would have been able to keep herself from doing much the same, considering Arthur Dinsdale's release from custody, had she been in Prudence's position.

The postmistress swiftly tucked her feather duster under a counter as Edwina and Beryl entered the shop.

"How may I help you ladies today?" Prudence said, taking a step away from the window.

"I would like to place an advertisement in the newspapers," Edwina said.

Prudence's slim nose twitched, as if she had caught sense of something intriguing. "Certainly. Which papers did you have in mind? The local ones or something further afield—London, say?"

"I should like to start with the local papers, please," Edwina said, stepping toward the end of the long counter where such requests were fulfilled. She remembered the humiliation she had endured in the past when she had stepped up to the very same counter to place an advertisement for a lodger. Her financial situation had been dire, and although it had come as a last resort, she had been forced to humble herself to do it. How much had changed in the few months since those dark times. In fact, it was a sign of how different things were that Prudence made no caustic comment in reference to those dreadful days. She simply retrieved a pad of paper from beneath the counter to jot down Edwina's request. Prudence was in charge of passing along such things to the newspaper office, as it was not a newspaper that was staffed full-time. In fact, it would be a fortunate thing should her advertisement make it into that week's edition of the newspaper.

Beryl stood close enough to peek over Edwina's shoulder as she carefully printed out her request. She read it through three times to ensure it was worded just as she preferred before passing it back to Prudence.

The postmistress arched a slim eyebrow before leaning across the counter eagerly. "So, you're looking for a nanny. Does that mean Charles has entrusted you with the responsibility for hiring one?" Prudence asked.

"I'm assisting him wherever possible. After all, we have been dear friends for a great number of years," Edwina said.

"So it would seem," Prudence said. She offered Edwina a knowing smile that left her stomach feeling slightly queasy. As if sensing her discomfort, Beryl stepped closer.

"I suppose you've heard about Arthur Dinsdale being released from custody," Beryl said.

Prudence swiveled her gaze from Edwina to Beryl. "I did hear something about that, of course. I knew that poor man had been wrongly accused."

"Are you a believer in his wife's abilities?" Beryl asked.

Prudence tipped her head to one side, as if considering the question carefully. "I can't say that I am convinced of such connection with those who have passed on, but he does seem to be a man of quality."

"You hadn't heard that the reason he was able to be released was because Bernard Stevens gave him an iron-clad alibi?" Beryl asked.

"Yes, of course, I knew that he was with Mr. Stevens. What of it?"

Beryl turned toward Edwina and sighed deeply. She went so far as to click her tongue loudly. If she had been British, Edwina thought it would have been the point at which she commenced tut-tutting.

"How sad to have been so utterly deceived. Do you not think so, Edwina?" Beryl asked.

Edwina nodded. "Yes, I'm afraid the Dinsdales did take in many unsuspecting souls with their scheming. Although I am rather surprised that someone as worldly-wise as you would have fallen for it as well," she said, turning toward Prudence.

Prudence's face infused with blood. "I most certainly did not. It would be a fine thing indeed for someone to pull the wool over my eyes."

"You said you thought they were outstanding people and you welcomed them to the village. Surely you could not have known, if you were to say such things."

Edwina heard Prudence stamp her foot on the floor behind the counter. "Although I certainly did not wish to cast aspersions on newcomers to our community, I'll have you know I was more than convinced of their fraudulent behavior. After all, have you heard of me going to one of their silly séances?" Prudence asked.

Beryl and Edwina exchanged a glance.

"I can't say as I remember hearing that you had attended any of the gatherings," Beryl said.

"Why would I? After all, I know when someone is trying to snoop for information," Prudence said.

"Really? What sort of information?" Beryl asked.

"Yes, that seems surprising, considering everyone knows how subtle and sophisticated those Dinsdales happen to be," Edwina said.

Prudence stomped her foot again. "I'll have you know, Edwina, that I told them all about Polly Watkins's murder, Chester White's interest in horse racing, Phyllis Linton's dead dog, Hattie's dead sweetheart, and even a bit of information about you."

Edwina's heart sank in her chest. "Information about me?"

"How do you think she knew to tell you that you would be a success in literary ventures? You don't think that the address on that brown-paper-wrapped parcel, which is attached to a publishing house, failed to attract my notice, now do you?" she said.

Beryl slapped her hand down on the counter in front of her and jolted Prudence into silence.

"Are you telling me that you purposely shared information with those two charlatans in order to pull one over on your fellow villagers?" Beryl asked.

Prudence began to shake. "It wasn't quite like that exactly. Really, they were very chatty, and it all just sort of came out. It wasn't until after people started coming back from their sessions with them that I put two and two together and realized that I was the source of the information they used in their sessions," Prudence said.

"Do you realize the amount of damage you could have done?" Beryl asked. "You could be the reason that Hazel is dead. Did you say anything that might have caused someone to harm her?"

"I'm sure I didn't say anything about Hazel," Prudence said. Her voice quaked as if she was far less convinced than she tried to let on.

"What about Minnie and Clarence?" Edwina asked, feeling her blood beginning to boil.

If Prudence and her gossip had caused someone to do violence, she was not quite sure she would manage to control her temper. She rarely felt anger, but when it did happen to bubble up inside her, she found it truly difficult to control. The idea that someone as harmless as Minnie might have been goaded into something as drastic as murder because of idle chatter boiled her blood. Had Prudence learned nothing after the incident with the poison-pen letters? That rash of disruption had ended in one tragedy and narrowly missed a second.

Prudence took a step backward, as if creating a greater distance between herself and her accusers.

"I may have said something about it, although I cannot recall for sure," she said, hanging her head. Edwina never thought to see the day that Prudence seemed ashamed of her actions. It was the one thing that might have put a damper on her rage.

"I hope you will let this be a lesson to you not to meddle in the affairs of others or go about spreading gossip in the future. You are a person of consequence and authority in this village, and the things you say matter," Edwina said. "It's a position of responsibility, and we all count on you to discharge it with discernment."

Prudence lifted her gaze from the floor and looked onto Edwina's face. Her lower lip trembled as she took a deep breath.

"I think that's possibly the kindest thing anyone has ever said to me. I had no idea my position carried so much weight in the eyes of anyone here in Walmsley Parva."

Edwina felt her anger slide out through her body and drain down through her feet. She knew what it meant to be someone the world seemed to dismiss. She understood being the sort of woman that society did not value. She looked over at Beryl, who nodded as though she also could comprehend why Prudence felt so moved. Edwina reached across the counter and squeezed Prudence's hand.

"Of course, it does. We should let you get back to work."

With proof positive that the Dinsdales were, at least on some level, outright frauds, Beryl felt it was time to pay a visit to their client. Edwina hastily agreed, and they left directly from the post office for the vicarage. Given the mild weather that day, it was no surprise to find Muriel standing in the churchyard dressed in a floppy gardening hat and work gloves. Even for someone as little interested in all things herbaceous as Beryl, she could see that the plot of ground surrounding the church was neatly cared for, likely due to Muriel's energetic attentions. As she observed the vicar's wife more closely, however, it appeared as though she were attending to the task with more than her usual vigor.

A wheelbarrow sat nearby, heaped high with clipped greenery. A pair of hedge shears sat nearby, and from the look of the unfortunate shrubbery dotting the church grounds, it appeared that Muriel had attacked them savagely and with little skill. Beryl heard Edwina's sharp intake of breath as they drew close to what had once been, even to Beryl's undiscerning eye, a rather lovely evergreen tree. Alas, the poor thing had been carved into a shape one might see splotched out by an avant-garde artist claiming to be making a statement. Beryl eyed the hedge shears, and as she did so, an uncomfortable thought occurred to her. Were they not very similar to the weapon described by the doctor at the inquest? Although the amount of physical strength required to run someone through, as the murderer had done, was considerable, Muriel seemed to fit the bill. Beryl watched as she tossed another armload of hedge clippings onto the already replete wheelbarrow before smacking her palms together, sending clouds of dirt and dust up into the air.

Beryl wondered if Edwina had had the same thought occur to her. She noticed that her friend had taken a step closer toward her side as Muriel approached them. Although it seems difficult to reconcile the notion of someone with the moral compass often attributed to a vicar's wife with a murderer, stranger things had, of course, happened. Still, they owed their client a report, and the report she should get. Even if she did turn out to be the one responsible for Hazel's death, she still had the right to know that the Dinsdales were, in fact, the frauds she had suspected them of being.

"I hope you're bringing me some good news for a change," Muriel said. "This week has been nothing but one disaster after another."

"I'm sorry to hear that. Has something happened with the vicar?" Edwina asked. Although Muriel was one of those stridently productive and brusque women, she had a very soft spot for her husband. Beryl thought it might have something to do with the fact that their children were grown, and she no longer had the caretaking of them as one outlet for her boundless energy. Sometimes Beryl felt sorry for the vicar and wondered if she ought to invite him out to the pub to join her and Simpkins in a bit of a tipple. If anyone in the village could use one, she suspected it was Vicar Lowethorpe. Even Beryl found his wife exhausting.

"I should say that it has. The poor man is simply beside himself with what has happened to the music program. Mrs. Corby is simply not to be believed," Muriel said, stripping off her gloves and slapping them rhythmically against her gardening apron.

"She can be a bit strident, I have noticed," Edwina said.

Muriel snorted. "That's one word for it. Another would be abrasive, and a third would be insufferable. Wilfred has taken to hiding out in his study any time she appears at the door or on the telephone. Which I can tell you means he's in his study most of the livelong day."

"Oh dear, I suppose that means even more of the church workload has fallen on your own shoulders," Edwina said.

"As a matter of fact, it has. If things don't improve shortly, I'm afraid I'll be the one giving the sermon this Sunday," Muriel said. "I've half a mind to learn to play the organ myself. I know I shouldn't be saying so, but I would have to admit that I feel the wrong person entirely ended up in that sarcophagus."

Beryl thought that was just the opportunity she needed to announce the reason for their visit.

"Then we shouldn't take up any more of your time than necessary, given your increased responsibilities. We did think we ought to come by and give you an update as to your case," she said.

Muriel widened her stance and crossed her arms over her chest. She looked like a woman bracing herself for more bad news.

"Don't tell me you weren't able to find anything out," she said.

"As a matter of fact, it's just the opposite," Edwina said. Her voice was taking on a cheerful note that Beryl always associated with parents speaking to overwrought children or nurses in psychiatric wings of hospitals. She thought, once again, about Muriel's potential as a murderer and wished she had thought to bring along her pistol.

"Is that right? Well, do tell. I could use a bit of cheering up, I can tell you," she said. She gestured toward a bench under a shady tree in the churchyard and bid them follow her. They did so, at Muriel's characteristic breakneck pace, Beryl nearly breaking an ankle as they traipsed swiftly across the lumpy ground of the cemetery. She placed herself between Muriel and Edwina, who was physically so much smaller than she. She stretched out her long legs as an additional form of barrier and launched into the report.

"We have managed to uncover the source of information that the Dinsdales have been using to appear as though they were passing on messages from the spirit realm to their sitters," Beryl said.

"Just one source?" Muriel asked.

"Just one source was all that was needed to fuel the entire operation, I'm afraid," Edwina said.

"Let me guess, Prudence Rathbone," Muriel said.

"You're absolutely correct," Beryl said. "She seems to have provided information in passing and hadn't really realized what had happened until people started streaming in and sharing with her exactly the kinds of messages they had been receiving from what appeared to be the great beyond."

"Prudence felt just awful about the whole thing and in no way meant to be complicit in fraud," Edwina said.

"No, I'm sure she didn't mean to aid and abet something so overtly egregious, but she absolutely meant to gossip, which is nearly as bad," Muriel said. "Although I suppose I should not be saying such critical things of one of the members of Wilfred's flock."

"She does feel quite remorseful about it all. Beryl did mention that it was possible she was responsible for driving someone to murder Hazel, after all," Edwina said.

Muriel raised an eyebrow and gave Beryl a slight smile. From the vicar's wife, that was tantamount to a hearty slap on the back. If she had been as inclined to blush as her friend, she might have done so. As she was not, she simply took the compliment in stride.

"But that wasn't the only thing we discovered," Beryl said.

"Really?" Muriel said, leaning forward slightly.

"It seems that not only were they using Prudence for information, but they had also roped Bernard Stevens into creating a line of props for their séances and doctored photographs that made it appear ghostly apparitions of loved ones were appearing in new images taken more recently," Beryl said.

Muriel sucked in her breath quickly. "But that's monstrous. Bernard has always been such a mild-mannered sort of person who one would not suspect of comporting himself in such a way. Were they blackmailing him or some such thing?" she asked.

"No, I'm afraid not. It really did just come down to a matter of money," Edwina said.

"Well, I suppose one can hardly blame the man, considering how the economy continues to slide further and further into a pit of despair. Still, it does speak to the corrupting influence of those occultists," Muriel said.

"Unfortunately, our findings don't solve your overarching problem, however," Beryl said. "After all, you're still out your organist."

"Yes, I'm afraid that's true. However, I would not say things have turned out badly after all. As much as Mrs. Corby is a thorn in the side of our small congregation, she is nothing in comparison with the worry that the church members might turn away in droves to follow a false doctrine. Wilfred will be

back to his old self in no time with this news, I assure you."
Muriel hopped to her feet and started whistling under her
breath.

"Does this mean you consider the case closed?" Edwina
asked.

Muriel waved a broad hand above her head. "Done and
dusted. Be sure to send me a final invoice at your earliest convenience." She strode away with her usual vigor and grasped
the handles of the wheelbarrow, pushing it swiftly toward the
side of the church.

"It's not the end of the case, though, is it?" Edwina asked.

As Beryl watched Muriel round the corner of the building,
she thought of the hedge shears once more and poor Hazel's
body wedged into the sarcophagus.

"No, it assuredly is not."

Chapter 31

They had been back at The Beeches for less than an hour when Beddoes appeared in the summerhouse, where the two sleuths were taking their ease after their considerable labors on the case at hand. She was encumbered by a large parcel and announced it had arrived care of Bernard Stevens's photography studio. Edwina seemed baffled by the package, but Beryl was pleased to see it. Although she was disappointed with Bernard's willingness to participate in the Dinsdales' underhanded schemes, she could not fault his speed concerning delivery.

"Wait until you see what I've got here," Beryl said, taking the package from Beddoes's outstretched hands. She placed it on the table in front of Edwina and untied the string. "I bet you'll never guess what it is."

"I doubt very much it is an elephant," Edwina said. She never was one for guessing games, Beryl had found to her chagrin.

"It's not even an elephant tusk," Beryl said, reaching into the box and pausing as she wrapped her hands around the object she sought. "Close your eyes."

Edwina did as she was bid and sat up primly, her hands folded neatly in her lap. Beryl reached out and placed the object on the settee beside her.

"Go ahead and look now," Beryl said. She sat down in the chair opposite Edwina in order to best take in the look of surprise on her friend's face.

"Why, it's a camera," Edwina said. She looked at Beryl with her head tipped to one side, looking remarkably like Crumpet when he was straining to pick out some of his favorite words from conversation swirling about him.

"But what kind of camera is it?" Beryl asked.

Edwina turned it over carefully, inspecting it in minute detail. "I really couldn't say. It's not quite like anything I've ever seen before."

"I would very much doubt that you had. It's a highly specialized piece of equipment that I thought might intrigue you," Beryl said.

Edwina held it up and looked through the viewfinder. "I confess I am intrigued, but I am not sure what it's for in the least."

"It's an aerial-photography camera. I went into Bernard's shop to ask for one as a cover for questioning him, never guessing he would actually have one in stock," Beryl said.

Edwina leaned back against the settee and placed the camera gently in her lap. Beryl could see conflicting emotions flitting across her friend's small face. Worry and curiosity seemed to be battling one another valiantly. Beryl was an optimist and thus rooted silently for curiosity. Maybe, just maybe, Edwina would take the bait.

"Aerial photography. Does this have something to do with the airplane?" she asked.

"That's the best way to put it to use, at least here in the village. I suppose that it might do some good from a skyscraper in metropolises like London or New York, but even the bell tower on top of the church would hardly be tall enough to warrant it here in the village," Beryl said.

"Does it really take photographs of things as far away as one can see from an airplane?" Edwina asked. Clearly, her curiosity was getting the better of her. Although she still bit on her lip, she did lean forward with her hands clutched tightly around the new piece of equipment. Perhaps Beryl might get her up in the air.

"It most certainly does. As a matter of fact, here in the box I have a few examples of aerial photography to show you just what this can do," she said, digging around once more. She lifted a small stack of prints from the carton and handed them to Edwina. She watched her face carefully as she thumbed through the different images, her eyes widening with surprise as she moved from one to the next.

"But this is miraculous. Who would have thought such clarity would be possible from such a great distance?" she said, looking back at Beryl. "It's really quite fascinating."

"I understand that it isn't something just every photographer becomes accomplished at. It's rather a specialty area, considering most people do not have access to an airplane in order to practice their skills."

"Yes, I can see how that would be quite a hindrance to the avid amateur photographer," Edwina said. She looked through the stack of photographs a second time before speaking again. "I suppose it really would be rather a waste to have a camera like this and the opportunity to practice with it and to refuse to do so."

"I suppose that's one way of looking at it. After all, I doubt very much that there are many aerial photographers in the whole of England. I doubt even more that there are any who are women. Wouldn't it be interesting to be the first?" Beryl asked.

She hoped that might be the final push Edwina needed. Although her friend was content for Beryl to be the one who was a celebrity, attracting fame in magazines and newspapers, she knew that Edwina enjoyed being seen as someone who also was accomplished in her own ways. Being one of the few women magistrates in the country had been something in which she took enormous pride. And, certainly, their shared venture as female private-enquiry agents had given her a sense of extreme satisfaction. Adding aerial photographer to her list of accomplishments would certainly be appealing.

"I suppose, since you put it that way, I'm almost beholden to put aside my fears and give it a try for women everywhere."

"It would be practically criminal not to," Beryl said.

Edwina got to her feet and carefully clutched the camera to her chest. "You know, it would give me a very good excuse to try that new leather helmet that Desmond sent me," she said.

With that, she turned toward the house and moved so swiftly across the luxuriant green lawn that Beryl could hardly keep up.

Her knuckles were white as she clutched the camera tightly. From her seat directly behind Beryl's, some of her view of the unfolding events was blocked from her sight. That did little to dampen her sense of foreboding as the airplane's tires bumped along the pasture on the way out of the village proper. Two or three times, she fought back an overwhelming desire to call out to Beryl, begging her to stop before they even truly got started. But she chided herself for her fears and kept her lips firmly clenched together. Not only was she concerned about going back on her word, but it had occurred to her that she did not particularly wish to swallow any insects.

And then, suddenly, the rumbling beneath them entirely ceased. A strange lightening sensation swept through her stomach and on up to her throat as she realized they had lifted from the ground. A tiny gasp escaped, despite her best efforts, and she forced herself to turn her head to the side and observe the rapidly receding patchwork of fields and hedgerows spread out beneath them. Mr. Watkins's herd of cows tipped their heads skyward as they passed overhead but did not seem disturbed in the least by the ruckus. As they flew higher and higher, Edwina was startled to discover she was not one bit bothered by the motion of the airplane. In fact, it was altogether preferable to exploits in the motorcar. She leaned eagerly forward and tapped Beryl on the shoulder.

"Is it always like this?" she shouted as loudly as she could, hoping to be understood.

Beryl leaned backward and shouted back. "Sometimes it's even better. I knew that you would love it, Ed," she said.

If there was one thing about Beryl that Edwina appreciated, it was the fact that she was never one to gloat about being right. She truly did just want to share the best of her experiences with others, even if, like she so often was, they were reluctant to give it a try. She looked to her right and spotted the steeple of the village church. It gave her a bit of a turn to consider how far above it instead of beneath it that she happened to be. She wondered if anyone else in the village besides Beryl had ever seen it from this angle and thus lifted the camera in order to attempt to photograph it. She imagined an exhibition of aerial photographs hanging at the Women's Institute for anyone in the village to peruse. She clicked the shutter as they passed, then turned the camera to a new target.

There, spread below them, lay The Beeches. From above, she could see how elegant were the lines of her beloved family home and how beautifully it was nestled into the surrounding grounds. Even from such a great height, all of the loving care that she and Simpkins had poured into restoring the gardens was clear to see. Her heart swelled with pride at the thought that her home stood up to scrutiny, even at this distance. She snapped several more photos of the place from a variety of angles. Beryl seemed to sense her interest in that particular set of photographs and circled the area repeatedly, allowing her to take her time in framing the shots.

Perhaps emboldened a bit by Edwina's equanimity, Beryl tilted the plane slightly to the side and swooped farther away. They glided over Pershing Magna, along the train tracks that connected village after village, and even went so far as to offer just the slightest glimmer of what Edwina suspected was the sea. She could not believe their speed in arriving at its edge so quickly. But before they went out over the water, Beryl turned the airplane back around, and before Edwina could believe it, they had arrived once more over the far side of the village. Before long, she recognized the edge of the property Hazel had rented to the Lintons, but as she looked at it through her viewfinder, something strange caught her attention. She tapped Beryl on the shoulder once more.

"Can you take us a bit lower?" She pointed in the general direction of The Swallows' Nest.

Looking through the viewfinder once more, she became even more puzzled. Hazel had been one of the most enthusiastic members of the garden club and took great pride in the appearance of her properties, whether she lived in them or rented them to others. The Lintons seemed like a pleasant young couple and not the sort bent on destruction. Why then did it appear that the entire back area of Hazel's lovely garden was pockmarked with holes and piles of soil?

Edwina could not imagine Hazel giving permission for her tenants to wreak such havoc on her lovely garden. And certainly, had she been aware of it, Hazel would have made mention of the damage. After all, she and Edwina had enjoyed many chats on the subject of their respective gardens over the years, swapping plants and seeds and paying visits back and forth to admire things that had come into bloom. Edwina leaned forward once more.

She cupped her hands around her mouth to make sure that Beryl could hear her request. "Could you set us down over there?" she asked, gesturing toward the field on the other side of a small copse of trees separating Hazel's property from the next one over. Beryl nodded and banked the airplane once more. Edwina's stomach felt topsy-turvy as they circled, then lowered enough to jounce to a stop after rolling across the lumpy field. Beryl shifted in her seat as the engine's sound died away and pulled off her scarlet leather aviator's helmet.

"What is it, Ed? Are you feeling unwell?" Beryl asked.

"No, it's not that. Did you notice Hazel's back garden?" she asked.

"I can't say that I could tell you which one belongs to Hazel," Beryl said.

Her friend had never been interested in accompanying her to visit any of the local gardens in the height of their seasonal glory. She'd always opted to stay behind to keep Simpkins company in the potting shed or to go out for a drive in her motorcar. Besides, she had not been in the village long enough to have quite such a thorough memory of which person owned which property, especially someone like Hazel, who was the mistress of more than one.

"It's the one on the other side of this copse of trees."

"The one with lawn all torn up?" Beryl said.

"Exactly. And for no good reason that I can think of," Edwina said, removing her own leather helmet. She placed the camera carefully on the seat beside her.

"Shall we go check it out then?" Beryl asked.

"That's what I was thinking," Edwina said.

She followed Beryl out of the plane, and the two of them moved silently through the stand of trees. From above, it had not appeared as though the grove was quite as wide as it seemed while traversing it. Edwina took the opportunity to consider what could possibly be the reason for all the digging. Nothing whatsoever came to mind. From high above, no pattern had appeared that might suggest some sort of ornate planting like a labyrinth or a formal hedge. The spacing did not seem adequate for specimen trees. Nor did any of it seem to be the sort of holes one might dig to support the foundation for an outbuilding. She was put in mind briefly of a comedic film she had seen once with someone who was convinced that a piece of property contained oil and had set about digging test spots over and over to no avail.

As they reached the edge of the wood, Beryl paused behind a broad-trunked tree and motioned for Edwina to halt. They peeked out from behind it and peered into the garden, looking for signs of occupancy. It was easy to see, from the way Beryl moved, that she had spent many a day moving quietly in the hopes of not being seen by man or beast. Edwina shuddered to think of her friend deploying those skills behind enemy lines, as she was convinced she must have done during the Great War. Beryl never spoke about it, but now and again something she did allowed an inadvertent glimpse into her past. Edwina followed as closely as she could on Beryl's heels as they slipped into the garden and began to move from gaping hole to gaping hole.

"What do you think is going on here?" Edwina asked.

"How many dogs did you say the Lintons had that died?" Beryl asked.

Edwina felt her limbs grow cold. Could it possibly be that the Lintons were conducting some sort of horrid experiments on animals? It seemed the sort of thing that might grace the pages of a sensational penny dreadful rather than the back garden of a country cottage. Surely that could not be the reason for the destruction. She was quite certain Phyllis Linton had been entirely bereaved by the loss of her dog, and she could not imagine her participating in anything that would harm some other sort of creature.

"I'm sure that can't be it. They are rather new to gardening. Perhaps they had in mind to plant a great many tulip and daffodil bulbs," she said.

But as the words left her mouth, she noticed a bit of fabric fluttering in the breeze above another hole. She made her way steadily toward it, glancing around as she did so. It would be very awkward to explain their presence to the Lintons. As she came to a stop, Beryl reached her side, and they both stared down into a very large disturbed area covered in a canvas tarpaulin. It was weighted down along its edges with stones the size of a stewing hen. Edwina bent down and removed several, freeing the edge of the tarpaulin. Beryl grasped the corner of the sturdy fabric and pulled it back, revealing the items protected beneath.

If Edwina had not been kneeling down, she likely would have fallen over. Beryl squatted at the other side of the hole and whistled long and low.

"Well, that explains the holes, now, doesn't it?" she said.

Edwina nodded, having difficulty finding her voice. Although everything was besmirched from centuries of being laid in the ground, it was still clear to see that the Lintons had stumbled upon something of great value. Bits of jewelry, a helmet, buckles, bracelets, and even a drinking cup could all be clearly seen jutting out of the overturned soil. Scattered over all of it were dozens and dozens of gold and silver coins. There, in Hazel's back garden, was a Saxon hoard.

Chapter 32

Beryl had not seen anything like it outside of an extraordinary visit to Egypt. To think that something as awe-inspiring as that could be found in little Walmsley Parva. She felt the swell of pride in her chest for her adopted hometown and an even greater sense of pleasure on Edwina's behalf. The look of wonder on Edwina's face was something to remember. She wished that she was the one who had her hands on a camera in order to preserve the moment in time. That said, it did not seem prudent to remain hanging about the place long enough to be discovered. She got to her feet and, as she did so, caught a glimmer of movement out of the corner of her eye.

Her many years spent out on one sort of expedition or another had taught her to react with speed to any sudden change in the environment. She spun about just in time to see Anthony Linton rushing toward them, a garden spade held aloft like a cricket bat. She heard Edwina cry out as he closed the gap between them at an alarming rate. Just as he came within striking range, Beryl whipped her trusty pistol from her coat pocket and pointed it straight at his chest. She thought it likely her skill with firearms was good enough to have aimed at his head, but she did not want to leave Edwina at risk should she miss.

She noticed Edwina scrambling to her feet as Anthony came to a full stop.

"I suggest you drop that, if you know what's good for you," Beryl said. It was the sort of tone she rarely needed to trot out and use, but on the rare occasion she did so, it was satisfyingly effective. Anthony released the spade, and it clattered to the ground beneath him, banging the metal portion against one of the rocks pinning down the tarpaulin before skittering down into the hole.

"I assume this is your doing," Edwina said, gesturing toward the pockmarked garden stretched out before them.

Anthony seemed reluctant to speak until Beryl took a step closer and waggled the pistol in his general direction.

"Yes, I'm the one responsible for all the digging," Anthony said.

Edwina, seemingly emboldened by Beryl's upper hand in the situation, had rounded the edge of the hole, coming closer to Anthony's side. Not close enough, mind, that he might have grabbed her or put her in harm's way should Beryl need to avail herself of her firearm, but closer, nonetheless. Beryl had found that Edwina did generally inch closer to her prey whenever she was attempting to get to the truth of the matter. Perhaps it was minute facial expressions or subtle shifts in tone of voice that helped her to ferret out lying, but ferret she did.

"I can't imagine that Hazel would have looked kindly upon this type of destruction in her garden. And since she never mentioned such riches being unearthed on her very own property, I have a sneaking suspicion she did not have the opportunity to tell anyone, did she?"

Anthony's shoulders sagged, and his head hung slightly. "It was the dog that started it all," he said.

"The dog?" Beryl asked.

Anthony gestured to the ground at his side. "When Phyllis's dog died, I came out here to dig a hole to properly bury it. And that's when I unearthed a cache of gold coins." He glanced over at the largest of the holes before continuing. "After I found the one bag, I assumed it was possible there were more to discover, so I began digging test holes all around the property."

"How soon did you find the burial site?" Beryl asked.

"That was what I was working on when Hazel discovered what we were up to."

Beryl turned her face slightly and exchanged a glance with Edwina. "I assume things did not go well, did they?" Edwina asked.

"No, they did not. Hazel came by unannounced with the news that she had decided to donate this entire property to the Dinsdales in order that they might open a spiritualist center. She told me she had thought at first that she would leave the property to them in her will but had decided to tear it up since she might outlive them. She determined to make a gift of it to them as soon as she could turn us out."

"That must have unsettled you," Beryl said.

"Unsettled is too mild a term for it. There was no way we could have completed the excavating in the amount of time she gave us to vacate."

"And it didn't occur to you to simply call a historical or archaeological society and get them involved with this extraordinary find?" Edwina asked.

Sometimes Beryl thought that her friend was a bit too high-minded to be believed. Although she could absolutely imagine Edwina immediately turning over such a windfall to the local authorities, she knew that the vast majority of people would be tempted to do otherwise.

"No, I'm afraid it did not. Phyllis and I have managed somehow to keep body and soul together since the economy has taken a knock, but it hasn't been the sort of life we expected to lead. I thought that this was just fate's way of finally delivering on the sort of future I had hoped for us when I asked Phyllis to be my wife."

"Couldn't you simply have fobbed Hazel off, hauled out all the loot, and covered up the holes?" Beryl asked. "I assume that things turned violent, but I don't understand exactly why that had to happen."

"It wasn't just that she appeared to give us notice. She also insisted on inspecting the property in order to catalog it for the Dinsdales. And, of course, she insisted on viewing the grounds. She was utterly devoted to her gardens, whether she paid much attention to them when it came to the weeding and watering or not."

"Knowing Hazel, she would have been utterly dismayed by what she found had happened to her beloved property," Edwina said. Beryl could hear the tremble of outrage in her friend's voice. Knowing how strongly Edwina felt about her own garden, Beryl supposed that she was incensed on Hazel's behalf.

"She stumbled around, squawking and flapping her hands, until she came across what you see here," Anthony said, gesturing toward the sprawling burial site partially hidden beneath the tarpaulin. "Then her outrage morphed into utter disbelief at the magnitude of my discovery. She announced that she would head off immediately to contact the proper authorities, and she turned her back on me. She really ought not to have done that."

"What did you kill her with?" Edwina asked.

Beryl did not quite like how white Edwina's face had gone. She hoped her friend would not grow faint and tumble down into the hole. There was no telling what sort of damage might be done from that sort of fall into a pit filled with so many hard and jagged objects.

"I had just removed a spear that was buried here in the mound when Hazel arrived. When she said that she was going to call the authorities, I simply lost my head. I bent down, picked it up, and ran her through." With each word Anthony spoke, his voice grew softer and softer, as though, just by telling it, the entire ghastly ordeal was seeping away. She wondered if perhaps her concern had been misplaced and that Anthony might be the one on the verge of collapse.

"But you couldn't allow her body to be found here, now, could you?" Edwina asked.

"No. When Phyllis came out to check on us and saw what had happened, she took charge of the operation. We decided that the best place to put her would be in the sarcophagus. That way, the scene of the crime could not be connected with this property and would not draw unwanted attention before we could complete our excavations."

"The Dinsdales were the perfect people to cast the blame onto, weren't they?" Beryl asked. "After all, charlatans like them might be up to any form of no good."

"Exactly. They're not generally thought of as the most outstanding of characters. Besides, if they hadn't convinced Hazel to give them the property, none of this would've happened in the first place," Anthony said. "Their silly dagger made it even easier to point the blame at them."

"Nonsense," Edwina said. "This happened because you were greedy and selfish. Hazel may have had the wool pulled over her eyes by the Dinsdales, but fooling her and others like her are the only things they are guilty of."

"Where is Phyllis now?" Beryl asked.

"She went back to the reading room in the village to pick up some more information about local history. The collection there has been most helpful in identifying some of the artifacts that we collected."

Suddenly Beryl had another question. "Were you, by any chance, the one who sabotaged the airplane?" she asked.

"Yes, that was me too. I didn't want you to be able to see anything that we are up to from above, so as soon as the opportunity presented itself, I messed about a bit with the engine and whatever else I could get my hands on. I don't know much about mechanical things, but I figured I could do enough damage to keep you grounded at least for a little while."

Beryl felt her hackles raise ever so slightly. The arrogance of the man, thinking that his amateurish efforts would keep someone like her grounded for long. But Edwina spoke up before she could respond.

"What an utterly despicable thing to do. We've solved quite a number of cases at this point, and you, sir, have the most deplorable excuse of any of the culprits we have caught. Beryl, will you please keep him subdued while I go and telephone for Constable Gibbs?" Without waiting for an answer, she stomped off across the lawn and headed for the house.

Chapter 33

Edwina looked around the dining room, feeling bathed in a contented glow. Simpkins placed her favorite crystal cake stand directly in front of her and lifted off the glass dome with a flourish.

"I thought that we would finish off our evening of celebration with something I created especially in your honor," he said, sketching a slight bow.

She looked at the generously frosted, slightly lopsided cake bedecked with autumn pansies and mint leaves. Georgie sat next to her and clapped his chubby hands together with glee at the sight of the dessert. Crumpet, who should have been too full even to stagger about from the quantity of food the toddler had dropped to him throughout the course of the meal, capered about as if cake were his favorite treat.

"You really didn't need to go to so much trouble," she said, looking up at Simpkins with a shimmer of tears in her eyes.

"Nonsense. It was my pleasure." He handed her a cake knife before sitting at her other side. Truly, he had gone to enormous trouble with the meal. Between the five courses he had prepared and the fact that three of them contained new recipes he was trialing for Colonel Kimberly's Condiment Company, he had been slaving away in the kitchen ever since her letter of acceptance from the publishing house had arrived two days earlier. In fact, she had the precious envelope tucked away in her pocket as she sat at the table, enjoying the company of her most beloved friends.

Beryl and Beddoes had come to enough of a truce that they had worked together that afternoon in secret to hang bunting and to fill the room with bouquets of flowers from the garden. Edwina had been completely surprised when called to dinner and escorted to her chair at the head of the dining room table, where they had placed a wreath of roses for her to wear on her head. She lifted the cake knife and sliced through the layers to the cheers of the others. As she neatly cut the slices and passed them along down the table, her heart filled with gratitude. Charles beamed at her as she looked down to where he sat at Beryl's side.

She would never have guessed, less than a year before, that her lonely life in an empty house—which, truth be told, had started to fall down around her ears—could transform into one filled with innumerable successes, both personal and professional, or that her home would become a sanctuary for so many. None of it would have happened if Beryl had not whirled back into her life like the hurricane in human form she so truly was. Not only did she bring her energy and enthusiasm to Edwina's orbit, but she also helped her to see the wonderful things that were already there.

Simpkins had gone from someone she considered a persistent but necessary nuisance to something of a father figure. Charles, with his steady support and quiet admiration, had become a trusted adviser and perhaps something more. Small Georgie, although new to the household, filled a longing in Edwina she had barely been willing to acknowledge. Even Beddoes, with her traditional sensibilities, gave Edwina a strong sense that all was right in the world, even when she knew it was not.

Their business was flourishing, she had learned to drive a motorcar, she discovered she enjoyed flying about in airplanes. Even her lifelong dream of becoming a published author was about to come true. And what was more, she had so many with whom to share it all.

No, she could not have guessed how life would change, and as she slipped her hand inside her pocket and ran her fingers across the finely textured envelope, her heart swelled even more. After all, if life had become so interesting so quickly, who knew what was in store in the future? She hardly dared to guess, but she could also hardly wait to find out.